CONTENTS

Title Page	iii
1. Bella	1
2. Ethan	13
3. Bella	18
4. Ethan	28
5. Bella	33
6. Ethan	42
7. Bella	51
8. Ethan	65
9. Bella	76
10. Ethan	85
11. Bella	97
12. Bella	104
13. Ethan	118
14. Bella	128
15. Ethan	140
16. Bella	151
17. Ethan	159
18. Bella	166
19. Bella	169
20. Bella	175
21. Ethan	184
22. Bella	190
23. Ethan	196
24. Bella	203
25. Ethan	213
Bella	222
Author's note	233
About Olivia	235

COPYRIGHT © 2020 OLIVIA HAYLE

All rights reserved. No part of this publication may be distributed or transmitted without the prior consent of the publisher, except in case of brief quotations embodied in articles or reviews.

All characters and events depicted in this book are entirely fictitious. Any similarity to actual events or persons, living or dead, is coincidental.

The following story contains mature themes, strong language and explicit scenes, and is intended for mature readers.

Cover by by Sarah Armitage Design
Edited by Stephanie Parent
www.oliviahayle.com

BILLION DOLLAR CATCH

"Have enough courage to trust love one more time and always one more time."

- *Maya Angelou*

1

BELLA

"You're going to be staying *here* all summer?" Trina's voice echoes through the dining room. She rounds the chandelier-topped table, large enough to seat King Arthur and all his knights.

"Yes," I say, twirling in the adjoining hallway. Even with my arms extended, I don't touch any of the walls. "It's amazing, isn't it?"

"Amazing? It's mental. It should be a crime. *You* should be the one paying *them*."

Laughing, I grab her arm and pull her into the kitchen. It's an expanse of marble and gray cabinets, of artfully arranged copper pots hanging over a six-plated stove.

"Look at this place!"

She reaches for her phone. "I have to take a picture of this."

"It's so beautiful." I open a set of the cabinet doors carefully. We can marvel, but it's still not *my* home. It's just mine for the summer. "I can't wait to cook in this kitchen. The things I'll be able to make…"

"I volunteer as a taster," Trina says. "If you need one."

"You're always welcome, as long as you—"

"Yes, yes, I know. Take off my shoes and don't touch any glass surfaces." She gives me a mock salute, but behind her glasses, her eyes are glittering. "I'm still in shock that you found this job, if you can even call it that. I'm happy for you."

"So am I. It's an immense relief, actually." When my ex had come home and announced he'd found someone else, I hadn't wanted to spend another minute in our apartment. But that left me with nowhere to stay and not enough money to find a good short-term solution.

So when this opportunity appeared on my screen—a Seattle-based company looking for house-sitters for the ultra rich—I'd applied at the speed of light.

"Come out here!" Wilma calls. "You have *got* to see this!"

Trina is out the back door immediately, following the voice of our third friend. Already guessing what she's spotted, I follow along, grinning.

Wilma is standing on the patio with a stunned Trina at her side. They're facing the backyard, if that's even the right word for it. A giant swimming pool glitters in the early summer sun. Four lounge chairs form a beautiful half-circle around an adjacent jacuzzi. Beyond it spreads a lawn impressively green even by Emerald City standards, neatly framed with a large hedge. We're in a walled paradise.

It's Eden.

"Bella," Trina demands. "I need a link to the company who gave you this job, and I need it stat."

Wilma's tone is urgent. "I need more than that. I need guaranteed visitation rights this summer. Every day off I'll be here, using this pool, and there's no way you can stop me. I'll give you anything."

"Yes, anything," Trina agrees. "I'll proofread the final draft of your thesis."

"You've already agreed to do that," I point out. "I'm reading yours at the moment!"

"Damn, that's right."

Wilma sinks down on one of the patio chairs. Her voice is dreamy. "I can't understand why these people would leave their house all summer. They're really gone until the end of August?"

"Yes, for three straight months."

"But why?" She sweeps an arm out to the luscious surroundings, the scent of freshly mowed grass wonderfully thick in the air.

"I have no idea," I say. "I'm guessing the Amalfi Coast beckoned? Who knows why the wealthy do what they do? I'm just happy they do. Now I have a place to stay and an extra income."

Trina stretches out on the other patio chair, a hand over her eyes to guard from the sun. "Not to mention a beautiful neighborhood. Have you seen your neighbors yet? This is your chance to get in with high society, you know."

I roll my eyes. "Yes, because I'd fit right in."

"Hey, none of that attitude here. It's not worthy of this house."

"You're right." Cocking my hip, I look down my nose at her. "And speaking of attitude, I'm not liking yours. Where's my Aperol Spritz?"

She grins at me. "That's more like it."

"Well, I've kind of already met my neighbor."

"You have?"

"Yeah." I nod to the hedge on the right side of us. Thick and green and high, the only thing visible beyond it is the shingles of the roof. "The man who lives there. At least, I *think* it was him."

Wilma, like a bloodhound when she scents a good story, straightens. "What happened?"

"I was out here yesterday," I say, nodding to the pool. "My first day here. And the sun was so gorgeous, how could I *not* be out here swimming, you know?"

"Of course," Trina says. "Anything else would have been a crime."

"A cardinal sin," Wilma agrees.

"And the hedges *are* very tall here. So I thought, maybe this summer will be the one where I'll *finally* manage to avoid any tan lines?"

"You didn't!"

3

"I was in my own garden!" I say. "Well, *my* is perhaps not the right word, but at the moment it is. So I took off my bikini top."

Trina's eyes are scanning the hedge, even as Wilma looks at me with wide eyes, like she can't believe I'd do such a thing. "There are no holes in those bushes," Trina says resolutely. "I'm guessing where this story will go, but he can't have seen you."

"He wasn't looking through the hedge, Trina. He was in that tree." I point to the large, curved oak that rises from the property on the other side. "I looked over and there he was, sitting on a bough. I could see the top of a ladder, too."

Wilma's eyes grow even rounder. "And he was watching you?"

"At that moment at least, yes, he was. Our eyes met." A flush rises to my cheeks at the memory. Even across the distance, I'd seen the wide smile on his face. He looked older than me, but probably not by much. And he'd been… well. Attractive.

"On purpose?"

"I doubt it," I say. "He had a yardstick and a saw in hand. Probably working on the tree."

"Was he hot?"

"Did he wave?"

"Yes, and no. I covered up and hurried inside. He'd gone when I got back out."

"Holy shit." Wilma sits back, nodding to herself. "This is a golden opportunity, Bella. You have to see that."

"Opportunity?"

"Hot neighbor, check. An *interested* hot neighbor, check. A single Bella, check check check!"

"There is no way anything will happen," I say. "Besides, we don't know if he lives there. He might have been the gardener."

Even as I say it, it seems unlikely. There had been something familiar in the set of his features, something in the smile… where had I seen that before?

"Or not," Trina says, pulling up her phone. "Now, I know pretty much everyone who lives in this area…"

"You mean you know *of* them," Wilma corrects, shooting me

a wide smile. I return it. Trina is the queen of gossip.

She rolls her eyes. "Yes, fine, of them. Greenwood Hills has all of Seattle's tech royalty. You know they check the plates of our cars out here, right? There's like twenty-four-hour security in this entire area. All the moguls and developers and the secretly rich live here. And the ostentatiously rich. They all have docks down on Lake Washington."

I snap my fingers. "That's it. Tech. He might work in tech. I recognized his face, but I couldn't place it."

"Tech?"

"Yes. God, he might have been a guest lecturer at the university. Is that where I remember him from?"

"Are you sure?"

"Not at all," I say. "That's just what he looked like, and only from a distance…" My mind searches through the countless hours of lectures I'd sat through. As a PhD student of systems engineering, there had been quite a few during my academic career. But there was one, while I'd been an undergraduate…

"Carter!" I say. "His last name is Carter."

Trina's fingers fly over her phone. "Carter…. Ethan Carter?"

"Yes!"

"This is him." She holds up her phone. The picture is of a man in his mid-thirties, dressed in a suit, green eyes staring into the camera. He's not smiling, but his mirth is there nonetheless, lurking in the corners of his mouth and at odds with the furrow between his brows.

"That *is* him." I press my hands to my hot cheeks. "Dear God, he's brilliant, and he saw me topless."

"He's your neighbor, Bella, holy shit!"

Rising from the chair, I shake my head at them. "That's it. No more topless sunbathing out here."

"No, *even more* topless sunbathing out here!" Wilma exclaims. "Lose the bottoms, too!"

I cross my arms over my chest. "Absolutely not. God, I might want to work at his company one day!"

Trina's face is worse. It's filled with speculation. "Remember two weeks ago, at my birthday party?"

I have no idea where she's going. "Yes?"

"And we played that silly truth-or-dare game that Toby brought. It turned out quite fun."

"It did," I say, narrowing my eyes at her. Wilma is grinning.

"We dared you to—"

"I remember."

"And you didn't do it. Fair enough," she says, palms up. "I totally get that. It was too much. But remember how you said *rain check?*"

Damn it.

Why do I have the friends I do?

"I remember."

"Well then, this is it. We're going to cash that in today," she announces. "Look, your neighbor is a good-looking guy, yes. But he's also a goddamn expert in his field. You've taken a class with him!"

"A guest lecture."

"You're new to the neighborhood. So here's the dare—bake some of your amazing muffins."

"Or your blueberry pie," Wilma interjects. "Or the cinnamon buns!"

"Any one of those," Trina agrees. "And you make enough for your two best friends to taste. And *after* that, you go over and introduce yourself. Give him the goods. Say sorry for the little mishap in the garden. And tell him what you study." She grins, pleased with her own brilliance.

I stare back at her. As dares go, it's not the worst, but it's more daunting than any I've done before. Seeing me waver, she holds up the picture of Ethan Carter again. It's the smile hidden in the corner of his lips that convinces me, and not the stark line of his jaw or the handsome set of his eyes.

A man who smiles like he does wouldn't slam the door in my face.

"All right," I say, sounding braver than I feel. "I'll do it. But there's no way you two will be here when I do."

6

Immediate howls of protest.

"No, I mean it. Now come on. We have brownies to bake."

"Brownies?"

"Yes. This is a high-risk mission. I can't afford to experiment, not here, not now. Men like chocolate."

"They do," Trina confirms.

"Everyone does," Wilma adds.

Steel in my spine, I march into the pristine kitchen and its five-thousand-dollar oven. "Bring out the mixing bowls," I declare. "We have eggs to beat."

The dramatic moment is undercut when we all stand there, staring at the beautiful knob-less cupboards. None of us have a clue where things are, not to mention how to open some of the melt-into-the-wall pantry doors. But just like we figured out our Orientation Week, we'll figure out this kitchen—together.

It's late afternoon by the time we have the perfect batch of brownies cooling on a tray. "They look delicious," Wilma says.

"You can have one," I say. "Actually, take a few."

"You don't have to say that twice." Trina leans against the kitchen island, a plastic binder in her hands. "So these are your instructions?"

"Yes, the house-sitting manual. It has all the information about this place." Winking, I snatch it out of her hands. "Including confidential information."

She grins at me. "I didn't see anything important. Well, apart from the preferred pH-value in the pool. But I promise I'll take the information to my grave."

A soft meow echoes in the kitchen. "Ah! There you are!" I crouch down, moving slowly toward the sleek, gray cat. "My roommate!"

The cat looks unimpressed.

"You're a cat-sitter too?"

"Yes. That's part of why they wanted someone here, to keep him company."

"What's his name?"

Giving up on trying to pet the cat—he's flicking his tail and looks ready to bolt—I reach for the manual. "It must be in here somewhere. It was on the page with feeding instructions. Toast!"

"Toast?"

"That's his name."

We look at the cat, now stretched out on the carpet, his tawny eyes staring back at us.

"Rich people," Wilma declares, as if that explains everything. "And speaking of rich people... it's time for us to leave and for you to knock on a certain someone's door."

I give a mock groan. "I can't. I've forgotten how to knock."

"Bella, you promised."

So I did.

Ethan Carter. I'm just going to go say hi to Ethan Carter, my neighbor. One of Seattle's most impressive tech icons. A pioneer in the field of technical mechanics. Who just happens to be my neighbor for the next three months.

And who has seen me topless.

"I did promise," I say. "And that means you have to go now, before I completely lose my nerve."

Wilma jumps down from the barstool and Trina gives me a nod, the kind a team player gives to another in the heat of the game. "You got this," she says.

"Thanks."

Reaching over, she smooths my fringe into place. The curtain bangs had been a complete impulse decision just two weeks ago, but I like them. They frame my face. They're a change. New hair, new me.

"You look gorgeous," she says. "Nice choice of dress."

Glancing down at the sundress I'd put on this morning, I have to agree. It's probably the one thing I own that has spaghetti straps. "Thank you."

"Text us the second after you're done, and tell us everything," Wilma says. "Oh! I almost forgot, I brought you those pills you asked for."

"The herbal sleeping aids?" I ask. Across the counter, Trina raises an eyebrow at me. We'd had an intense discussion last time we were together about whether Wilma's new fascination with herbs had any scientific basis.

"Yes." She puts a bottle down on the counter, a picture of leaves on the front. "They'll help you sleep, I promise."

I turn it over in my hand. "I'm willing to try," I say. "I can't handle having to lie awake for hours much longer."

"Consequence of your break-up," Trina points out.

"Yes, but an annoyingly persistent one." Searching through the pantry for a large platter, I start arranging the brownie slices. "Thanks, Wilma."

They leave with good-luck wishes and the roar of an old engine. Looking at myself in the gold-framed mirror in the larger-than-life hallway, I decide I look pretty good. Presentable. The girl-next-door, I think, smiling at my own little joke. A big plate of brownies in hand and nerves dancing in my stomach.

As much as I might groan, Trina had been spot-on with this dare.

Locking the giant door behind me, I leave one imposing house for another. My neighbor's house is just as large.

A white villa rises up behind the gates. Gray shutters. A large porch. That's pretty much all I can see through the fence.

The curb appeal in this area is seriously high, *if* your particular thing is fences and gates.

I press the button to the intercom with a heart that threatens to gallop off and leave me behind in the dust.

A softly accented voice answers. "Hello?"

"Hi. I'm Bella, I just moved in next door and wanted to introduce myself. I brought brownies." Stupidly, I lift the plate up high to the miniscule camera, as if the sight of gooey chocolate might help my case.

Silence stretches on.

God, I've miscalculated. These people don't do things like this. They don't have yard sales or exchange baked goods, and they sure as hell don't let strangers into their gated little slices of paradise. Greenwood Hills doesn't work like this.

But then microphone static reaches me, and the same female

voice rings out. "Come on up to the main door, sweetheart."

The wrought-iron gate swings open.

That must have been his wife. Stupidly, the realization hits with faint disappointment. The thought of the smile playing along the edge of his lips had been intriguing. How would you draw it out? What would be the right joke?

I stop outside a beautifully carved wooden door. It seems a shame to have houses this beautiful when nobody can see them from the curb.

The door swings open and I'm greeted by a smiling, black-clad lady in her mid-fifties. Her dark hair is pulled back in a bun. "Hello," she says. "Bella?"

"Yes. I'm sorry to just come knocking like this. I moved in just yesterday, and I—"

"I know. I saw you unpacking." The lady waves me into the hallway. "Welcome to the neighborhood."

"Thank you," I say, a sigh of relief escaping me. "It's a beautiful place."

"It really is. I'm Maria," she says, "and I work for Mr. Carter. He'll be with you in just a bit."

"Here he is!" The voice is rich, expansive. It fits perfectly with the man I'd seen the picture of just a few hours ago. He comes striding down the hallway.

The years since I'd sat in the lecture hall and listened to him speak have made him even more impressive, the soft fabric of his sweater clinging to a wider chest.

And his smile.

It's there, lurking at the edge of his mouth and playing in the depths of intelligent eyes. Yes, he remembers me. The topless girl next door. To my horror, my cheeks heat up.

"Mr. Carter," Maria says. "This is the girl you told me to let in."

"Bella Simmons," I say, extending a hand and trying not to drop the giant plate of brownies. Why had I decided to bring so many? It looks like I'm supplying a bakery.

"Ethan Carter." He gives my hand a firm shake, his skin

warm. "Welcome to the neighborhood."

"Thank you," I breathe, relief sweeping through me. "I'll be honest, I wasn't sure if this was common practice here. Saying hi to your neighbors when you're new and all. I'm sorry if I've just committed an unspeakable faux pas."

His eyes flick down to the plate in my arms. "We usually execute people on sight for this, but you brought brownies, so I'll make an exception."

If I wasn't still so nervous, I'd be laughing at that. "Consider it a peace offering, then."

"Getting heavy?" He reaches out and takes the plate from me.

"A bit. Thank you."

"Although I suppose I should be the one with a peace offering." Holding the plate in one arm, Ethan reaches up and runs a hand through his hair. The smile lurking on his lips is more pronounced now. "I hope you know I wasn't in that tree to spy on you."

My cheeks flare up. "Right. I didn't think you were. I mean, you had a measuring tape."

"Flimsy evidence, but I'm glad you believe me." His smile is wide now. "I was location scouting for a treehouse."

"Really? That's lovely."

"I'm glad you think that. I'm not sure what your—parents? Aunt and uncle?—will think when they get back. It'll overlook their property."

My response slips out before I can stop it. Caught in his gaze, soothed by the deep tenor of his voice, there's no way I can tell this multi-billionaire that I'm a homeless house-sitter. "Aunt and uncle," I say. "I'm watching the house for them this summer. Three months."

"That's very nice of you," he comments.

"Well, it's a very nice house."

Ethan's grin widens. "Good point."

Up close, he's somehow more imposing at the same time as he's less so. He's flesh and blood, tanned skin and curving lips and smile lines around his eyes. But he's also clearly a *man*, one who wears cologne and a twenty-thousand-dollar watch and manages a billion-dollar business.

"So," he says, snapping me out of my admiration, "do you work around here? Or do you—"

A childish shriek sounds somewhere in the background. It echoes down the hall to us, followed by padding feet and Maria's low voice. Somewhere in the house, a door slams.

Ethan sighs. "I'd better go. My oldest just learned how to dramatically shut doors from some TV show."

"Ouch," I say.

"Yes. I'd have a choice word with the writer of that kids' show if I could."

I head back to the front door, unable to let him go yet. "Kids, huh? That's who the treehouse is for?"

The ever-lurking smile breaks out, spreading across his features. It transforms him. He's welcoming and strong and why had I been nervous for this?

"Yes," he says. "I'm not planning on building one for myself, Bella."

"Oh, thank God," I say, the teasing words escaping me. "That would have made you seem like a professional peeper."

"Thankfully not a profession I've ever wanted to pursue."

Another shriek echoes down the hallway, and he looks over his shoulder. I open the front door and step outside. "Sorry, I'll leave. See you around, and thank you."

His smile is indulgent now. Am I rambling? "Bye, Bella," he says, the deep voice washing over me. "Thank you for the brownies."

I make it back to my giant house in an awestruck daze. Toast meows for food at my feet. "Yes," I tell him. "Right. We have a job to do here."

And I do. House-sit. Make money. Finish PhD thesis. Figure out my future.

Developing a pointless crush on my no-doubts-already-taken neighbor is nowhere on that list.

2

ETHAN

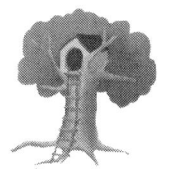

"There's no way," Cole says. "No way at all. You *have* the time to get out there. You have a nanny, right?"

"Yes," I say, looking at my friend over the rim of my whiskey glass. For Cole Porter, who has a three-month-old infant, a nanny likely seems like the perfect solution. But when your kids are six and three, they need a bit more interaction.

"So use her," he insists. "You need to get out there. Life shouldn't be lived alone, man."

"Mhm," I say. "And this is coming from happily-married and soon-to-be-married over there?"

Nick grimaces at that. The man is a renowned commitment-phobe, but over the last couple of months he's settled into an unconventional relationship with Cole's little sister. Unconventional in that it's a relationship, period—and for Nicholas Park, that's a big thing.

"You don't have to find someone to marry," Nick says. "Hell, can you even have one-night stands as a single dad?"

I scowl into my drink. They mean well, but we're getting into territory I don't like to discuss. "You can," I say. "At out-of-town conferences."

"How emotionally fulfilling," Cole remarks.

"You need it regularly," Nick says.

I lean back in the leather chair and look at them through narrowed eyes. "And when did you two become such experts, anyway? You were both inveterate bachelors until a few years ago. Besides, I have kids. It's different for me."

Cole nods, like he's some goddamn expert after three months of fatherhood. "Sure is."

I shake my head at him. "You have a wife who thinks you walk on water and a host of staff."

He grins, unashamed. "Yes," he says, "and I'm loving every second of it. But with a bit of dating, that could be you."

Nick reaches over and touches his glass to mine. Taller than both Cole and me, and with a wolfish glint to his eyes, he's not a man to trifle with. "Don't listen to the man," he tells me. "He won the tennis match earlier. You know how he gets."

I give a sage nod, knowing it'll infuriate Cole. The competitive nature between us runs deep—and ever since I'd become a semi-regular at their tennis matches, that tension had only increased.

"I don't want to date," I say. "Another time commitment? Shoot me. Besides, I have no interest in the women who frequent your parties. No offense, Cole."

He grins. "None taken. I didn't fish from that pool myself either, so to speak."

"They're not all bad," Nick says, narrowing his eyes at Cole.

Predictably, he rolls his eyes. "I thought it was obvious that I didn't include my sister in that statement."

"Neither did I," I add, knowing from experience how defensive Nick is of Blair's reputation.

Cole turns his attention back to me. The setting sun bathes his backyard in golden light, a fellow Greenwood Hills resident. "All right," he says. "There's no one around but Nick and me. Be honest. When was the last time you got laid?"

I lean back in my chair. The sky is a beautiful deep orange as I look to the heavens for help. I receive none. "I'm not answering that."

"Talking about it might help," Nick points out, contained amusement in his voice. "That's what I'm told all the time these days. *Communication helps.*"

"I'm not holding a damn feeling stick and telling you two about my sex life." Or lack thereof. The last one-night stand had been… seven months ago on a business trip to New York. But they don't need more fodder for their amusement.

They continue talking like I'm not there. Cole wants to set me up with someone—something about an old college friend's cousin—and gets so far into planning that I'm forced to zone back into the conversation.

"Out of the question. I have my two girls and I'm perfectly happy with that." I drain my glass of whiskey and ignore the pang that accompanies the statement. I *am* more than happy with my daughters. I wouldn't trade them for anything in the world—not even the world itself. And yet, there is a small part of me that sees what Nick and Cole have, and thinks…

No. I've had too much to drink if I'm unraveling into self-pity like this.

"I'd better go," I say, rising from the lawn chair. "See you around, assholes. And the next time, I don't want to hear another word about how lonely you think I am."

I find my own way past Cole's house and onto the large driveway in the front. Shutting the gate behind me, I begin the short walk from his house to my own.

The lots in Greenwood Hills might be big, and the area heavily forested, but we're not many who live here. All that spaciousness makes for a beautiful environment to raise kids. That's why I'd bought the house originally, when Lyra had been pregnant with Haven.

I snort at the memory. My ex-wife had been disappointed that the house didn't have waterfront access to Lake Washington, and it hadn't helped when I told her those houses only go on the market once a century.

But then again, Lyra had only ever been after the money and

status I could provide. Getting pregnant had been an excellent method to get her hands on it.

Walking onto my cul-de-sac, I glance at the house next to mine. Bella Simmons's new home for the summer. She was infinitely preferable to her aunt and uncle, who had never once smiled or said hello in the years I'd lived here. Not that I'd ever made much of an effort back, to be fair. I couldn't really remember what they looked like.

But Bella, I remember perfectly.

Thick, brown hair and big doe eyes. Long legs, fair skin. It had been creamy in the sunlight, the day I'd seen her tanning. It had been from quite a distance, yes, but I'd have to be blind to be unmoved by the sight of her body in nothing but a pair of bikini bottoms. Soft-looking skin and pink nipples.

I shake my head at my own leering thoughts as I unlock the front gate to my property. I'm the one in the wrong. Spying on her from the tree, accidental or not. Having lustful thoughts.

Talking to her hadn't helped.

She'd stood right here in my hallway, her cheeks flushed, holding a tray of brownies made just for me. Rambling in her speech and gorgeous in her sundress. Sweet and young and clearly not for me.

Thou shalt not covet thy neighbor's niece, I think, snorting. Perhaps Nick and Cole had been on to something when they told me to find at least semi-regular female company. But where would I find the time?

The house is quiet when I open the front door. Haven and Evie had been sound asleep when I left, Maria reading in the room between theirs in case they needed anything. There are alarms and safety cameras aplenty. I'd just been across the street, too. But I don't fully relax until I walk past their bedrooms, peering in to see their small, sleeping forms.

I'd been right. There is no way I could have anything to do with dating, not when my heart—and my schedule—is already this full.

But that doesn't stop me from heading to the kitchen and grabbing one of those delicious chocolate squares to eat, my thoughts drifting to the beautiful brunette who'd made them.

A man could still fantasize, right?

3

BELLA

"No, you're staying here."

Toast looks up at me like my mere existence is a personal insult. I press my leg into the half-opened front door and remember exactly why I'm more of a dog person.

"You're not getting out. Not on my watch. They printed it in bold *and* underlined in the instructions I got."

Toast bumps his head against my leg, and not affectionately. "No," I say again. "Now, I'm going to pull my leg back to shut this door. Do you promise me you won't try to stick a paw in or something? I don't want you getting hurt. Just think of how much a visit to the vet would mess up your day."

Not to mention mine.

Toast sits down, looking up at me angelically. I'm not buying it. It might be a ploy.

"Okay now." I pull the door shut slowly, inch by inch. "I'll be back tonight. Don't break any vases."

And then, at the last second, a loud meow. But the door is shut. Breathing a sigh of relief, I lock it behind me.

"If this is to become a daily thing," I tell the shut door and the devious cat behind it, "then I think I deserve a raise."

There's no response. Hoisting my bag up higher on my

shoulder, I search through my pockets for my car keys. Should be here somewhere...

I find the keys and unlock the door to my 2007 Honda Civic. It's an old madam, this car. Possibly one of the *least* flashy cars this neighborhood—and this specific driveway—has ever seen.

Sliding into the driver's seat, I look down at my watch. I still have plenty of time. While there are no classes over the summer, I still have regular meetings with my supervisors, and they don't appreciate lateness.

I turn the key in the ignition.

Nothing happens. The nothingness is pretty spectacular, actually. Not the faintest sound of an engine.

"Not you too," I tell it, thinking of Toast's escapist stunts. "Behave."

I take a deep breath before I turn the key again.

The engine doesn't so much as make a peep.

Damn it. Why today, of all days? I try five more times and the car refuses to start each time. This happened once, a few months ago, when the battery ran out of charge. I'd been told by the insurance company to change the battery back then. Something about charging problems and faulty electrical drains and the ominous-sounding verdict of *it will likely die again*.

But it hadn't. And I'd forgotten all about those several hundreds of dollars I didn't have to spend on a new battery.

Getting out of the car, I aim a solid kick to a tire. It's ineffectual, but it makes me feel better.

"Damn it!"

Can I find someone with jumper cables? I hadn't been able to last time, and I'd paid for that mistake. I call Trina. Predictably, she doesn't answer. She's the queen of having her phone on silent.

Wilma doesn't pick up either, which means I'm shit out of luck. Calling my little brother Wyatt is out of the question, because he doesn't have a car.

I look over at the closed garage doors. Mr. and Mrs. Gardner's cars are in there, locked away while they're traveling this summer. I know where the keys are—that was one of the items in my house-sitting guide. Can I use them to jumpstart my own car?

Battling with indecision, I get out and pop the hood to my car. The engine is a mess of cables and steel and things that I'd likely break upon impact. I should have paid more attention the last time I saw someone do this.

"Is everything all right over there?"

I jump at the voice and the hood slams shut with the sound of steel on steel, narrowly missing my fingers.

"Shoot. You okay?" Standing on the other side of the fence is Ethan. I glimpse the shiny black lacquer of a car behind him.

He's in a suit.

For a second, that simple fact makes it difficult to craft a reply. How could I, when he looks as if he's poured into the fabric? No tie. Undone top button, a slice of tanned skin in view. Thick hair that's just as messy as it was the day before. And eyes that look increasingly concerned as I play mute.

Nodding, I force out a response. "Yes. Well, no, not really. My car won't start."

He runs a hand along his jaw. "Problem, that."

"Yes."

"Do you know why?"

"I *suspect* it's the battery," I say. "It's done this before. I was warned it would happen again. I didn't listen."

"Do you have jumper cables?"

"No."

"Right. Well, I'll be over in a second." He disappears from view, speaking to someone on the other side in too low a voice for me to make out.

This was not at all how I'd planned out our next interaction! After the brownie-hello two days ago, my mind had raced ahead to a summer of polite exchanges and charming smiles. To waving at him from the side of the pool as he worked on the treehouse. To potentially—sometime around week seven—slip

20

into conversation that I study system engineering. One of the few women at Washington Polytech doing that, in fact.

But no. Now I look unprepared at best and downright negligent at worst.

Ethan reappears at the bottom of my driveway, holding a set of cables, still clad in his suit. "I'll back up my own car," he says. "It should be a simple fix. Do you have somewhere you need to be today?"

"Yes, a meeting." I smooth a hand over my tailored slacks. "Thank you so much for helping me. Are you sure you have the time, though? I don't want to keep you from—"

He waves away my protest. "Not a problem. Besides, your brownies were excellent, so I owe you one. Let me be your knight in shining armor."

I lift up the hood to my car and he fastens the strut. Broad, tan hands grip the ends of the jumper cables. A white shirt peeks out from the sleeve of his suit jacket.

"Wait," I say, my hands flitting forward to grip his wrist before he can touch my engine. It's firm under my touch. "You might get grease on your shining armor."

His lips twitch. "You're right. A knight can't have that, can he?"

"It would look very unprofessional."

He shrugs off his suit jacket and I take it from him, folding it over my arm. It's warm from his body heat. And then the worst of all—he rolls up his shirtsleeves, unveiling inch after inch of muscled forearms.

"Better?" he asks.

"Uh-huh."

Still smiling, he bends to attach the cables to my engine. I watch this time, remembering where he's attaching them. It's bound to happen again. "You really know how to do this," I comment.

"I've had a fair bit of practice," he says. "Spent a lot of time with my head under the hood as a teenager."

"Oh."

"I take it you haven't, though?" Shaking his head briefly, he rests his fingers on a box-like thing in the engine. "You definitely need to change your battery."

"Oh, I know. I just never got around to it."

"There's a mechanic in Greenwood, down by the strip mall. He always has time for locals." Ethan bends over the engine again, a smile in his voice. "Though I can't think of a mechanic who wouldn't make time for *you*."

I blink at the broadness of his back. "Oh?"

"They love pretty faces."

My mind goes completely blank at that.

"Daddy!" a young voice calls. "Can we watch? Please?"

A little girl stands at the base of my driveway, hands clasped behind her back, bouncing on the balls of her feet. Her hair is a mess of curls, the exact same honey shade as Ethan's, minus the faint salt and pepper.

Ethan straightens. "Watch me jump-start a car?"

"Yes!"

He turns to me. "All the cartoons in the world, and this is more interesting," he comments, rubbing a hand over his neck.

"I get it," I say, because I do. He's far more interesting than any TV show.

"Haven," he says louder, "this is Bella. Bella is our new neighbor for the summer. She's the one who baked the brownies."

Haven dances forward, stopping beside her father. She can't be older than six. "Hello," she greets me.

"Hi," I say. "It's nice to meet you."

She smiles, revealing a gap where her front teeth should be. "Nice to meet you too. Your car's broken?"

"Yes. The battery is dead and your dad is helping me fix it."

"He's good at fixing things," she comments, rising up on her tiptoes to watch. "But he's terrible at braiding hair."

Ethan snorts. Valiantly, I stop myself from laughing by biting down on my tongue. "Is he?"

"Yes. Maria does our hair instead. You have really pretty hair," she tells me. Her voice is clear as a bell, no shyness at all.

"Thank you. So do you. I love the curls."

"Thanks," she says. "Could you teach me how to bake brownies some day? Yours were reeeally good."

Ethan puts a hand on her shoulder. "Bella might be busy," he says. "But maybe she can give you her recipe, if you ask nicely."

I smile at her. "I'd be happy to give you the recipe. And if you need help while you're baking, you're free to let me know. I'm here most days."

"You don't work?"

"*Haven,*" Ethan says.

I chuckle. "I do, but mostly from home. I'm a graduate student."

"Wait for meeee!" A second child comes chasing up my driveway on round little legs, her pigtails bouncing. "I want to see!"

She barrels into Ethan's leg and he gives me a glance that's half-apologetic, half-embarrassed. "Sorry," he says. "Seems this knight comes with quite the entourage."

"I don't mind," I say, smiling at the new little girl. She peers up at me. "And who is this?"

"This is Evie, my youngest," Ethan says, putting a hand on her shoulder. "And how did you escape, huh?"

Maria comes around the corner in the next second. "I'm sorry, she fooled me…" and then she scoops down and picks up the small girl. "We can watch from the other side of the fence," she says. "Your father has to back up the car."

Ethan nods. "That's right. This is not a place for kids. Haven, I want you on the other side of the fence as well."

"But—"

"Not a discussion." Steering her toward their house, Ethan gives me a crooked smile. "I'll park one of my cars here. We'll have yours started in no time."

"Thank you. You'll have an endless supply of brownies after this in thanks."

His smile widens at that. "I might hold you to that."

Mine fades as he parks his giant Jeep beside my little beaten-up Honda Civic. The difference between us couldn't be any starker. But he says nothing about it as he pops open his hood. It opens automatically, revealing an engine that's impressive even to a novice like me.

"Here we go..." he says, connecting wires, humming with life and competence. I'm still holding on to his suit jacket and the fabric is soft under my hands. Idly, I wonder what it would smell like. Does he wear cologne?

"What do you study?"

"Sorry?"

"You said you're a graduate student," he says. "What do you study?"

"I'm doctoring in systems engineering."

His gaze snaps up to mine. "You're a systems engineer?"

"Soon-to-be, yeah."

"What topic are you researching?"

"How model-based project strategies provide greater efficiency."

He nods to himself. "Very interesting," he says, and there's no artifice in his voice.

A small glow of pride starts in my chest. Ethan Carter, a pioneer in the tech industry for his work on nano-research and its commercial implications. For a second, I feel like the undergrad student who had sat second row during his guest lecture.

"We'll have to talk about that," he murmurs, walking around to the driver's seat of his car. "Very interesting indeed. And you'll be here all summer?"

"Yes."

"Good." He slides into the driver's seat. "Get in your car, but don't start it until I tell you to, okay?"

"Okay."

The deep rumble of his engine roaring to life is the only sound, followed quickly by the cheers of two small girls across the fence. I smile as I sit in my driver's seat, the door open. There's a large coffee stain on the passenger seat. I'd never really noticed that before.

"Now!"

"All right," I tell my car quietly, hand on the car key. "I promise I'll buy you a new battery if you just start now. We have an audience."

And then I turn the key.

My engine growls to life in a far less flattering way than Ethan's state-of-the-art Jeep, but it's alive. "Thank you," I tell it, putting the gear in neutral and getting out, the car still on.

"That's it. All she needed was a jump." Ethan reaches out a hand to me, expectant. I stare at it for a second before I realize I'm still holding his jacket.

"Right. Here. Thank you so much for this. I don't know how to repay you."

"Yes, you do," he says, shrugging into his fitted suit jacket. "You already promised. Brownies in perpetuity."

"Of course. How could I have forgotten?"

"I don't know, but I'll keep reminding you. I have two kids to feed." And then he winks, bending over to remove the jumper cables from my still-roaring engine without pausing. "Now I want you to go get this car serviced, all right? First thing tomorrow."

"Sure, yes. And I'm sorry if I've made you late to some meeting."

"Oh, that's fine," he says. "They'll wait."

I swallow at the casual mention of such power. "Oh. Good."

He pauses with a hand on the front door to his car. "I work in tech, actually. We have a lot of system engineers at my company. I'm sure there are many who'd find your study interesting."

My head bobs like a doll's. "I know."

"You know?" A raise of both eyebrows.

"No, I mean, I know that you work in tech. I think you gave a guest lecture a couple of years back at Washington Polytech?"

A smile breaks across his face. "You were there? Among the students?"

"Yes. It was a great lecture," I say.

"Don't lie. I made it all up on the fly."

"All right, so it wasn't very structured," I admit, smiling back at him. "But it was even more interesting because of it."

"Now *that*, I believe."

"Your use of props was ingenious. The water bottle stunt? Ten out of ten."

His grin widens. "You really were there."

"Daddy!" An impatient voice on the other side of the fence. "Did you fix it?"

And then an older child's voice. "Of course he did, silly. Don't you hear the engine?"

An angry wail back, and then, "Stop it!"

"No, you stop it."

Ethan gives me a look that is both tired and apologetic. "Don't have kids," he tells me, but there's fondness in his voice. "It's a trap."

"I'll consider myself warned." My insides feel light—like I might float away at any moment, despite the engine running in my car or the meeting I'll surely be late to.

"I'll talk to you later," he says, shutting the front door and reversing with one hand on the steering wheel, a move men have somehow always perfected. He looks like sin doing it. On the other side of the fence, I hear Maria calm down the girls' fighting.

I slide into the front seat of my little Honda and reverse after his monster of a vehicle, shutting the gate with the automatic controller. The girls wave at me when I drive past. I wave back, watching how Ethan bends to hoist up the youngest.

Not for me, I tell myself. Those kids have a mother, someone who receives all of Ethan's smiles. Besides, I have more schoolwork than I can handle. We're from stratospherically different circumstances. Forget out of my league—Ethan Carter and I don't even play the same sport.

And yet, I spend the entire drive to Washington Polytech sorting through my memories. Had I seen him wear a wedding ring?

4

ETHAN

The asphalt is smooth under my feet. The sun's first rays haven't quite driven out the night yet, and the air is cool. A beautiful morning for a run.

I loop around Redfern Drive and head down to the park by Lake Washington. There's almost no one out—the best time of the day, this. No work calls. No duties. No one to compete with except the smartwatch on my wrist and yesterday's record.

No music in my ears, either, just blessed silence.

I glance down at the watch. Do I have time to run alongside the lake until Greenwood Hills ends? No. Haven and Evie will be up soon, and we always eat breakfast together. It'll be a shorter run today. I wouldn't trade mornings with my daughters for anything.

A woman comes jogging out of the adjacent street and onto the road in front of me. Few are the times I've seen other runners at this hour.

And there's something familiar about her form, the long hair pulled back into a ponytail, the fair legs under her runner's shorts…

I speed up. With each passing yard, it's getting clearer who it is.

"Bella?"

She glances to the left and then jumps, reaching up to tug at one of the Bluetooth earphones. "Christ," she says. "Ethan, hi."

"I keep scaring you. I'll have to work on that."

She shakes her head, her skin flushed from exertion. "Not at all."

"Do you run a lot?"

"Yes, but today's the first time in this neighborhood," she says, nodding for us to continue. We run side-by-side at a leisurely pace. Her skin glistens in the morning sunlight.

"It's a great place for runs. If you head east instead, from our houses, you get to a trailhead with quite a climb. Magnificent view over the lake."

"I'll try that some time." She pushes a loose strand of hair behind her ear, running at my side. "My car is running great, by the way. Thanks to you."

"I'm still waiting for my daily brownie delivery."

She laughs, shooting me a sideway glance. "I couldn't possibly do that to you. Think of all the calories. The sugar. The gluten. The chocolate."

"Delicious," I say. "Have you changed your battery yet?"

She shakes her head so the ponytail flies. I wonder what it would feel like wrapped around my hand. "Not yet. But I have a time with the mechanic for next Friday."

"Good. Not that I mind, you know, but I might not always be around with my trusty cables."

"Very true." She smiles again and looks over at me, and there's no way to stop myself from flirting when she looks like this. I have no right to make a move and no idea if she'd even be interested, but those are rational considerations, and I'm not in the mood for rationality.

"So, tell me something," I say. "Was it *very* obvious that I was unprepared?"

"For your lecture?"

"Yes. Be honest."

She laughs, our pace slowing down somewhat. "Yes, it was

obvious, but I don't think anyone minded. It was very charming."

"Charming? I was aiming for informative, but whatever works, I guess."

Her cheeks flush further. She's gorgeous, with her skin covered in a faint sheen and her eyes dancing. "You were informative," she says.

I put a hand over my heart. "Thank God. I'd hate to be told... what, four years after the fact that I embarrassed myself completely."

"Your dignity is intact."

"In that way at least," I say with a grin, and she smiles back. "So systems engineering, huh?"

She nods. "It's interesting."

"And very male-dominated," I say. It's impressive, what she's studying. Makes her even more intriguing. The watch on my arm gives me an annoying buzz to let me know the pace is too slow. I won't reach my target. I ignore it.

"Yes," Bella says. "I'm the only female PhD student in the department."

"I'm not surprised."

She gives me a crooked smile. "I'm brought out for every photoshoot the department has. It makes them look better."

I roll my eyes, annoyed on her behalf. "Of course it does. Want to head up here?"

She looks at where I'm pointing—Brownell Drive, which will eventually loop back to our street. "Lead the way," she says. "You know this area better than me."

"You're giving me too much credit. If I wasn't a runner I'd be lost."

"Yes, people don't really socialize here, do they? I haven't seen a single one of my neighbors. Apart from you," she says.

"Much obliged," I say and pretend to tip my hat at her. A silly gesture—one my eldest daughter enjoys—but Bella smiles at it. "People enjoy their privacy here."

"And to think I just barged into your house with brownies."

"Well, I think I violated your privacy first," I say, and because I'm awful and I can't resist, I look straight at her as I say it. She smiles at my teasing and looks away, biting into her lower lip.

"Lesson learned," she says. "And the worst part is, I can't pay you back in kind, either."

I blink. Twice. "No, I don't think you can. There's no tree on your side of the hedge."

"Shoot."

Does she mean—would she want to? Are we really joking about *her* seeing *me* undressed?

"And even if you had, I don't have a pool installed," I say. "So no such luck."

She snorts. "You've covered all your bases."

"It's what I do best."

We turn onto our street. The sun is completely up now, chasing away the dew still clinging to the greenery. "Do you often run this early?"

"No," she says. "I was woken up today by a very angry, very loud cat."

"Ouch."

"Yes. He doesn't like me yet, unfortunately. I'll have to get him some toys or treats." A thought hits her. "Do cats even like treats?"

I laugh at that. "Ask your aunt and uncle. They ought to know."

She looks away. "They probably do, yeah."

We're almost at our driveways before I find the courage to speak the words. They're partly for Haven, yes, but they're mostly for me. An excuse to spend time with her, although I have nothing to offer.

"What are your plans this Saturday?"

Her eyes shoot to mine. "I don't have any."

"How do you feel about attending a six-year-old's birthday party?"

Her eyes light up, and I want to kiss her for that reaction alone. "It's Haven's birthday?"

"Yes, we're throwing a party in the backyard. Bouncy castle, piñata, the whole thing." I shake my head at the thought of the extensive organization that's gone into it. Thank God I can pay people to handle those things for me. "Haven wanted to ask you to come."

Bella smiles, like she's genuinely touched by the invitation. "That's sweet."

"She told me yesterday that she didn't want you to see the balloons and think you weren't invited."

Bella laughs at that, and the sound is more gratifying than I'd expected. It makes me want to earn it again. "That's so thoughtful of her. Of course I'll swing by."

"Excellent. Have a piece of cake, get a balloon animal. It'll be fantastic," I say. "A real raver. All of Seattle's preschool elite will be there."

She nods, playing along. "I assume it's black tie?"

"It is, yes, thank you for asking. There'll be valet parking too, so don't worry about finding a spot to park."

She shakes her head, grinning wide now. "I'll be there."

"Looking forward to it," I say, like an idiot, stopping by my gate. "See you then."

"Wait, what about presents? What does she want for her birthday?"

I shake my head. "Good God, no present. She has more toys than any kid could ever need. No, don't get her anything."

"I can't show up empty-handed."

"Make brownies, then. You owe me some anyway."

Her smile is crooked. "All right. Until then."

"Until then," I echo, losing sight of her as she walks up her own driveway.

And later, when I look at my smartwatch and the statistics from my run, it doesn't surprise me at all that while I didn't reach my target speed, my heart rate had remained elevated the entire time.

5
BELLA

On Saturday, the commotion from Ethan's house starts early. So early, in fact, that the sound of men shouting orders at each other drags me out of sleep and not my trusty alarm.

The guest room window overlooks the hedge. I glimpse something very purple and very large on Ethan's lawn—is that a bouncy castle?—and smile. A kid's birthday party. I haven't been to one in… over a decade, probably. Not since I was a kid myself.

Toast winds his way through my legs when I enter the kitchen.

"I have arrived," I tell him grandly. "Food is imminent."

He looks up at me as I fetch his wet food. The second it hits his bowl, he's on it, devouring every morsel.

"Do you even taste it on the way down?"

There's no response, just the sound of his furious eating.

"We won't make a gourmand cat out of you," I tell him, mock-sadness in my voice. "That career path is ruled out for you."

He doesn't answer. Not very talkative, either. Sighing at my own silliness, I assemble my ingredients and mixing bowl on the giant kitchen island. Ethan had requested brownies, but I'm keen to make a different recipe… chocolate chip cookies. All kids like that, right?

It's one of many questions that whirl through my mind as I bake. The pressing list of things to do is never far away. A place to stay, financial aid applications, writing my thesis...

"Maybe you can help me, Toast," I say. "How many words do you type per minute with those paws?"

He looks at me over the empty rim of his bowl with wide, golden eyes. *You're on your own,* they say.

"Yeah. I figured."

A few hours later, in a dress and a pair of wedge heels, I head out to the front door. Music drifts over Ethan's side of the hedge, punctuated by children's excited shrieks.

The driveway is decked out with balloons, tied to every possible anchor. Pinks and blues and yellows. The front door is open and guests are milling beyond, adults and children alike.

I hold on to my basket of cookies like it's a lifeline and step inside. I'm nearly bowled over when two kids race past me, one chasing the other. A woman in heels runs after them. "Not upstairs!" she calls.

I weave through a few men in suits to get to the giant kitchen island I've spotted in the distance. Who wears a suit to a kid's birthday party?

The island is overflowing with presents and food. In the center is a giant chocolate cake, complete with two beloved sister-princesses on top. I put my basket of cookies down in between a plate of Rice Krispies Treats and watermelon slices.

Smiling at a child standing on the other side, I walk through the open-landscaped living room to the patio. Ah. So the purple thing I'd seen that morning *had* been a bouncy castle. And a popular one, judging by the number of kids currently on it.

I don't see Haven, Ethan or Evie anywhere, nor Maria. But I do see a host of parents and kids and a few servers, too, walking around with trays of lemonade.

To my right I overhear two men debating stock options, and to my left a few women discuss an ongoing renovation project. *They promised me it would be done in five months!*

I feel spectacularly out of place, and except for the kids themselves, like the youngest person there.

I spot Ethan at the far end of the lawn. He's hoisting Haven up in the air as she screams with laughter. He throws her into the bouncy castle so she—and the kids around her—all fly up from the impact. She bounces back, arms raised, and he does it again. And again. The sight makes me smile.

After a lap around the party—I catch snippets of conversations about dance recitals and summer vacations—I sneak back out and retreat up my own driveway. Mingling has never been my strong suit, and not at a party like that. Ethan had only been half-joking when he said Seattle's preschool elite would be there.

It's late that evening when my doorbell rings. I've long since swapped out my dress for a pair of sweats, my makeup off, an old movie playing on the massive TV in the living room.

After a moment of deliberation, I press down the *answer* button on the intercom system. The camera flicks to life. "Hello?"

It's Ethan, a bottle of wine in one hand, the basket I'd delivered cookies in clasped in the other. "I'm here to return your basket," he says, and the deep timbre of his voice is impressive even through the static. "Open up, Bella."

And God help me, but I do. The gate swings open and I rush to the mirror, running a hand through my hair. My sweatpants aren't that bad. But the T-shirt? It has the old Washington Polytech logo on it and it's two sizes too big.

"Damn it, damn it…" Do I have time to run upstairs and pull on a camisole? A sweater? Anything that doesn't have a hole in it?

A knock on the front door.

My time has run out.

"Toast! Not now!" The damn cat is pressing close to the front door, looking up at my hand on the doorknob. The intent in his eyes is clear. *Escape!*

I scoop down and lift him up in my arms. I'd discovered just yesterday that he very much dislikes being carried. Tonight's no different. He lets out a grumpy meow and squirms.

I pull open the door. "Ethan, hi."

"Hey." Ethan's still in his chinos and shirt, now unbuttoned at the top. "Is that the famous cat?"

"Yes. Come in, please, before he gets out. He's an escape artist, this one."

Ethan pushes the door shut with his foot and Toast leaps onto the floor. After a brief moment of hesitation, he winds his way around Ethan's legs.

"And disloyal, apparently," I say. "He never does that to me."

Ethan's warm laughter fills the hallway, and it's a pretty large hallway, so that's saying a lot. He bends down to scratch the cat. "He's just friendly," he says. "Which is more than I can say for you."

"Oh?"

His gaze turns teasing. "You thought you'd just leave your cookies and sneak out of there without saying hello?"

"Oh, I'm sorry about that. You looked busy, and Haven looked like she was having an absolute blast."

"She most certainly was. She's out like a light now."

"That's good. Come on, let's head inside…" I lead him into the kitchen, accepting the basket he hands out to me. "How did you know they were my cookies?"

Ethan raises an eyebrow. "I would recognize your baking anywhere."

I swear, my heart does a double-take at that.

"The basket is labeled," he says. *Property of the Gardners*, written in the bottom. Your aunt and uncle are proper folk, it seems."

I put it down on the counter. "Did you like them?"

"I wish I could say. Unfortunately, they were *very* popular. I saw plenty of kids who looked like they enjoyed them, though."

"Yeah, there were a lot of guests there."

"Too many." He tugs at the collar of his shirt again, putting down the bottle of red wine in front of him. "I've spoken about nothing but school districts and vaccination schedules all day. Would you like a glass of wine and a discussion about something that's not even remotely kid-related?"

There's no way I can resist that, regardless of my sweats, my lack of makeup, or the cheesy romantic comedy still playing in the background.

"I can do you one better," I say, reaching for the cookie tin on the middle of the kitchen counter. Removing the lid, I push it toward him. "I saved a few. One for you, if you'd like."

Ethan stares at them for a long moment. "When did you say your aunt and uncle are coming back?"

"End of August."

"Is there some way to extend their trip?" His eyes dance as he grabs one of the cookies. "I could get used to this level of neighborly camaraderie."

I laugh. It's breathless, both from the compliment and the white lie that has somehow become bigger and bigger. It had seemed so innocent just a few days ago.

"I'll see what I can do," I promise, grabbing two wineglasses from the cupboard. "Why don't you pour and I'll just turn off the TV…"

He does just that, his voice reaching me in the living room. "I can't remember the last time I watched a non-animated film."

"Hey now," I tell him. "That's kid-related talk. I thought you issued a moratorium."

"And I broke it myself," he says. "How pathetic."

I slide onto the barstool opposite him. "Perhaps you're being a tad too harsh on yourself."

"Here," he says, handing me a glass of wine. "I very much appreciate the outfit, by the way."

I glance down at my Washington Polytech T-shirt. "I'm glad you see it that way," I say. "I wasn't really expecting visitors."

"I *am* sorry about just coming over and demanding company. You can kick me out at any time."

"Good to know," I say, making my voice teasing. It's been a while since I flirted like this—and it's *never* been with a man quite like him. There's virtually nothing about Ethan Carter that's *not* intimidating to me, from his charismatic way with people to the tailored fit of his shirt. He has a solid grip on life, it seems. It's not happening to him—he's happening to it.

I wish I could feel like that.

He takes a deep sip of his wine. "It *is* late," he admits. "It was presumptuous of me to barge in like this."

"You didn't barge," I say. "You knocked."

He gives a small smile. "Factual. You really are an engineering student, aren't you?"

"Guilty as charged."

"It's been a long time since I spoke to a student," he says.

I take a sip of my wine. "You were a PhD student yourself, not too long ago."

He snorts, looking away from me. His hair looks even more mussed than usual—like he's been running his hand through it repeatedly in the last few hours. There's a furrow between his brows. "Well, it's been a solid decade since I finished that."

"A very productive decade."

He sighs, looking down at his wine. "Far too productive," he says. "I feel like I've lived three lifetimes in ten years."

I put my head in my hands, leaning forward on the counter. "You do?"

"Yeah. All the shit that's happened, the company, the kids…" He shakes his head and gives me a crooked smile. It feels more real than any he's given me before, somehow. Wry and authentic. "Listen to me. Self-pity is the lowest of emotions."

I smile. "You're not being self-pitying."

"I'm not?"

"No. You just sound tired."

"That's it. Tired of talking to all those parents today," he says, raising his glass accusingly at me. "You were supposed to be there, you know. I was banking on having at least some non-kid related conversation."

Laughing, I nod at the cookie in front of him. "You'll just have to accept that as an apology."

He takes a bite, drawing out the wait, before he gives a solemn nod. "Apology accepted."

"Good." I sink back down onto my stool and take another sip of the red wine. It tastes good—rich and heavy. No doubt expensive.

"So," he says, the green of his eyes inviting. "Tell me about your studies."

So I do. I launch into the details of my thesis with one of the few people who'd actually understand, thrilled when he asks relevant questions. Ethan Carter, listening to me. Ethan Carter, giving advice. It's a pinch-me moment.

We're both deep into our second glass of wine when he shakes his head with a smile. "So the Gardners were hiding a talented systems engineer from me all this time. Who knew?"

The words warm me. "Who knew you were their neighbor?"

"Indeed," he says, looking down at his hands resting on the counter. There's no wedding ring on the left one. "I haven't been much of a neighbor at all in the last few years. There hasn't been time."

"The three-lives-in-a-decade thing?"

"Exactly."

Without the liquid courage, I'd never have been bold enough to ask what I do next. "I can't help but notice... you're raising the girls on your own?"

He nods, eyes still on his wine. "Yes. With Maria's invaluable help, of course, as well as my mother's. But their mother isn't really in the picture."

"I'm sorry," I say.

But Ethan just snorts. "I'm certainly not. I'm *thrilled* not to be married anymore."

"That bad, huh?"

"That bad," he agrees. "But I got two brilliant kids out of the deal, so I can't seem to find it in myself to have any regrets."

I raise my glass, meeting his heavy gaze with my own. There's more he's not saying—and his eyes aren't entirely without bitterness. But I smile, wanting to raise his spirits. "To no regrets," I say.

"To no regrets," he agrees, our glasses touching with a soft *clink*. "And welcome to Greenwood."

The way he says it makes it easy to imagine him saying *welcome home* in that same deep, confident timbre. Something in my stomach flutters.

"Thank you." I take a sip of my wine and wish I was dressed in something different, that my hair wasn't in a braid, that I had put on mascara.

"Do your aunt and uncle often travel this long?" Ethan's gaze is on the kitchen beyond, taking in the pristine countertops. I'm dedicated to keeping the house as clean as possible.

The question bites. "Fairly often, I think."

He looks down at his wine, the thickness of his hair in view. Would he be upset if I admitted it was a silly white lie, one I didn't think would hurt? Would we laugh about it?

"Well, I'm glad they do," he says. "No disrespect to them, but I much prefer your baked goods and engineering expertise."

I smile into my wineglass, twirling it around as if it holds all the answers. *Just tell him.* "Well, it's funny you should say that," I say. "Actually, you know them—"

I'm interrupted by the loud sound of an alarm. Ethan curses, fishing up his phone, and gives me an apologetic look.

"Damn. Sorry, but I have to go. It's around the time Haven often wakes up."

"Not a problem at all."

He stands, looking from his glass of red wine to me and back again. "This was nice. Even if I did barge in."

I slide off the barstool. "Barge in any day."

He smiles that wide, effortless, charming smile again, the one that seems to warm me from my head to my toes. "You might regret you said that," he warns.

"Maybe. But I doubt it."

His smile turns crooked. "Interesting," he remarks. "Well, I'll see you around, Bella."

"Good night."

And then he's gone, the front door shut behind him, and I'm left reeling in the hallway. Ethan Carter in my kitchen, coming over for casual conversation. Even if I never see him again after this very moment, he's made my summer.

I shouldn't have lied to him. I resolve to tell him my true reason for staying here the very next time I see him, running through potential ways of phrasing it in my head. Besides, my racing heart is definitely overthinking all the possible implications of this. There is no way he's interested in me, as a man to a woman.

I count out the reasons as I lie in bed, forcing a semblance of logic. One—he's twelve years older than me. He wouldn't want a student. Two—he has two kids under the age of ten. That's his priority, as it should be. Three—he's, well, *Ethan Carter*. He can have anyone. Why on earth would he want me?

They're good, sound reasons. And yet, I fall asleep to the image of his wide smile and the strength of his hands as he uncorked the wine bottle.

So yeah, I'm pretty screwed.

6

ETHAN

The coming days are an absolute mess.

Work is on the verge of madness—my chief engineer needs to take a few personal days a week before we launch our latest product—and I'm left trying to fit eighteen hours of work into a fourteen-hour day. Gone are the early morning runs, as are any social events after Haven and Evie have gone to bed. I'm at my computer for so long each night that I should just give up and propose to my MacBook. It's time we made it official, anyway. We've been living in sin for long enough.

It's late one such night when I see a man leaving Bella's house. In the dim lighting from the streetlamp, his face is young and unlined, his hair dark.

I can't see her, but he's holding a paper bag in hand. My mind immediately fills it to the brim with cookies or brownies or whatever else she might have given him. Her heart, perhaps.

The disappointment I feel at the sight is unwarranted. She's been nice. Neighborly and nice, and nothing more than that. Of course she has a boyfriend. A smart, beautiful young woman like her? Of course she does.

I shake my head at my own stupidity. Years without a relationship and months without a woman's touch have addled my brain. I could only hope that she didn't think I was a complete creep, coming over unannounced with a bottle of wine like that after my kids were asleep.

Remembering some of the things I'd said... embarrassment burns. I'd mentioned my ex-wife. My kids. Asked how long she'd be staying here this summer. Yes, she must have noted my interest.

When I finally shut my laptop, it's past midnight and my mind feels like it's turned to sludge. There are too few hours in the day, I have a million things to do, and yet my mine keeps replaying the image of the young man leaving her house.

It's not improving my mood.

The door to my home office is pushed open. Haven is standing there in her polka dot pajamas, blinking at the sharp light. I twist my desk lamp away.

"Daddy?"

"I'm here." I push my chair back and scoop down to pick her up. She fits easily against my side, her hands on my neck.

"You weren't in your bed."

"No, I'm sorry." Shutting the door to my study, I walk with her over to my bedroom. It's rare that she comes over at night anymore. "Did you have a bad dream?"

She nods. "Can't remember it now."

"That's good. We don't need to remember bad things."

Turning on the dimmed lights in my bedroom, I pull back the covers with one hand and put her down with the other. She stretches out like a cat before curling up on her side.

Her hand won't let go of my shirt. "I'll be back, baby girl," I tell her. "Just give me a minute."

"S'kay."

When I return, teeth brushed and in a clean T-shirt, she's so quiet and still that I'm sure she's asleep. But she turns to face me across the wide expanse of my bed.

"What is it?"

Her voice is a whisper. "When will Mom visit?"

Ah. She knows I don't like this question, though I've always tried to be nothing but civil when my ex-wife is discussed. I could bear it if Lyra's flakiness only extended to me. But to our daughters? It makes my hands knuckle into fists.

"Daddy?"

I scoot closer and run a hand over her soft hair. "I don't know," I reply. I've always tried to be honest with my kids. Don't know if it's the right strategy, but it's the best one I have. "She comes and goes as she wants, a bit. I know you miss her."

Haven shakes her head at that. "Don't miss her. Not at all."

The denial cuts. "It's okay if you do and it's okay if you don't. You can feel whatever you like about Mom. About me too, for that matter."

She nods and nestles her head against my hand, her breath evening out. When she speaks again, it's so soft that I barely hear the words.

"You liked those brownies. The ones the neighbor made."

What on earth?

"Yes," I murmur, "I did. Why?"

"No reason."

There's no further explanation and within a minute, Haven's breathing calm, her form limp beside me. I stare up at the dark ceiling and try to trace the conversational paths that led her to that question, but I can't find any.

Kids.

―――

Haven's master plan is revealed the next day.

Because when I open the front door to my house, home with time to spare before dinner, there aren't three girls in my house. There are four.

Bella is standing by my kitchen island with one of my daughters on either side of her, Evie kneeling on a chair to be able to reach. Maria is sitting opposite them, smiling as she watches.

"And then we crack the eggs… yes, just like that," Bella instructs Haven. "Be careful not to get any shells in the mix."

"I want to try! Me!" Evie holds on to the edge of the counter and bounces in a way that makes me very nervous she'll slip off.

"Of course you do. Here, why don't you try in this bowl…"

She hands Evie three eggs and a much smaller bowl. My youngest immediately busies herself with smashing them against the rim, fierce concentration on her small, ruddy face.

"What's this?" I ask. "Have you started a cooking channel?"

Bella jumps at my appearance and I curse myself for scaring her, *again*. One of my many talents, it seems.

"Daddy!" Haven runs around the kitchen island, heedless of the flour on her hands as she hugs my legs. "Surprise!"

I put a hand on the back of her head. "Surprise indeed. What's this?"

Bella's gaze is chagrined, looking from me to Haven. My eldest doesn't notice. "You've been so busy," she says, "working working working. So we're making brownies for you. So you feel better."

"That's really kind," I say, wondering how much is for me and how much Haven just wanted to learn how to make them. It doesn't matter. The gesture is sweet.

She grabs hold of my hand and tugs me toward the kitchen island. I follow obediently, my eyes on Bella as she stands rosy-eyed and purposeful, whisking away. How had she been talked into this?

"Bake with us," Haven says.

"I should change."

Bella looks at my clothes. "It might be too late for that suit."

"Right." Looking down, I take in the flour stains and the trace of batter from Haven's hug. "Rest in peace, old guy. We had a good run."

From the corner of my eye, I see Maria slip off the barstool and head out of the kitchen. Had that been a smile on her lips?

I lift Evie up and she squeals with delight as I place her on the counter. She's rarely allowed to sit up here. "So," I tell them. "What are we making?"

The next hour sees perhaps the most uncoordinated baking

ever done by mankind. Turns out my kids aren't brilliant at following orders, and Bella is timid about issuing them.

"Listen to Bella," I tell Haven once. "You wanted to learn how to make brownies, didn't you?"

She nods. "Yes. Sorry, Bella."

My neighbor's lovely niece smiles, the same soft, kind smile she'd given me the other night. "Not a problem. Do you want to help me add the chocolate bits?"

"Yes!" she says. "Can I taste a few?"

"Me too!" This is Evie, of course.

Bella laughs, and I laugh with her. "It's hopeless," I tell her. "Ambitions run high, but the follow-through is weak with kids under eight."

"So I'm learning," she says, her eyes lingering on mine for just a moment too long. It's such a stunning combination, brown hair and blue eyes. A killer combo. Even with the apron on, the form of her body is clear. Like clockwork, the memory of her topless and sunbathing resurfaces.

And my mind is back on Impossible Avenue, bypassing Never-Gonna-Happen Street and veering dangerously close to Creep Gutter.

I try to focus on the task at hand—*you're baking with your daughters, man*—but the awareness of Bella as soft and warm and womanly stays with me.

She's off-limits, I tell myself. *Remember the man who left her place? She's taken.*

The kids watch in fascinated silence as Bella opens the oven and puts in the baking pan. I hold them back, a hand on each of their shoulders.

"Hot," I tell them. "No touching."

Haven sighs. She's been told that a thousand times by now. But Evie still loves doing what she's not supposed to do, and it doesn't help that she's mischievous to the nth degree.

"That's it!" Bella says. "Now we wait for twenty-five minutes."

Evie groans, but not Haven. She claps her hand. "And *then* we eat."

"Yes. Well, after they've cooled for a bit."

"And *then* you'll be happy, Daddy."

I blink at that. I didn't think they'd noticed how stressed I'd been this past week... or did she mean longer than that? "Thank you," I murmur, avoiding Bella's gaze.

"Boring," Evie announces, skipping away from watching the oven. "I want to play."

Haven dances after her sister into the living room—which serves as a playroom, more often than not, given that I never have visitors. *Usually.*

Bella looks over at me and silence falls thick between us. "I'm sorry," she says. "For being here when you got home. You didn't know... I thought you did. That this was your idea."

I wave her excuse away. "Coming home to three beautiful girls baking? I can think of worse things."

She looks down, a blush on her cheeks. "All right. Good."

Damn it, there I go again, saying things that I shouldn't be. I'd completely lost my game *and* I'm too eager, somehow both at the same time.

"I'm curious, though," I continue. "How did they rope you in? Bribes? Blackmail?"

Bella chuckles, reaching up to secure her ponytail. Long tendrils—are they called side bangs?—frame her face. "Nothing so malicious. Maria and Haven came over and asked if I was free to help. They said it was okay with you... I assumed you knew."

"I get it," I say, wondering why they'd done that—and why Maria had agreed to it. No doubt it was Haven's idea. "You did nothing wrong. Neither did they, for that matter. You're always welcome."

"Thank you."

"Not that I'm sure why you'd *want* to. They can be a handful."

She smiles, and it's soft again. "They're brilliant kids. Very smart, too."

Christ. It's not enough that I want her with an almost physical ache—I really need to get laid, holy shit—but now she's complimenting my children too. How had the Gardners kept her away all these years? How had I never met her before?

I would have remembered.

"They are."

She bends to look at the brownies in the oven, revealing the soft nape of her neck. "A while longer, I think. And then they'll make Daddy happy again?"

I give an exaggerated groan at that and she laughs, just as I'd hoped she would. "The things kids say," I complain. "I have no idea where she got that from."

"You don't?"

Perhaps it's the spark in her eyes—teasing and kind at the same time. But I answer her, regardless. "There's a lot at work right now. There's always a lot, but this week…"

"I've heard about your latest launch," Bella says.

My eyebrows shoot high at that. "You have?"

"I study engineering with classmates who are just a tad obsessed with these sorts of things, so yes, I've heard about it."

"Classmates, huh?"

She leans against the kitchen counter. "Yeah. We have an online group. There's always a ton of discussion."

Classmates her own age, which translates to guys her own age. I feel a million years old suddenly, with this giant house and kids and no time at all to give a girl like her what she deserves and expects. Dating and going out and having fun, flirty adventures together. Between my kids and my work, I'm already splitting myself in twos. I don't have threes.

But there I go again. *She's taken.*

"Sounds fun," I say. "Planning on throwing massive student parties out here?"

She chuckles. "God, no."

"Your aunt and uncle would likely have your head," I say, thinking about the small label attached to the bottom of the basket she'd brought cookies in last weekend. It seemed a tad, well, neurotic.

"Oh, they would." She runs a hand over her neck. "But about that, Ethan… it's so stupid. But I need to say it. When we first met, I actually—"

"No need." I don't think I could bear to hear the words, the kind phrasing. Because that's what'll hurt the most—the kindness in her voice as she gently turns me down. "I know you have a boyfriend, and you don't have to worry about any designs or expectations from me. I just want to be friends." I hold up my hands to drive the point home, hoping she won't elaborate.

Bella looks down. A fierce blush colors her cheeks, advancing down her neck. "All right."

"I'm sorry if I've come off like I… well. I'm sorry," I say.

She nods. "Okay. You haven't, you know, but that's good to know. And just for the record, I don't actually have a boyfriend."

Oh.

Fuck.

"That's what I get for assuming, I guess. I saw a man leaving your house late the other night."

She looks up, embarrassment clear in her eyes, and I want to sink through the floor. I've just done it again—put my foot in my mouth. I'm not just off my game, I've lost it completely.

"Never mind," I add. "It's not my business. I shouldn't have assumed, or asked. You do you."

"No, it's okay," she hurries, kind as always, trying to put *me* at ease when I'm the one who's throwing around implications. "It was my brother."

Ethan, you colossal idiot.

"Your brother?"

"Yes. He came over for dinner. It's not…" She shakes her head, her voice quiet now. "I don't have a boyfriend."

Silence between us again. It's not comfortable this time. My words, spoken harshly in defense earlier, seem to hang between us. *No expectations or designs. Just friends.*

"But that's all right," she adds, like the silence is too much to bear. "I'd like to be friends, too."

"Good," I say. "Awesome."

The padding of feet is the only warning before Haven throws herself at my legs. "Are they done?" she asks Bella. "It's been *forever.*"

Bella's face is wiped clean of any tension, her eyes serene as she gazes down at my daughter. I watch through a daze as they inspect the brownies, as they take them out from the oven, even as I obligingly *ooh* and *aah* at the finished result. And when Bella leaves soon thereafter, giving Haven a high five and promising to return some other day, there's only one thought left.

I've blown everything.

7

BELLA

So he wanted to be just friends.

The memory alone is enough to make my cheeks scald. Had my awestruck interest been that obvious to him, that he felt he had to tell me that?

I suppose he must be used to it, though. A man like Ethan Carter probably has women throwing themselves at him daily, if not for his money than for his status. Or for his looks—they're quite enough in their own right. He's a catch in every imaginable way.

"Bella?" my brother asks. "Are you even listening?"

"Yes, I'm sorry."

A sigh. "I can't wait until you're done with your thesis and actually get back down to earth," he says. "You're always off somewhere else at the moment."

I step onto the patio and into the late afternoon sun. This garden truly is something to behold—I'd give up the house gladly as long as I had access to this kind of paradise daily. "I'm just a bit distracted."

"That's what I mean." Wyatt sighs again. "And you're *sure* I can't come stay in that massive house of yours? I don't get why I can't. I'd be in that pool *daily.*"

It hurts to stay firm, but I do it. "You know why I said no. No one else is staying over, either. Wilma and Trina aren't."

"But I'm your brother."

Yes, and with a habit of always bringing his friends around, of breaking vases, of leaving a trail of Cheetos dust in his wake…

"I'm not allowed to have stay-over guests," I say firmly. "It's explicitly stated in the agreement I signed."

"They'd never know."

"You don't think a place like this has cameras and stuff?" I stop at the edge of the pool and dip my bare toes into the water. Cool and lovely.

"You're such a bore, Bella," Wyatt complains. "If *I* had a mansion for the summer, I'd invite *you* to stay for as long as you'd like."

He's playing on my conscience now. My little brother is excellent at doing that. "Stop it," I tell him. "I've already told you no, and explained my reasons. It's not personal. I'm like… like a steward here. And I can't screw it up. Besides, you have a place to stay."

"Fine." Wyatt's sigh across the line is flippant now. "I get it, I get it."

Sure he does. "Good. But you know you're welcome to visit on occasion. Just you, though."

"I know. Thanks."

Something moves in my peripheral vision. No, *someone*. Ethan is in the oak tree again. He's not alone this time, as a second man sits higher up in an adjacent tree.

Ethan gives a wave.

"Bella?" Wyatt asks.

"Yes, I'm still here. Sorry, but I have to go."

"Is your thesis calling?" Kyle teases. Now that he's asked his question, *again,* and I've told him no, *again,* the tension is gone between us.

When he visited last week for dinner, he'd walked around and marveled, going so far as to open closets in the master bedroom. That was when I'd shoved him down the hallway and pointed at the stairs.

"Yes. Words don't write themselves, you know."

"Talk to you later, Bells."

"Love you."

"Love you too."

Slipping the phone into the back pocket of my jean shorts, I head to where Ethan is perched on the bough. A trace of faint humiliation still burns, but I force it down. Surely we can discuss a few nice, neighborly things, like the weather. Just keep it friendly.

I rock back on my heels. "Are you making it a habit? Sitting up there?"

"Better cell phone reception," he says. "Who knew?"

I bite my lip to keep from smiling. "Right."

"I didn't mean to overhear your conversation."

"That's okay. What are you doing, though?"

He glances over at the man in the other tree, currently measuring the width of the trunk at different intervals. "I'm a terrible father," he says.

"I very much doubt that."

His smile becomes crooked again. "I'm hiring a company to build the treehouse. Actual professionals. Go ahead, tell me I'm a copout."

I pretend to consider, furrowing my brow. "It is definitely a strike against you," I deadpan. "I *might* consider calling social services."

He nods gravely. "You take your civic duty seriously. I can respect that."

I laugh. "In truth, I don't think it's bad at all. Professionals know what they're doing, right?"

"And I don't," he says, smile wide. "Not to mention this is meant to be a surprise, and my hammering away out here an hour every evening won't exactly be… inconspicuous."

"Sure won't." I glance from Ethan to the man in the neighboring tree, still hard at work examining branches and boughs. "It'll be big?"

Ethan shrugs. "No idea. I told them to design whatever will fit and make it special."

"I had a treehouse growing up."

"You did?"

"Yes. It was filled with cushions and in the summer my mother hung string lights inside."

Ethan's eyes widen. "Damn. I hadn't thought of that."

"Of what would be inside it?"

"No, not at all."

And he looks so... I can't resist. "I can help with that. If you need help, I mean. Picking out pillows and a throw rug and maybe hanging lights... if it's meant to be a surprise. For Haven and Evie?"

Nice, Bella. Very eloquent.

But Ethan gives a grateful nod. "I'd appreciate that."

"Of course. Just let me know when you want to look at it."

"Is it terrible of me to suggest right now?" he asks. "My mother has Haven and Evie today, and that doesn't happen all that often."

I smooth a hand over my shorts. "Of course! It's a Saturday—I wasn't planning on working anyway."

"And no plans with all those student friends of yours?" he teases. "I haven't heard you throw a rager yet."

"And you won't," I say. "Should I come over? I can bring my laptop and we could, I don't know, order some stuff?"

His shoulders relax a tad. "Perfect. Yes, let's do that."

Fifteen minutes later we're sitting on his giant patio, side by side on a sofa, looking at pictures of treehouses. Google has served us a smorgasbord from the quaint to the outlandish.

Ethan laughs as I scroll over images that are clearly not for us. "Bathtubs... Wall-mounted TVs... people really go all out," he says. "Wait. What about that?"

The image is of a small treehouse with child-size wooden chairs. A throw rug on the floor. A hammock attached in the background. Lights running over the ceiling in a zigzag pattern.

"That's perfect," I say.

"Did yours look like that?"

"Yes," I say, "if you imagine a crooked floor and far less space. The do-it-yourself version of this."

He shifts closer, the heat of his thigh pressing against mine. "That sounds idyllic."

"It was, at times."

"At times?"

His voice is too soft and too close. It's hard to think. "Yes. I... my younger brother was often in trouble and my father wasn't always around. I spent most of my childhood with my head buried in my schoolbooks."

"That sounds familiar," he murmurs.

"The schoolbook part?"

"The entire thing," he says. "You're the eldest?"

"Yes. You are as well?"

"Most definitely." Ethan smiles, and it's the same crooked thing that he'd given me in my kitchen, the one that's wry and amused and genuine at the same time. Maybe that's how he meets all of life's challenges, with a smile and boundless competence.

I wet my lips. "We should order the stuff online."

"I can do that," he says. "Two chairs, small table, a bunch of pillows and lights."

"You got it. Awesome."

"Thanks for suggesting this. Without you they would have raced up the ladder and found the place empty."

"Oh, I doubt that. You would have figured something out." I twist away from the heat of his skin on mine, meeting his gaze. "You're not actually a bad father."

He doesn't respond to that. He looks down instead, gaze on my bare shoulder. "I'm sorry for the other day."

"The other day?"

"For assuming you had a boyfriend. And then for assuming... well." Ethan's not smiling now, a furrow in his brow. "I was out of line."

"That's okay," I murmur. This close, his green eyes have hazel flecks in them.

He shakes his head. "It was presumptuous, what I said."

"I understand."

He glances down, the thick honey-brown of his hair coming into view. It's the first time I've seen him struggle to find his wording. "Even so, I would like to clear the air."

The doorbell rings out loudly behind us. Ethan curses and looks down at the thick watch on his wrist.

"Damn."

"Everything okay?"

"Yes. Please give me a moment."

He strides back into the house. I gently shut my laptop, clasping it to my chest. There is real danger here. I'd felt it from the beginning, but then it had been a foolish dream, a crush like the ones I'd had on actors and singers as a teenager. Distant and harmless. Now I feel like I'm standing on the edge of tumbling into something deeper and far more hopeless.

When Ethan returns, I'm already standing, prepared to leave.

"Bella, I'm sorry. I have a dinner tonight, and the chef just arrived to prepare."

"I understand."

"A few friends are coming over." He gives me another one of those smiles—crooked, hesitant, genuine. "You said you had nothing planned today. Why don't you stay?"

I have no idea what to say to that. Can't even form the words.

"Feel free to leave whenever," he adds. "But there will be great food."

And great company, I think, my treacherous mouth almost uttering the words aloud. "Thank you, that sounds great."

His smile widens. "Perfect. They should be here in... ah, about half an hour. Let me just finish up out here with the contractor and hop into the shower."

"Oh! Yes, of course. I'll do the same—I'll be back."

"Excellent." He pauses on the steps off the patio, looking back at me. The sunlight gilds his hair. "I'm glad you're staying."

The words make me feel like I'm floating all the way back into my larger-than-life house and the three-person-sized shower. Wilma and Trina would have a fit if I told them about this.

Perhaps that's why I haven't. Ethan feels like my secret, like a potential friend that's too good and too elusive to talk about. It's as if the second I speak about him, he'll disappear, the magic spell broken.

Nerves make my throat dry and I clear it twice, standing outside his front door and waiting for him to open it. The dress I'm wearing had felt appropriate—knee-length, black, sleeveless—but I have no idea how he's dressed.

On impulse, I'd grabbed a bottle out of the Gardners' wine fridge and taken a picture of the label to later replace it, praying it's not a thousand-dollar bottle. I clasp it in front of me like armor.

He opens the door with a flourish, eyes sweeping over my form. "Bella," he says. Thankfully, he's not in black tie, but wearing a pair of dark trousers and a button-down.

"Ethan." I hold up the wine bottle. "I didn't have time to bake, so…"

He smiles, accepting the bottle. "This will do. A good vintage, too. Do you know wine?"

"A little." A very, very little. "I know I like to drink it."

He snorts, leading me in through the kitchen. A focused young woman in white is preparing what looks like lamb chops. He wasn't joking when he said a chef had arrived.

"The others are outside," he tells me. "Let me introduce you."

We step out onto the patio and the bubbling conversation between the guests stills. Four pairs of eyes turn to me.

"Hello," I say, giving a little wave, my gaze moving across each of the guests in turn. My stomach sinks as I take in the familiar faces. He hasn't just invited a few friends—he's invited some of the city's most famous.

There's Cole Porter, whose face is regularly in the news for some building project or another. His sister is here too. I'd once seen her on a morning talk show discussing fall fashion trends. She's looking at me curiously now, impeccably dressed.

By her side... oh. The man is vaguely familiar in an almost threatening way. Dark hair and dark eyes narrow in on me.

But Ethan just stops by the table like this group of people is nothing out of the ordinary for him, because of course it isn't. He fits right in.

"This is Bella Simmons," he says. "She's my neighbor's niece, living next door over the summer."

I nod obediently as my stupid, stupid lie is repeated in front of the city's elite. "That's me," I add another nail to the coffin.

"Bella, meet Cole, Skye, Nick and Blair." He gestures in turn, as if I don't already know.

"It's a pleasure to meet you," the short brunette says—Skye. She's the only one I've never seen before. "Come on over, have a seat."

I do, sinking down in the chair next to her. "It's lovely to meet all of you."

"So you're Ethan's new neighbor?" Cole says. He looks exactly like he does in the newspapers. Somehow that makes it easier to respond, as if I'm talking to the image of him rather than the man himself.

"Yes, at least for the summer."

Ethan takes the chair opposite me, handing me a glass of wine. "Bella's a PhD student," he adds. "In systems engineering."

Blair gives me a wide smile. With her golden hair and socialite status, I feel like I've been hit by the sun. "Engineering? That's very impressive," she says. "I'm pretty sure I failed math in high school."

"You did," her brother supplies. "I remember."

Nick drapes an arm behind her chair. "You've done fine without it," he says. "Ethan, thanks for finally inviting us 'round."

"I figured I had to pay back eventually," Ethan says. "Lord knows I've eaten enough meals at yours."

"We haven't been keeping score," Skye says.

"Yes we have," Cole interjects. "This is nice, but you're still in the red."

Faced with their banter and obvious familiarity, some of my nerves lessen. The wine helps—as does Skye's soft questions at my side. Turns out she's an author, but she wasn't famous or influential at all before she married Cole. Her kind smile tells me she understands that they can all be a bit… well, intimidating.

"Ethan's such a great guy," she tells me in an aside during dessert. "But I'm sure you've already figured that out."

I nod, swallowing the delicious bite of tiramisu I'd just taken. Across the table, Ethan's eyes glance toward us.

"I have," I say carefully.

"So are his daughters. Evie is a few years older than our son, but I hope they'll be playmates one day." Her smile warms. "He's very smart, too."

"Your son?"

"No, Ethan." Skye laughs, glancing briefly at her husband, consumed in some discussion with the others. "Although Isaac rolled over onto his tummy the other day, quite early too, at three-and-a-half months. Cole is convinced that means he's a genius in the making."

The obvious fondness in her voice makes me smile. "I'm sure he is, with parents like you."

"Do you want kids?"

I nod. "One day, yes."

"Ethan," Skye says, involving him in our conversation. "How about you? Do you want to have more kids?"

Oh no. Has she assumed Ethan and I are…?

Ethan takes a sip of his wine, the picture of ease. "Maybe," he says. "Although at the moment it's a very distant priority, I have to say."

"Understandable," she says.

"I stepped on Legos just yesterday and vowed never again. But who knows?"

"Who knows indeed," Cole adds, showing that he's been listening to the whole conversation. A look passes between him and Nick. "Not to mention a man like you isn't made for single life."

I watch, wide-eyed, as Ethan lets out a groan. "Not this again. Not in my own house, damn it."

Nick raises his hands. "We won't."

"Even if we're all thinking it," Blair adds.

"But we won't," Nick says again, more firmly.

A smile breaks across my face. So they've been pestering him about his single-hood for a while? "If it makes you feel any better," I tell Ethan, "I'm told the same thing by most of my friends too."

Blair's eyes go round. "How perfect."

"Are they equally annoying?" Ethan asks me, ignoring the others.

I respond in kind, focusing only on him. "More, I think. They don't know when to stop."

"Oh, neither do we," Cole says. A second later, someone slaps him on the shoulder—I hear the sound and the muffled *ow*.

Ethan's eyes blaze and his smile is private, one that ignores the people around us. It sends a shiver down my spine. "Interesting," he murmurs.

I look down at my dessert and try to hide the blush on my cheeks. It's always been the thing to give me away, like a giant, heat-infused billboard. *Look! Bella cares!*

Cole and Skye leave shortly after that. "We can't be away from Isaac for too long," they say, almost in unison. Blair and Nick decide it's time to head out too, Blair mentioning something about an early morning as she kisses Ethan on the cheek.

"It was so nice to meet you," Blair tells me, giving me a hug. "I'm already looking forward to the next time."

And then they're all gone, leaving so quickly that I don't

have the time to follow them out the front door. "Wow," I say, leaning against a wall in the hallway. "Were they in a rush?"

"Of a sorts, I think," Ethan says darkly. But then he sighs, and the furrow in his brow smooths out. "Do you want a glass of wine to finish the night?"

"I'd like that, yes. My commute home is pretty short, you know."

"Oh, I know."

I sink down on the barstool in the kitchen and watch as he uncorks another bottle. "She smells nice," I say.

His lips twitch. "Who?"

"Blair. I've only ever seen her on TV before, or in magazines."

"She's in a fair bit of those," Ethan says, handing me a glass. He leans against the kitchen island next to me—close, but not touching.

Nerves dance in my stomach at the proximity. "Not to mention... well, the others. Impressive friends."

He raises an eyebrow. "But annoying."

"But annoying," I agree, wondering if it's all the wine or his nearness that's making my tongue this loose. "My friends are the same way. They see being single as wrong, somehow. An unnatural state that has to be fixed at all costs."

He gives a slow nod. "But it's one you prefer?"

I look away from his gaze. "*Prefer* is a strong word. Accept might be better. I'm not opposed to it. You have to find the right person—and that's not easy."

"No," he says, "it's not. I'd rather be single the rest of my life than together with the wrong person."

"Cheers to that," I say, holding up my glass. He toasts it gently. "Is that how you felt about your marriage?"

The words are out before I can stop them. It's a presumptuous question, but it doesn't explode between us. It fizzles instead as Ethan regards me. The furrow between his brows is back, making him look older than thirty-six.

"Yes," he says. "It was wrong from start to finish."

There's more I want to ask. Why go through with it at all,

then? But he shifts closer and the scent of him, of faint cologne and wine and man, hits me.

"Not that I have the time now," he says, eyes on mine. "Not to myself, and not to date. None of the others understand that."

"I get it," I say, wetting my lips. "You have other priorities."

"I do," he agrees.

"Makes sense."

"It does." His hand shifts closer on the kitchen island, our fingers touching. His index finger against my pinky. All my senses narrow to that brief contact. I'm back on the precipice, hovering right on the edge. *Flee or fight.* Stay or run.

"About the other day," I say. "You told me... well, you were very clear."

He exhales. "I was a fool. I didn't mean what I said."

"You didn't mean it?" My eyes are on our hands. I move my fingers over his—long, broad-knuckled, tan. A man's hands. His skin is warm to the touch.

"No," he murmurs, "I didn't."

My entire body tightens at what I see on his face. Gone is the carefree smile or the teasing glint in his eyes. No, his features are focused. I tilt my face upwards—it's a natural response to his gaze, my body reacting on instinct.

And he takes what I offer.

He bends his head and presses his lips against mine. Once, twice. Tentative kisses, but there's leashed strength behind it. Like he's not sure how I'll respond or if this is allowed, but he just has to try.

It's allowed, I kiss back. *It's encouraged.* And when he cups the side of my face and tilts my head back further, I sigh against his lips. Maybe that was the sign he was looking for, the permission he needed. Because he deepens the kiss, my lips opening for him, a warm sweep of his tongue over my lower lip.

Oh, dear Lord. My hands find a grip on his shirt, tugging, and he's pulling me up and out of the chair. His hand settles on my lower back, flattening, pushing me more firmly against the solid length of his body. I keep my grip on his shirt, though—for good measure.

And all the while Ethan continues to kiss me deeply, leisurely, expertly. Nothing else matters now except that single fact. My head feels dizzy and I clasp my arms around his neck to be sure I'm not floating away.

My hands find their own path up his neck, twisting in his hair and tugging. He groans at that. "Too much?" I mumble, but he swallows the words before they're fully out.

"Not enough," he murmurs back. There's such longing in his kiss—such need and want and strong, sure confidence. *Trust me,* it says. *I know what to do. Let me do it.*

I kiss him back with the same surety. His hands on my body, one sliding up to grip my hair and the other down to the curve of my ass. Tearing my lips away from his, I kiss along the rough edge of his jaw. I've wanted to do that since I'd first seen him.

His hands fist in the fabric of my dress. "Bella…"

"Mmm?"

"I have nothing to offer you."

I force my gaze back to his, away from the tanned, warm skin of his neck. His eyes are on fire.

But he must have seen the confusion in mine, because he steps back, breaking the warm, close contact between us. It feels like a loss. "There were a lot of jokes about how I'm single tonight," he murmurs, "but I *am* single for a reason. I meant what I said. I don't have time."

"I know." Heat and shame rises on my cheeks. Is he rebuffing me again? Twice in a week must be a record.

"I can't offer you what I should be able to. Time to do this properly."

"Seemed like you were doing it properly to me."

"Beautiful girl," he says with a smile. "Yes, that part I know how to do."

"I get it, you know." I put my hand on his on the kitchen counter and try to focus my scattered thoughts. "You have your daughters. And your business. And your treehouse."

"Yes, don't forget the treehouse."

"I'm not asking for anything," I say, pulling my hand away from his. "Thank you for a lovely evening, and for the nightcap."

"Thank you for staying," he says, just as quietly. "And Bella…"

I pause in the hallway. "Yeah?"

"I wish I had the time to date you properly."

"Well, for what it's worth," I murmur, "so do I."

8
ETHAN

I'd told Bella I didn't have the time to date her. To give her what she deserved. Which made it *very* unfair that she didn't give me the same space. No, the taste of her is on my tongue from morning to evening, the feel of her body branded in my palms.

If I'd craved female company before, the brief brush of her breasts against my chest hadn't helped. What had been a steady flame now feels like a raging wildfire of need.

At work, my assistant asks me what's wrong—that's how irritable I've become. And when Cole texts me to say thanks for dinner and ask how "the cute neighbor girl is doing," I contemplate ghosting him.

Had I blown it? Destroyed both the budding attraction and the cautious, kind friendship that had been growing between us? In the last few weeks, that had felt like something special.

I shake my head at my own dithering. *You can't offer her anything—just a few nights in your bed, and she's worth more than that. Stop considering it.* But then my body would remember the feel of hers against it and the cycle began anew again.

I don't see her for the rest of the week, forcing myself to focus on my work and my kids and nothing in between. I'm not a little proud of that, either. Keeping myself from knocking on her door feels like a Herculean feat.

"Can Bella come over?" Haven asked mid-week, which made my resolution falter. "Maybe she can teach us how to make muffins!"

"Muwwfins!" Evie had exclaimed.

Miraculously, I'd stood firm. I told them Bella was busy studying but they were free to ask Maria if she could teach them to make something. A minor victory for mankind, perhaps, but a giant one for me.

It all ends Friday evening. Coming home from work, my mind fracturing at the seams from hard day of work I'd had, I see her.

Bella is talking to Maria on my driveway, a glittery football in her hands. She's just as stunning as I remembered.

The shirtdress she's wearing is tied around her waist, highlighting her form, the late evening sunlight gilding her long brown hair. A soft smile plays on her features.

I park, getting out of the car with a hand on the roof. "Hey."

"Hi," she says, looking from me to Maria. "Well, that was it, really. Sorry about the delay in getting it back to you. I didn't notice it at first."

Maria shakes her head. "They haven't missed it," she says with a nod in my direction. "They have more toys than they need."

"Oh, far too many," I agree.

She smiles at us both and heads back into the house, football in hand, leaving me and Bella alone. The silence is awkward. It's never been awkward before.

"I'm sorry," Bella says. "Haven or Evie kicked a football onto my lawn and I was just returning it. I didn't mean to—"

"Don't apologize," I say. I think I could stand anything but that. "They're always kicking things over—I'm surprised your aunt and uncle haven't formally complained yet. Thank you."

She runs a hand over the back of her neck. "It's not a problem."

"Good," I say. "I don't want things to be…"

"Weird? Odd?" Bella smiles, the unusual mix of humor and

kindness in her eyes that so disarms me. "It doesn't have to be. I understood your point the other night."

At the moment, it's very difficult to remember exactly why I'd been so insistent on making that very point. "All right. Good," I say. "Just so you know that it's not... Jesus, Bella, it's not for a lack of wanting."

That's it, the shade of her cheeks is my new favorite color. "All right," she echoes. "Good. Me neither, for the record."

I force myself to clear my throat and *not* focus on that admission, not right now, or I'd kiss her right here for all to see. "It's good I have you here, actually," I say. "The treehouse installation is tomorrow. I'm sure they'll be making a fair bit of noise."

Her eyes light up. "That's lovely! The kids are gone for the day?"

"They're staying at my mother's this weekend, to give me time to set it all up." I clear my throat again. "Anyway, just so you know."

She backs away, her smile slanted. "Let me know if you need help with anything. I'm home all weekend."

"Thank you." Oh, what a dangerous offer. Watching her retreat up her driveway, my mind refocuses on the words she'd spoken earlier. I play them over and over in her soft voice. *Me neither.* She wants me too, and it's getting harder and harder to accept that I just don't have the time she deserves.

The next day is the summer's hottest on record for the year. Sweat runs down my back at ten a.m., and the humidity is not helping. Nor is a scheduled treehouse installation with ten men working in the heat.

I bring my laptop out onto the patio and reply to emails while I watch them work. An organized team with all the measurements and materials already prepared offsite, it's a joy to watch them assemble it all.

I wonder what Bella is seeing on the other side. Is she lying by the side of the pool in the same bikini I'd first seen her in? Are the workers enjoying the view?

No, Ethan, abort that train of thought. *Cut it right off.* Valiantly, I manage to only circle back to it a *few* dozen times throughout the day. By late afternoon, the treehouse is complete. Beautiful redwood shingles on the roof, with windows and an ascending ladder. The contractor had spoken about adding a deck at a later stage—I'd said no, not now… maybe when the kids got bigger.

I bid the workers goodbye and climb up into the structure. It holds under my weight. I'm here to inspect it, but I can't fool myself as to why I look out the east-facing window first.

Ah, blessed relief—Bella's there.

Sitting by the pool, a skirt and a bikini top on, her hair unbound. She has a book in hand. I've gone and given my kids the best view of the entire property.

Shaking my head at my thoughts, I look around the space. It'll be good with the bits and bobs Bella helped me to order. Haven and Evie will be over the moon when they see it.

"Ethan?"

I look back out the window to see Bella shading her eyes and looking in my direction.

I lean out the open window. "What do you think?"

"It's beautiful!" she calls back. "Well, the part I can see from here!"

"It's quite spacious," I say. "Maybe I can rent it out to college students after the girls are gone."

"A bit of extra income."

"Every penny counts."

She fans herself with the book, her thumb stuck in to keep her place. "It's terribly hot today."

"The worst," I agree. "I'm regretting not putting in a pool right about now."

Her fanning abruptly stops. "Well, why don't you come over and swim in mine?"

What an offer.

There are a hundred reasons why I shouldn't, but not one of them seems convincing at the moment. Not with her smiling up at me in nothing but a bikini top and a short skirt. The water behind her beckons.

"Come on, Rapunzel," she teases. "Let down your hair."

That does it. "How can I resist, with an invitation like that?"

Ten minutes later she opens the gate for me, now in my swim trunks, a towel over my shoulder. She's slipped out of her skirt—greeting me clad in nothing but her dark-blue bikini and the fall of her long hair.

"Lifesaver," I tell her, my hand opening and closing at my side. The taste of her bursts forth on my tongue again, a reminder of our kiss—of having someone to hold in my arms again.

"I'm just glad for the company," she says, shooting me a look under her bangs. It's impossible to decipher. "I never realized quite how far Greenwood is from the center of Seattle. My friends complain about the drive."

"It's not even twenty minutes."

"They're lazy." She heads to the shallow end of the pool, stepping carefully into the water. The sunlight across the water sends rippling reflections over her fair skin.

It's damn near impossible to look away from the curves of her body. My mind catalogues it all on instinct, filing it away without my agreement. Round, firm breasts that would fit perfectly in my palm. A waist that's begging for my arm around it. Soft thighs and curved hips.

"Are you coming?" Bella asks, shading her eyes again. Her smile is wide.

I toss the towel on a nearby chair and join her in the water, wading into the depths. "I should have installed one of these ages ago."

She dips her head back, rising up like a seal, hair slick around her face. "Why haven't you?"

"The kids. Evie needs to be older before I feel comfortable with a death trap in the yard," I say, looking away from her to the treehouse beyond. The kids, who are my priority, even though I want nothing more than to sweep this woman off her feet.

"Mhm," she says. "I bet there are a ton of decisions you've made over the past few years that haven't been for you. You do a lot for them, don't you?"

"Sure. That's what it means to be a parent," I say. "I can't remember when I've had a day like this to myself, without the kids or work. It's been forever."

I turn on my back and float in the water. The sky above is a deep, cerulean blue. Here with her, it's easy to ignore all the responsibilities that beckon.

"Freedom," she says.

"Yeah."

"I feel like that too, sometimes. And I don't even have kids."

I snort. "I thought so too, before they arrived."

"In between my thesis, networking for jobs, applying for fellowships, trying to create a plan for the future… It's all so much."

"I remember that."

"You do?"

"Feeling like you're falling behind with every passing day? Yeah."

She snorts, turning around and swimming past me. I follow her, both of us drifting into the deep end. "Somehow I doubt that," she says. "You must have been running laps around your fellow classmates."

"What, because of my later success?"

"Yeah."

"Want to know a secret?"

Bella swims closer, droplets glittering in her long eyelashes. "Tell me."

"I was late to practically every lecture. Had average grades, nothing spectacular. *Barely* got accepted into graduate school."

"You're not serious."

"I am," I say, smiling. "So I'm guessing you're already way ahead of twenty-five-year-old me on that score."

She bites her lip. "Ah."

"What?"

"I'm twenty-four."

I groan. "Of course you are."

"Is that a problem?"

"You're making me feel even more of a cradle-robber than I already do." The words slip out—no taking them back.

"A cradle-robber?" She swims closer, flicking her hand and blasting me with water. It's cool, washing over my head. "I'm a grown woman!"

"Oh, I know that," I say. "But it was still wrong of me to come on to you in the kitchen."

Bella shakes her head, swimming away from me toward the shallower end. I follow her languidly, my arms cutting through the water.

"Ethan?"

"Yeah?"

"When was the last time you had a relationship with a woman?"

I tread water, watching as she reaches a place where her feet touch the bottom. She steadies herself against the edge of the pool.

"A while," I say.

Her eyes are level on mine. "How long?"

I swim toward her, the words dragged out of me. I'm finding it harder and harder to keep up my usual easygoing, charming personality around Bella, at least when she asks me questions like this. "Well, my marriage was the last one."

Her eyes widen and I hate what's there, what she's no doubt thinking. So I look away instead. The last thing I want is to be pitied.

"And that ended…?"

"Right after Evie was born," I say. "So three years ago."

"So let me get this straight. The reason you said we couldn't keep… well, *kissing*, was because you don't feel you have the time for any form of commitment."

I drift closer to her. Jesus, but it's hard to think with her this close. "Yes, that's pretty much it."

Her smile is half timid, half brave. "So as long as we establish that this is… consensual and fun and entirely without expectations… there shouldn't be an issue?"

"You're approaching this very logically," I point out.

She smiles. "Engineering student."

"I get it," I say. "Engineer, here."

"So what do you think?"

"If I had to approach this logically?"

Bella moves closer, nodding. I lose the fight with my self-control, reaching up to slide wet fingers over her cheek. It's just as soft as it looks. "I'm having a difficult time thinking at all," I confess.

And damn it, but Bella flushes again, her smile a beautiful thing. "You could, you know, *not*," she breathes.

"Not think?"

"Mhm."

I bend my head and savor the moment—the sight of her lips opening for me and her eyes fluttering closed. Just like I'd tried to in the kitchen, I kiss her softly. Properly.

The taste of her lips is like honey, sweet and overwhelming. It draws me in. Soon, cupping her cheeks isn't enough, and my hands venture down under the surface to close around her waist.

Bella sighs into my mouth. It's a soft, trusting sound, one that speaks of surrender, and damn if my body doesn't ache to receive all she might have to offer.

"See?" she murmurs, stepping close enough that our bodies are flush below the surface. "Look at me having no expectations. I'm doing it so well."

I pull back long enough to chuckle, my fingers digging into her hips. "I don't want you to have *none*."

Heat flashes in her eyes, brief and fiery, and then a shy smile spreads across her face. It would take a far stronger man than me to resist. I can't, it's that simple. So I kiss her again, luxuriating in the feel of her against my lips. The taste of her against my tongue.

It's nothing at all to lift up her up and tell her to wrap her legs around my waist. To reach under her, gripping her thighs to keep her secure.

Bella twines her arms around my neck like I'm all the support she needs, like she trusts me. And damn it, for so long I'd thought I was tired of being the one people leaned on—in my business, my family, my relationships. But here with her, it makes me feel like I can do anything at all, just because this beautiful young woman trusts my strength.

"Damn," I murmur, breaking off long enough to kiss her cheek. "I came over for a dip in your pool."

Her smile widens and I hear my own words back, groaning. "That's not how I meant that."

"It's okay," she murmurs, pressing warm, open-mouthed kisses to my neck. It's making it very, very hard to focus on keeping my hands where they are and not sliding them down. The desire to tug her bikini out of—no. That's not me. *Shouldn't be*, at least.

"Bella," I breathe, my fingers digging into the supple skin beneath my hands. "The last time I had a moment to myself was years ago."

"I know," she murmurs again, her hands now buried in my hair. She does some sort of sorcery with her fingers, twisting and tugging, and I lose all train of thought. No one has touched me like that in a long, long time. Perhaps ever. "This is good though, isn't it?"

"Yeah," I groan. "Very."

There's a smile in her voice, speaking between soft, feathery kisses. "We're adults. We can make adult decisions."

"God help us, yes we can."

Her hands rake down my back and the shivers that explode over my skin are heavenly, they're magnetic, and it's impossible to not take control of the kiss. I can't resist sliding a hand down to her ass and squeezing.

The water might be cool but there's a fire raging below, in the space between our bodies, pressed so close together. Bella bites into my lower lip and *holy shit,* I don't think a woman has ever done that before. I palm one of her tits through the thin, flimsy fabric of her bikini top.

Somehow, the string tie comes undone, and then my hand is the only thing covering the soft swell. A taut nipple tickles my palm.

My poor, shattered self-control frays further.

"Sorry," I murmur. Bella glances down, her chest now bare as the top floats uselessly between us. I look down, too, and she's fucking perfect. "So much better up close."

Bella laughs, leaning in to hug me. It hides her tits from view, but now they're pressed tight against my chest, and that's definitely not *less* distracting. "Whoops," she breathes.

I smooth a hand over her back. Had that been nervous laughter? "Truly unintentional," I say. "I can close my eyes while you cover back up."

Another chuckle, more genuine this time. "Nothing you haven't seen before."

"At quite some distance," I point out.

"That's true." Her lips briefly touch my shoulder. "But I *did* notice that you put a window in the treehouse facing this way."

I grip her tightly and wade toward the edge of the pool. "A construction error," I say. "I'll make sure it has shutters."

Another laugh. "Don't worry. I've started covering up."

"Practically a crime," I tease, and she relaxes entirely in my arms, leaning back again. I don't look down at her chest again. It takes willpower, and probably gives me a few new gray hairs, but somehow I manage.

"So," she says, knotting her fingers behind my neck. If the kisses hadn't already, the look in her eyes alone would break down my resolve. It's soft and shy and kind, all at once, as she gazes at me like I'm a man without baggage and burdens, a man she likes.

"So," I echo. "*Clearly, I* want to spend time with you, despite not having much time at all. Do you think I can manufacture some? Invent a machine for that?"

"You'd make a fortune," she says, "but I think we'll manage without it, too."

"Somehow," I say. "Because I do want to eat a proper dinner with you. Just the two of us. Though God knows when we'll manage that."

"Tonight?" she asks, glancing toward my side of the hedge. "Your mother still has the girls, right?"

I frown. "She does. But I promised to have dinner with my brother." Could I cancel? Liam never came to town, the bastard, but Bella is warm and half-naked in my arms…

"Oh, of course you should do that. I'll be here."

"That doesn't incentivize me to go," I say, releasing my hold on her. I close my eyes and keep them that way.

Bella laughs. "You *can* look, you know."

"Not if we're going to get out of this pool and go our separate ways I can't."

"Right," she says. "As if I'm irresistible."

"You have no idea." Complete honesty fills my voice. "Can I open my eyes now?"

"Yes." She's flushed and wet and gorgeous, all covered up again. "When are you meeting him?"

"Far too soon, probably."

She chuckles. "Poor brother. You seem so excited about it."

I kiss her again, taking my time. It's a kiss to savor, now that I know there's more of this to come. I can't wait. "I'd better go," I say. "Want to help me set up the inside of the treehouse tomorrow? I have about forty-five minutes of kid-free time."

Bella laughs, waving me away. "Go. And yes, I'll help. I can't wait."

And judging by the tone of her voice, she means it, too.

9

BELLA

I knock on Ethan's door the next day, right on time. I'm not the least bit nervous, nor has the memory of yesterday been playing on repeat—of being in his arms, our bodies pressed together underwater, his warm, demanding mouth on mine...

No, I'm unaffected. And if I could only tell myself that enough times, it might become true.

I'd said I had no expectations, but after he kissed me, well... That's not entirely true now, not when I know what he's capable of. And if he only had time for me every other week, that would be okay, if only he'd kiss me like that. Like he wanted me more than he wanted air, his hands gripping me like I was desire itself.

I press the heels of my hands against my burning cheeks. Until a few months ago, I'd been six years into a relationship with my ex and content. He was still the only man I'd ever slept with. Who was this new me who made out in pools with attractive older men?

Ethan's front door opens. "Sorry for the wait," he says. "I was on the phone. Come on in."

"Thanks." Our arms brush as I step past him inside. There's a hint of him, of soap and linen and man, in the air between us.

"No, thank you," he says, shutting the door firmly behind me. "For helping me with the treehouse. For coming over whenever we need you. Brownies, interior decorating... you know everything."

"That's me, at your service."

Ethan's eyes lighten. He reaches out and braces a hand against the wall on either side of me. "At my service?"

I'm not sure if I'm breathing. "Yes."

He bends to press a warm kiss to my neck, right below my jaw. A shudder runs through me at the contact. "And now I have you here all alone," he murmurs.

"So it's it was all a ruse? You never wanted my treehouse decorating skills."

His lips trail up to meet mine. It's slow, tentative, languid. Drawing me out and into the kiss until I'm drowning in it. He doesn't stop when I'm struggling for breath. No, Ethan just returns to my neck, continuing down, turning back the edge of my shirt to reach my collarbone.

I grip his shoulders. "Eager?" I murmur, but I'm talking about myself here, because I'm shivering all over.

Ethan smiles against my skin. His kisses slow, returning to my mouth. His hands dig into my waist. "Yes. I can't help it," he says. "After yesterday, well..."

I run soft fingers over his cheek. He hasn't shaved today, the stubble sharp against my fingers. It's wrong to compare, but my mind goes there anyway. He's different in every possible way from the only man I've been with before.

"I get it," I whisper. "I feel it too."

Ethan groans and rests his forehead against mine. "Where did you come from?"

"Route 520," I murmur. "From central Seattle. Took the exit over by Evergreen Plaza, and then east into Greenwood."

He gives me his wide smile, the one that takes my breath away. It speaks of days in the sun and arms strong enough to carry both your groceries and your troubles. He kisses me again, and I have the distinct feeling of being swept off my feet, of flying further and further away from the Bella who takes things slowly and methodically and who—

Ethan's phone rings. He breaks away from me, his hand sliding from my waist to his pocket in search of the offender.

He raises the phone to his ear, his smile gone. "Hi."

I wrap my arms around myself and follow him, at his insistence, into the living room. Boxes of items he'd ordered are spread out on the hardwood floor. I look through a massive box of throw pillows and listen to Ethan's conversation.

"No, that's not acceptable. I've told you this before. I want at least a week's advance notice, and I want you to send me a copy of the flight details."

His voice is unlike I've ever heard it before.

"I'm not keeping you from them. I'm just holding you to two very simple rules. Do you want me to write them down?"

I grab a box of the outdoor lights and contemplate heading out into the garden. This is a personal conversation.

"I remember," he mutters. "And if you think it'll make me more likely to… No… Yes, and anyway, it's simple. Let me know more than a week in advance and *I'll* be the one to tell them."

Yeah, I should be out of here. I clutch the box of lights tight and head toward the patio door.

"I won't put them on." His voice softens, but it's not with kindness. It feels almost threatening. "Lyra, that tactic won't work either. Let me know when you've booked your flight."

I've *just* gotten the patio doors open when Ethan clicks off the phone. After taking a deep breath, he picks up two of the miniature wooden chairs, one under each arm, and heads toward me.

"Trying to make an escape?" he asks, but the genuine humor in his voice is gone. It's been replaced by that furrow in his brow, the one that makes him look older than he is. Funny, what a difference expressions make.

"Yes," I say. "That sounded personal. I didn't want to intrude."

We walk in silence across his lawn toward the treehouse in the corner. It's beyond anything I'd imagined—shingles and a stepladder and a tiny balcony. Small window-boxes have been installed, too. It's kid heaven. Rich kid heaven, perhaps. It looks like a dream.

I pause on the lawn. Ethan stops too, looking from me to the treehouse. His face lightens somewhat. "Impressed?"

"*Wildly,*" I say. "Can I move in? I promise I won't play loud music. I'll be the model tenant."

He snorts. "Tempting, but I'm not sure that would comply with housing regulations. It doesn't have any heating. Not to mention it's tiny. Like, miniscule."

"Don't knock my new house."

Ethan chuckles, putting the chairs down by the ladder. "Just wait till you see the patio add-on the company sent me sketches of."

"Wow."

He runs a hand over his neck. "And you weren't intruding."

"I wasn't?"

"It was my ex-wife." His jaw works, looking away from me toward the house. "She likes to talk a big game about coming to visit, but she rarely does. The girls get worked up about her coming only to be disappointed when she bails."

"Ah. That's why you've set rules?"

"Yes. Someone has to." He shakes his head, motioning me to join him as he heads back to the house. I pick up another box of pillows and he grabs the child-sized table.

My mind is reeling with questions as I follow him back across the lawn. Why, how, when, who? There's a story here, but like all stories, it'll have to be told at its own pace.

Ethan sets the child-sized table down with an exhale. "Damn it," he mutters. "She's not even here, and she's still ruining this."

"Don't let her," I tell him. That's what I'd had to realize the last few months after the break-up with Ryan. I could let his actions haunt me and consume me and make my day miserable… or I could shut them out altogether.

His smile is slanted. "Truer words have never been spoken. Come on, I want you to see the inside."

I climb up the ladder and peer inside the treehouse, the smell of fresh wood in my nostrils. More spacious than it looked, the treehouse is gorgeous, with carved details in the ceiling and a built-in bookcase alongside one wall.

"Yep, I'll take it," I say.

Ethan laughs. "Still not for sale."

"I'll make you an offer you can't refuse." Turning around, I stretch my arms out. "Come on. Hand me the chairs."

Piece by piece, we decorate the interior, Ethan helping me as I hang up the lights. They fall in lovely draping lines from the ceiling and down around the eaves. When he connects them to the outdoor electricity system… well, it's beautiful.

I sink down onto the heap of cushions we've built in one corner, right by the bookcase. "Haven and Evie will love it."

"They'll want to sleep out here tonight," Ethan says, settling himself beside me. "I can already see us having the argument."

I smile, reaching out to dislodge a piece of errant sawdust caught in his hair. "You win some, you lose some," I murmur.

Ethan stills, shifting closer. "Do that again."

"This?" I run my fingers through his hair, less careful now. It's like coarse silk against my skin.

"Yes."

It's very easy to oblige. I lean against the wall and gently scrape my nails against his scalp.

Ethan groans. "Continue like this and I might actually let you move in here."

"Do you allow pets?" I ask. "Because Toast needs a human keeper."

"Not usually, but I'll make an exception for you." A muscular arm reaches out and settles across my legs, a hand coming to rest on my bare thigh.

Not once have I been so physically aware of a man—of where our bodies touch, of *his* physicality, of the very air that separates us.

"You are almost too good to be true," he says.

"How so?"

"I tell you I can't offer you anything, and instead of running, you just accept it. You make no demands. I'm trying to figure out your angle."

"My angle?"

"Yes. Nobody can be this kind and smart, not to mention unbelievably hot."

My laughter is shaky. Maybe Ethan notices that, because he turns, an eyebrow raised. "You don't believe me?"

"I've been called many things, but not hot."

His brow furrows. "What kind of morons have you dated?"

More shaky laughter. I can play it off with a joke, but he'd just spoken about his ex-wife, and here in the small space with him…

"Just the one," I say. "He had his moronic moments, though."

"The one?"

"Yes."

Ethan's hand on my thigh moves, smoothing up and down, even as he turns to face me fully. "Tell me."

I put a hand on his chest and play with the buttons. The slide into sensuality is effortless, with both of us reclined here on the pillows. "We were together for a long time," I say. "Six years."

"Six years?" he murmurs. "I wasn't even married that long."

"No?"

"Three and a half," he says. "But tell me more about you."

I drop my head back into the soft pillows. There's no way I can tell Ethan about how Ryan had walked out—about the words he'd spoken one morning over breakfast. *Pass me the butter. Oh, and I've found someone else.* "This wasn't supposed to become feelings o'clock."

Ethan's hands settle around my waist. "And all because I had the audacity to call you hot," he says. "It's okay. I won't do it again."

"Oh, thank you."

"I can use other words. Sexy, irresistible, a turn-on…"

Laughing, I pull his face down to mine. He obliges immediately, lips settling on mine. It's a long, long while before we break apart enough for me to speak, and when we do, I can barely remember the conversation.

"Charmer," I murmur, shifting so he can settle more comfortably against me. It's a simple enough movement—almost instinctual. But as my legs widen to make room, I can feel the hardness of him pressing against my thigh. All my attention narrows to that single point of contact, even as Ethan continues kissing me, as his hand slips under my shirt.

It's intoxicating and frightening and invigorating, my body tingling. Ethan wants me, and here is visceral proof of that. The idea of being hot and irresistible shifts from a foreign concept to something very real. A role he's cast me in—a role I'll play gladly. It doesn't even feel like acting.

He kisses down my neck, his hands working expertly along the length of my blouse. Button after button falls to his skill, his mouth there a second later.

"Like silk," he murmurs, his lips against my stomach.

Maybe it's those words. Maybe it's his touch. Or maybe I've hungered for this for so long, for touch that's uncomplicated and strong. There's no doubting his desire.

And it feels so good to be wanted.

So I reach down and undo the front clasp of my bra. The cups spring apart, and Ethan is there an instant later, wide hands caressing the fabric off.

"Nothing you haven't seen before." I aim for teasing, but my voice comes out breathless. "The first time from this very tree."

He hums low in his throat, staring down at my boobs like they contain all the answers, capable of curing cancer and restoring peace in the Middle East. His hands on my waist tighten into a bruising grip.

"All right," I murmur into the silence. "So I guess you're more of a boob man. Glad we have that settled."

Ethan laughs huskily, a hand coming up to cup and weigh and tease. "Recent convert," he says, bending to flick his tongue over a rapidly hardening nipple. The sensation makes me gasp, and when he settles his mouth and sucks…

Is it possible to shatter from this alone? I never have before, but as Ethan's mouth bites and licks, I think I just might. I wrap my legs more firmly around him and surrender to the touch.

And touch me he does. Hands on my waist, my hips, my neck, my nipples. Hands on the buttons to my shorts. I rise up on my elbows and shrug out of my shirt altogether. It suddenly feels like the easiest thing in the world to give in to the fire between us, to take off my clothes. His pleasure in my body is evident—why shouldn't I feel the same way?

Ethan kisses me, tongue against mine. I grip his shoulders as he breaks apart long enough to speak. "Tell me if it's too much," he murmurs, his hand smoothing down my stomach to stop at the waistband of my shorts.

Oh Lord.

His hand dives clean underneath the waistband of both shorts and panties, smoothing over skin and then he's there. I gasp as his fingers make contact.

Ethan groans. "Bella, holy shit."

We breathe in tandem as his fingers reach further down still and one slides deliciously deep inside. His groan is deeper this time.

"You're so wet."

Faint embarrassment, and then nothing, because his hand is parting and stroking and I need to get *him* out of his clothes, too. I want skin on skin on skin on skin.

Ethan's hand disappears. He grips my shorts and cotton panties instead and I lift my hips obediently. He tugs, tossing them to the side, and then I'm naked and covered at the same time—covered in his dark gaze as it rakes me from head to toe. Fire spreads through me as it cloaks, shields, driving away any hints of insecurity.

His eyes lock between my legs. A hand returns, circling, stroking, once easing inside and I arch up, staring blindly at the pinewood ceiling.

Ethan curses. "Fuck, Bella, I need you."

I reach for him.

His phone goes off.

"Why," he curses, "does this *always* happen?"

I laugh breathlessly and wrap both my arms and legs around him. He's still fully clothed, his jeans rough against my skin. "Don't go."

"I don't want to." He reaches for his phone, turning off the alarm.

"Will they be here soon?"

"In ten minutes," he says. "My mother is bringing them over, and I told her to be *very* punctual."

Gripping his shoulders, I press a kiss to his cheek—the only part of his face I can reach from this position. "In that case, you definitely need to let me get dressed."

"Let me take it under consideration."

Giggling, I wiggle against him. "And we need to get the flowers in here. And turn on the lights. And the plate of cookies."

"Whose side are you on?" he asks darkly, but he sits back on his heels and drags me up into sitting with him.

"Yours."

He hands me my clothes, running a hand over his face. "Holy shit. That was… intense."

I slide up my panties and shorts, feeling the exact same way. "You could say that."

He watches as I fasten my bra, eyes dark.

"It's not goodbye forever," I tell him.

"Thank God for the small mercies." He kisses me, hard and true. "Will you stay? Be here when they get back?"

"Of course I will, if that's okay."

He helps me down the ladder, hands on my waist and lifting me the last bit. "It absolutely is." Reaching down, he adjusts his trousers. "Although I'll have to stop myself from kissing you for a few minutes."

Laughing, I grab his hand, pulling him toward the house. My body feels too light and too heavy at the same time. "Come on. Let's fix the last things."

10

ETHAN

"But it's just so *pretty*," Haven says. It's the twentieth time she's made the same observation today. She's sitting cross-legged on one of the tiny kid-chairs, a book open in front of her, and the widest, happiest smile on her face.

"That was the idea," I say. I'm halfway up the ladder, leaning in through the door. "But you still can't sleep here tonight."

She blinks at me, eyes wide. "Why not, Daddy?"

"We've already discussed that."

Evie gives a dramatic sigh from her sprawl on the cushions. "I'm staying."

"Neither of you are." My voice is firm. "There are no beds here, no glass in the windows. It'll get cold and damp."

"It's summer," Evie says. Her voice is tiny but full of fiery determination.

"What happens when you need to pee at night?" I point out. "No bathroom out here."

That momentarily stumps them both.

But then Haven's eyes light up. "We'll just have to go back to the house. It's not that far."

I lean my head against the wooden doorframe. I'd really created my own monster with this one. "Mr. Snuggles lives in your room," I point out to Evie. "I don't think he would like sleeping out here. Elephants don't climb."

Her small face screws up with sudden consternation. This is a problem.

"You can carry him, or I could," Haven points out, displaying a rare bit of sisterly assistance. I'd be pleased at that, if she wasn't doing it to further her own goals.

Evie nods slowly. "Yes," she says. "But Mr. Snuggles doesn't like the dark."

"That's right. And it'll get very dark out here," I say. "No night lights."

Evie rises from the pillows, her mouth now set in a different kind of determination. She heads toward me. "Come on, Haven," she tells her big sister.

Victory!

"Want to jump?" I ask, holding my arms out to catch her. Squealing, she throws herself out of the treehouse and I catch her, spinning her around. Crazy to think that I won't *always* be able to do this. A few more years and she'll be too big. A few more years after that and she'll be asking to wear makeup or go on dates, and then college and—

"Faster!" she screams.

So I spin her around until my arms ache, until Haven rolls her eyes impatiently. But I ask her too, of course.

"Do you want to jump too?"

She hesitates only a moment before nodding. I catch her as well, and when I bend to pick up Evie, both of them give little hoots. It's been a long time since I carried both of them at the same time. My body reminds me exactly *why* I'd stopped, but I ignore the protesting muscles. Mind over matter.

"Daddy truck," Evie declares.

"Yes," I grunt. Haven pushes the patio door open and I set them both down on the living-room carpet, ignoring the protests. "Whoops," I say. "The Daddy truck ran out of gas."

Maria snorts from the kitchen, and I'm happy at least

someone appreciates my amazing jokes. "Dinner's almost ready," she calls.

Evie throws herself onto the couch and scrambles to arrange the pillows into a little fort. "Is Bella coming too?" she asks.

I blink at her. "No."

"But Bella was the one who fixed the treehouse," Haven says. "She should get dinner."

I rub the back of my neck, no idea at all how to respond. "I installed it," I say weakly. Well, technically I paid someone to, but the nuances of that seemed unimportant to explore with a six- and a three-year-old.

Maria joins the conversation. "Maybe she wants more than the occasional hello," she suggests. "She's been very kind to the girls."

I look at my housekeeper in surprise. Seeing my glance, she just clucks her tongue and shakes her head, turning back to plating. Her expression makes it clear that I'm being slow.

All right then. I clear my throat. "Would you like it if Bella came over for dinner tomorrow evening?"

Both girls cheer, Evie going so far as to break into a little impromptu dance, wiggling her butt.

Apprehension makes my stomach knot. The last thing I want is for them to get too attached to someone who isn't permanent. Lord knows their mother had already done enough damage on the trust front.

"I like it too," Maria says. "I'll make something special. I like having guests to cook for."

"Steak?" Evie asks hopefully. For some reason, she's gotten it into her head that steak is her favorite food, even though she only ever eats a few slices. It really is mine, though. Perhaps that's why she's adopted it too.

"Maybe," Maria says. "Or perhaps we'll make homemade pizza? You can all make your own? And afterwards you can show Bella your dance recital, Haven."

The girls launch into feverish practice at that suggestion, so energetic that I have to tell them off when it's time to get seated

87

for dinner. They're still excited when I put them to bed, even as I read them their favorite stories and stay for ten minutes extra to make sure they're truly out for the count.

And then I let my mind stray to the one thing it had wanted to obsess over since that morning. The memory has been nonstop knocking on my mental door, and now I let it in, reveling in it.

Bella, naked and smiling beneath me in the treehouse.

The feel of her body under my hands, the expanse of fair skin, smooth and rosy and freckled and dear God, the slick heat of her… The mental image makes my body ache with need. If only I could've buried myself inside of her and felt her arms around me, her body shuddering…

What had come over me? I'd practically mauled her in my children's new treehouse, for Christ's sake. The more I think about it, the more aroused I get, and the more aroused I get, the more the guilt grows.

So when the house is quiet, when I've made sure everyone is asleep, I softly shut the door to my bedroom and give her a call.

She answers on the second signal. "Ethan?"

"Hey," I say. "Sorry for calling so late."

"It's not late. It's not even nine o'clock."

"Right. I suppose I'm on a different schedule," I say. "Everyone's asleep here."

She gives a soft laugh. "How'd it go after I left? Did they play in it the whole day?"

"Yes," I say. "I had to convince them not to sleep in it, too."

"You were right."

"I usually am."

Her breathless laughter sounds indecently husky to my ear. "So humble, too."

"The humblest," I say. "But Bella, about earlier…"

"Yes?"

"I don't know what came over me. Just yesterday I told you I wanted to take you to dinner, and today I practically attack you."

"You didn't," she protests. "I was equally involved."

The image of her absolutely unreal body rears its glorious head again. I think it might keep hitting me in regular intervals from now on, for the rest of my life, never lessening in potency.

There are worse fates.

"You were," I say. "I'm glad we were interrupted about as much as I hate that we were."

"I wouldn't have stopped you."

"I wouldn't have stopped," I vow.

Bella's sigh is a tad shaky. "What are you doing now?"

"Right now?"

"Yes."

"I'm lying on my bed. I've just put two very excited children to bed. I'm actually on the phone right now."

"Oh, you are?"

"Yes. With my neighbors' young, ridiculously hot niece. She's moved in for the summer."

"Is she nice?"

"Very," I say. "Too nice, actually. She comes over with baked goods and helpful ideas and is very understanding about my role as single dad. It's almost too much."

"Gosh," Bella says. "She sounds awful."

"Oh, she's the worst," I agree. "I keep hoping she'll have some flaw, *something* humanizing, but I come up short every time."

"No one's that perfect. You'll just have to keep digging," Bella suggests.

"Regarding that," I say. "Would you let me dig tomorrow?"

A brief pause. "What kind of digging are we talking about here?"

"It wasn't an innuendo. That's a bit on the nose, even for me." I run a hand through my hair. Do I sound too excited at the prospect? "No, I was wondering if you'd like to come over for dinner."

"Oh! I'd love to!"

"The girls would be here too. They were the ones who suggested it, actually."

Her voice turns playful. "I see. You were pressured into making me an offer."

"Yes," I say. "They have water guns aimed at my head as we speak."

"Do you need to be rescued?"

"Think you could handle them if I said yes?"

She snorts. "Handle? Please. I can do one better than that. I can offer to teach them how to bake cookies in exchange for handing over their weapons."

"You're right," I admit. "They'd cave in an instant."

Bella laughs again. It's a beautiful sound, feminine and happy. A sound I want to be responsible for drawing out again and again. "I'll be there," she says. "Anything to save you from being forced to make advances under duress."

"Thank you. But just so we're clear, none of my advances to you have been under any kind of duress."

Quite the opposite. I can't seem to stay away.

"Well," she says, voice dropping low. "I'm glad to hear that, although, after today… I didn't really think they were."

My laughter comes out a bit hoarse. "No, I was pretty forward."

"I enjoyed it. And maybe tomorrow evening, after the girls have gone to bed, I could stay for a little while?"

Holy shit. Just those words, just the promise of it, and my body reacts. The image of her naked resurfaces in my mind like clockwork. Fucking hell.

No less potent.

"Ethan?"

And my name, whispered… "You should definitely stay after they've gone to bed."

"Okay, good." A smile in her voice. I can see it in front of me —kind, tentative, playful, shy, all of those things rolled up in one. This woman is driving me insane. "Goodnight then."

"Goodnight, Bella."

But it's a long time until my body has finally calmed down enough to settle for sleep, and only after I've taken the edge off with my own right hand.

Tomorrow couldn't come fast enough.

———

"This movie is really good," Evie tells Bella. "The *best*."

"It's okay." Haven slumps against the giant cushion fortress she's built in front of the TV, her little sister lying down beside her.

"Only okay?" Bella asks, not seeing the not-so-subtle shake of my head. This is thorny territory.

Haven jumps on the chance to complain. "Yes, because it doesn't have a prince in it!"

"No prince!" Evie chimes in happily. A familiar logo appears on the TV in front of us.

"Ah," Bella says tactfully. Yeah, this movie is a frequent source of conflict in this household—as are all decisions. But I'd implemented a system. The kids each get to choose what to watch every other day. Simple. Fair. An elegant solution.

And always met with complaints.

"But movies without princes are great too," Bella says. "After all, every movie can't have a prince in it. And not all princesses *need* a prince."

Evie grins, not at all tactful in her victory. "Exactly."

It's a great message. Could she also tell them never to date? Like, ever?

Bella glances back at me, smiling.

"Great answer," I tell her.

She pretends to wipe sweat off her forehead and settles back on the couch next to me. "Felt tricky," she stage-whispers.

There's no need to. Once the movie is playing, both of the girls zone out entirely. Bombs could be falling around the house and they wouldn't hear a thing.

Although, I'm somehow certain that if I yelled *who wants ice cream*, they'd find a way to break that trance.

I barely watch the film—I've seen it enough times. No, Bella is the interesting show here. Stretching my arm out, I drape it over the back of the couch. Just enough that I can curl my fingers over her shoulder.

Bella glances up at me, a smile in her eyes. "Hello," she whispers.

"Hi," I murmur back. "No need for a prince, huh?"

She pushes her thigh against mine. Playful, but my body is on hair-trigger alert, and my other hand lands on her leg. "Not actively looking for one, at least," she teases. "But if you happen to find one along the way…"

"Ah." My thumb rubs circles on the smooth skin of her knee. Thank God for summer and dresses. "An accidental prince."

"Something like that."

"Picked up along your own adventure," I say. Her hair has slipped forward, blocking her cheek from view, and she pushes it back with a slim hand.

"I think I'd be more interested in finding someone to go on adventures *with*."

"Interesting," I say, keeping my voice light. Of course she wants to make her mark on the world. Perhaps travel the globe, meet interesting people. And my adventuring days are if not over, at the very least put on indefinite pause.

Bella's hand finds its way up to my head and then her fingers are twining in my hair. My eyes flit closed of their own accord. "Damn it," I murmur. "Sorcery."

How can something so simple feel so good? I crack open one eye to see if the girls are still preoccupied—yes, they're glued to the movie—and close my eyes again.

"Nobody does this for you, huh?"

"No," I say. "We can't all be princesses with castles and butlers."

"No, some of us just have mansions and staff."

I bark a laugh at that. Evie glances back and gives a sharp

"*Shh, Daddy!*" before turning back around. No sign at all that she'd even registered my arm around Bella.

But there is being reckless and there is being plain stupid. So I force iron-clad will through my veins and remove my hand from her knee. It isn't easy. The awareness of her body against mine is more than a physical thing. It feels like a force, urgent and pressing, and I'm entirely caught in its grip.

It's a relief when the movie comes to its predictable end. I extricate myself from Bella, though it feels like losing a limb, and tell Haven and Evie it's time to go to bed.

Haven accepts her fate stoically—this happens once a day, after all—but Evie puts up a fight. All the usual tactics fail, until it becomes clear she's just biding for time.

"Bella?" she asks. There's a rare note of shyness in her voice.

"Yes, Evie?"

"Will you read to me?"

My heart kicks into overdrive. They're getting too attached, they're getting too attached…

"Of course I will." Bella takes Evie's hand in hers and my daughter pulls her toward her room, almost skipping. The sight is enough to still the quiet panic in my head.

"Daddy?" Haven asks from her bedroom, a book in her hand.

"I'm coming."

It takes twenty minutes for Haven to fall asleep. I close the door gently behind me, only to see that Evie's is still open. When I peek inside, Bella is sitting beside my daughter's bed, the book closed in her lap.

Evie is fast asleep.

Bella motions questioningly. *Can I leave?*

It makes me chuckle. "Yeah, come on."

She tiptoes out of the bedroom and I close that door, too.

"She was out like a light."

"And sleeps like a baby."

"Very fitting."

I motion with my head and we walk down the stairs. "Thank you for staying. For reading to her."

"I enjoyed it," Bella says. "I don't have any nieces and nephews, no kids around me… I tried doing voices. I don't know if it worked."

"Oh, I'm sure it did. I never have the patience for that. No, it's safe to say you have two new members of the Bella Simmons fan club."

She walks ahead of me into the kitchen, leaning against the kitchen island. "Just two?"

"Yes. I'm already a fan."

"You are?"

"Have been for weeks," I say. "Did you like the movie?"

In the dark, her eyes are almost black. "I didn't catch a word."

"Funny," I say. "Neither did I."

"What do you want to do now?"

"I think I have games. We could drink wine and play."

She nods slowly. "Games."

"Yes. Most of them are for kids. I have Twister. Operation. Forty-piece puzzles."

"Exciting."

"Very. But I might have Yahtzee somewhere." Potentially in the garage. Or the attic. It seems very unimportant.

Bella steps closer, wetting her lips. "I don't want to play Yahtzee."

"It's not that good of a game," I agree.

"Too much math," she says.

I reach up and run my fingers along her cheek, down to her chin, tipping her head back. Her skin is like silk, and now I know that it's like that *everywhere*. "Says the engineering student."

"To the engineer." Her voice is a soft exhale against me.

"There is *one* game we could play."

"Oh?"

"It doesn't have a good name," I admit. "Repeat-of-what happened-in-the-treehouse is the working title."

"But without interruptions?"

"But without interruptions, yeah."

Her hands flatten against my chest. It's nothing at all to dip my head a bit further, to press my lips against hers, to feel the sweet thrill of her mouth opening to me. So I do.

Bella kisses me back like she wants me just as much. No pretension, no deception. Just warm acceptance and heat.

She wraps her arms around me. The simple act presses her body tight against mine, soft in all the right places, and my previous resolution to go slow disappears entirely. *Poof, gone.*

My hands grip her thighs and lift her up on the kitchen island. Bella laughs breathlessly, but I cut it off with a kiss. Her hands rake through my hair just the way I like, and fucking hell I want this woman. More than I've ever wanted anything.

My hands find the hem of her shirt and slip under, smoothing over the soft skin of her waist and hips. Moving higher still.

Bella pulls away from my lips enough to speak. I don't pause, switching my attention to her neck instead. "Ethan…"

"Yes?" I think I might shatter if she tells me to stop. I'll obey, of course, but damn how I hope she won't.

"This can't be a total repeat of the treehouse," she says.

I grip her waist like I need her to survive. At the moment, it's pretty damn close. I should respond, but she's soft and warm and so sweet against my lips. It's far easier to surrender than to converse.

I force myself to form the words. "Oh?"

"This time, I can't be the only one nude."

The words barrel through me, and just like that, I'm drowning in need. There's no resurfacing.

I lift her up and head down the hallway to my bedroom. Thank God for someone—the interior decorator?—putting it on the ground floor.

Bella giggles. "Where are we going?"

"I'm taking you on our first adventure." I push open the door to the master suite. "Ta-da."

She laughs again, but it's huskier this time, breathless and tinged with anticipation and desire. "Unchartered territory," she says.

I set her down on the bed. She scoots back immediately and opens her arms, welcoming me on top of her. Forcing myself to go slow, I kiss down her neck, folding her dress up inch by inch, kissing her stomach and chest and teasing her nipples through the fabric.

Bella is the one to take off her bra. "So impatient," I murmur. Dimly, I wonder if I'm really speaking to her at all, or to the painful ache in my jeans. The desire to bury myself inside of her feels all-consuming. I'm like my kids with that movie—nothing else could get my attention now, not even ice cream.

She reaches for my shirt and I pull it off. For a moment, she only looks at me, reaching out to run a hand tentatively over my bare chest. Her fingers rake through the hair on my chest.

A brief flash of self-consciousness hits. I'm not in my twenties anymore. I certainly stay in shape, but the days I had the time to maintain carefully sculpted abs are gone.

But then Bella arches her back and any thoughts of my own physique evaporate. There's no room for that, not when rosy, pink nipples beckon and firm, round tits. Fuck, I've missed tits.

I bury my face against her chest, using my mouth to kiss and suck. Bella laughs, but it turns into a gasp when I bite a nipple. "Too rough?" I murmur.

"No." The word is whispered. "Do it again."

Smiling, I give her other nipple the same treatment. She arches up, her leg locking behind my hip. The movement brushes right over my hard-as-steel cock.

That's it. I tug off her dress altogether and run my hands over the fair, silky skin on display. I pause when I get to her cotton panties, unbearably sexy in their simplicity. "Do you want me to slow down?" I ask.

Bella's dark hair is spread around her on the pillow, a halo, a crown. "I want you to speed up," she murmurs.

I comply.

11

BELLA

Ethan tugs my panties down my legs. A brief pang of shyness hits me as I'm once again naked and he's not, splayed out on the bed in front of him. It doesn't last, not as his gaze rakes over me. It drips with desire and deep primal admiration.

How could I *not* want him when he looks at me like that?

"You're just going to look?" I ask, my voice breathless with anticipation.

Strong hands settle on my knees, pushing them apart. "Taunting me right now is dangerous."

I can't form a witty response to that, nor even a coherent one, because he settles between my legs and unleashes heaven. That's what it feels like.

His mouth paints heat across my sensitive skin. I stare up at the ceiling and breathe through the pulsing need that sweeps through me with ever sweep of his tongue.

His hands don't stop, either. They roam my body as he works, twisting, teasing, caressing. My muscles relax, one after one, surrendering to his skill.

Only to lock up when his mouth settles on a sensitive spot. The touch feels like liquid fire.

"Right here?" he asks hoarsely, repeating with his finger.

I nod like a maniac. Yes, yes, yes yes *yes*. Ethan grins between my legs and bends to his work. It's not long until I collapse in on myself like an exploding star, my body arching upwards.

But he's relentless, continuing on past the point of no return. Past the point where I would have stopped touching myself if this was a solo thing. I twist my hips, trying to get away, but he's merciless as he worries my sensitive skin.

"Ethan," I mewl. If he continues, I'll rise and leap and fall again.

He finally lets me go, rising up on his knees. The satisfied grin on his face takes the little breath I had remaining right away. Thick hair and wide shoulders and so much masculine vitality that it almost pains me to look at him.

Breathtaking.

"Your turn to get undressed," I say, nodding to his offensive jeans. "Off."

"If you insist." He reaches for the zipper in his jeans and pulls them down. The length of him springs free and I can't tear my gaze away. Not even as he kicks off his jeans altogether, not as he gives his cock a slow stroke, not as he reaches for something in his bedside table.

My throat feels dry.

Other parts of me are… *not.*

Ethan rolls on a condom with expert precision, not the least bit bothered by me watching him.

"Ethan," I murmur, not knowing if it's a plea or a question. Perhaps it's a prayer. He kneels by my legs and spreads them apart further, a hand on his cock as he lines himself up.

Anticipation makes it hard to breathe.

He pushes into me in one deep thrust. Inch after inch after *inch* fills me up. "Fuck, Bella…"

Yes, I think in response. *Fuck Bella, and don't stop, not ever.*

It was never this gloriously uncomplicated with my ex. It's wrong to compare, but it's not really even a comparison, just knowledge. A certainty that sears through my brain. I won't be satisfied with anything less now. No awkwardness or shyness or overthinking.

Just pure action.

Ethan makes it simple. Faced with his want, there's nothing to do but to give in.

His hips move in deep, rolling thrusts, reaching deep inside me. Once. Twice. Fourteen times. And all the while he's staring down at me like I hold all the secrets—like this is everything he's ever wanted.

His gaze is the best thing I've ever worn.

"Touch yourself," he tells me, so I reach up and cup one of my breasts, flicking my nipple. "Fuck yes, just like that."

I give him a show at the same time as he gives me one, moving in powerful thrusts above me. The look in his eyes makes me heady with power. So heady that I reach down and touch myself, *there*, even as he moves inside me.

Ethan's green eyes burn even brighter. "Come around me?"

I don't know if I can. But as my finger circles, as he speeds up, as his hands dig into my thighs… I'm sensitive enough, pushed to the edge by his tongue before. And with him sliding in and out, stretching me apart…

My second orgasm spreads through my body like a shot of pleasure straight to the vein. I keep my eyes on Ethan the whole time, muscled above me, on his five-o'-clock shadow and burning intensity.

He shatters right after me. A deep, rumbling groan and rapid, erratic thrusts. He's pushing hard enough into me that my inner thighs might bruise, but it only strengthens the orgasm blazing through me.

Like a tree falling, Ethan settles on top of me, damp forehead against my neck. I wrap my arms and legs around him and struggle to find my way back to steady breathing.

"Holy fuck," he mumbles.

A tired chuckle spreads through my chest, into him, and he raises his head to give me a glazed look. *What?*

"It felt holy," I supply, hugging him tighter.

Ethan gives me a crooked smile. "Best review I could ask for," he says.

"I'll put in on Yelp?"

"Thanks," he says, easily breaking my stranglehold and guiding himself out, a hand on the base. He ties the condom off with a practiced flourish. "That was beyond," he says. "I can't… I haven't…"

"It's been a while?"

He stretches out next to me, lying on his back. "Was it that obvious?"

"Only a little bit," I say. The depth of his need feels flattering.

"Well, that's it. No more brownies."

I raise myself up on an elbow. "Why on earth did you think of that?"

"There's no way I can repay you for *that*. So no more baked goods. You'll just make the balance even more uneven."

I reach out and smooth a hand through his hair, and his eyes close. "You can repay me by doing that again, some time," I say.

"Oh, I plan to." He puts a large hand on my thigh, comforting and warm. "When was your last time?"

"A few months ago, with my ex."

"The one you told me about? The moron?" Ethan sounds pleased at the thought, or perhaps the epitaph.

"Yeah."

But then his hand tenses on my thigh. "You said he was the only relationship you've ever had."

"Yes."

"And you don't strike me as someone who has one-night stands." He turns his head to look at me. "Don't tell me I was your second."

"All right."

"All right what?"

"All right, I won't tell you that."

He groans, shifting onto his stomach and wrapping an arm around me. "I was?"

I bury my face into the bed. "This is a great comforter," I say finally. "What's the thread count?"

"Bella."

"No, don't tell me. Five hundred? Has to be Egyptian cotton, too."

Ethan groans and I look at him. "Why does it matter?"

He's quiet for a beat, so I scoot over and run my hand through his hair again. Surefire tactic, that. "Tell me."

"I shouldn't."

"Tell me anyway."

He sighs. "It makes me feel worse. And awesome. And then worse again for feeling awesome."

"Why on Earth would it make you feel *bad?*" Had I seemed inexperienced? Just because I'd only had sex with one person didn't mean we hadn't done it many times.

He looks over at me with eyes that seem older than he is. The same ones I sometimes saw when he spoke about his ex-wife or his kids. "Like I'm taking advantage," he says.

I move closer, until I'm pressed against his side. "And what am I? Helpless? A victim?"

"Never that."

I slide my leg in between his and let my fingers graze through his chest hair. The sheer *manliness* of him will probably never stop thrilling me. It's like every inch of him screams genetic superiority, a neon billboard to women everywhere. *I'll give you great babies.*

"So? If you tell me *one* more time that you have nothing to offer me, I'll beat you," I warn.

He groans, but there's lightness to it—a hint of playfulness. So I reach down and run my fingers along the length of him, and it twitches to life at my touch. "Besides, I *know* you have something to offer."

Ethan pulls me closer. "Perhaps the only thing," he says, bucking his hips into my grasp for added effect. He's growing harder by the second.

"And very eager," I tease, tightening my grip. He hisses out a breath.

"And sensitive. And very, very keen on you." He flips me

over, lips on my neck as I continue to stroke him. He hardens in my hand.

"Ready again so soon?" I murmur, my breath speeding up as his lips find one of my nipples.

"I've thought a lot about how I want to take you," he says against my skin. "No time to spare."

But despite that, the second time is slower—Ethan takes his time, shifting me into different positions, coaxing me through it, always with the same glowing desire in his eyes. I collapse on his bed after we're done. Not for all the world could I move—not with the aftermath of that many orgasms coursing through my body.

A thump upstairs.

Ethan springs to life. One second he's sprawled with a leg over mine, the next he's standing, pulling on his clothes.

"Ethan?"

"Haven sometimes has nightmares. Evie sometimes wakes up. They might come down here."

I grip the comforter, pulling it up to cover me. Damn.

Ethan pauses by the door to his bedroom, glancing back to me. "Go check on them," I tell him. "I'll get dressed and slip out."

He frowns, clearly conflicted, but what I'm saying makes sense. "All right. I…"

"I know. We'll talk later."

Another nod, this time with a smile. "Text me when you're back home safe," he teases, slipping out and closing the door behind him.

I snort, reaching for my clothes. The walk is what, fifteen feet? But when I finally make it back to my oversized mansion of a house, Toast meowing his displeasure at his evening meal being late, I do just that.

Bella Simmons: *I've braved the streets of Greenwood Hills and made it home safely.*

Ethan Carter: *Thanks for letting me know. I've heard the gangs are notorious around here.*

I laugh quietly to myself, my body still tingly with residual pleasure.

Bella Simmons: *Was everything okay upstairs?*

Ethan Carter: *Yes. Haven had a nightmare and asked me to stay with her. I'm texting from the chair in her room now.*

Bella Simmons: *Poor thing. Good thing you're there. Thanks for tonight.*

Ethan Carter: *No, thank you. Sorry about how it ended.*

Bella Simmons: *No need to apologize. I'll sleep well now.*

Ethan Carter: *Good. I know I most definitely will. The coming days are a bit busy, but I want to see you again.*

My heart does a little double take at that.

Bella Simmons: *So do I. Let me know when it would suit you?*

Ethan Carter: *Will do. Sleep well, Bella. Dream of me.*

I put my phone down with a smile.

I have no idea where this is heading. He's clarified that he doesn't either, that he's busy, that he doesn't have the time for relationships.

And yet, I'm pretty sure I *will* dream of him.

12

BELLA

"Let me get this right," Trina says. "So not only did you *not* tell us that the two of you have become friends, you also *didn't* tell us that you kissed, even though it was days ago. You've also now slept with him? And you're telling us *two days after?*"

"Inexcusable," Wilma says. "This is grounds for excommunication."

Laughing, I arrange the ingredients I need on the giant kitchen island. "I wasn't sure where it was heading, or if it was even heading anywhere at all. I couldn't jinx it!"

A derisive snort comes through the phone—Trina. After years of friendship, we've perfected these three-way conference calls.

"Look," Wilma says, and it's clear in her tone that she's not talking to me. "You can be upset with Bella *later*. For now, we have so many more important things to ask."

I groan. "Don't."

"I have to! How was it? Who initiated it? Do you want to sleep with him again? What does this mean? Are you two dating? How big was he?"

"Wilma!"

"Sorry," she demurs. "I mean, was he *well-endowed?*"

Laughing, I start measuring out the ingredients for chocolate muffins. "I don't know."

"You don't *know?*" Trina says. "What, did you do it in the dark?"

"No, no, I know the answer to *that* question, and I'm not sharing it with you. I meant all the others. I have no idea what it means. He's made it very clear that he can't offer any kind of real relationship."

"Boo," Wilma says.

"No, no, it makes sense. He has two kids," I point out, scooping up a cup of flour.

"Exactly," Trina chimes in. "And Bella is far too young to become a stepmom."

I frown down at the mixing bowl. Stepmom. The word… wow. The idea hadn't occurred to me. "The girls have a mom," I say.

"Yeah, but one who's not around. Come on, Bella. Did you enjoy it? Do you like him? Tell us something at least."

"I do like him," I say. Probably too much. Definitely more than he likes me. "And I did enjoy it. But I'm trying very, very hard not to get my hopes up or get my emotions *too* involved."

"Smart," Trina notes. "No repeat of this spring."

"No, I can't have that," I say. They'd been by my side all through the hellish time, when my ex had said those disastrous four words. *I've met someone else.* I don't know if it's better or worse when there's no warning and no time to adjust. Trina and Wilma had been there throughout that emotional roller-coaster ride.

"But what has he actually *said?*" Wilma insists. "Give us cold, hard facts."

I reach for the baking soda. "Well, he's said several times that he can't offer me anything, that he doesn't have time to date. He's also mentioned that his divorce was a bad one, and he's not on good terms with his ex-wife."

"He's likely scarred by that," Trina says. "Perhaps unwilling to trust again. Focuses on his children and work instead of relationships."

"They're his shield," Wilma agrees. "Perhaps he even thinks

he can't keep a woman? That no one would *want* a man with two young kids and no time?"

Trina hums in agreement. "That must be it, too," she says. "Although the fact that a multi-millionaire mogul can get scared and self-conscious does *not* bode well for the rest of us."

"Not at all," Wilma says. "Bella will just have to help him overcome his trust issues."

"Hold on, hold on," I demand. "When did you two become therapists, huh? Where did all this psychoanalysis come from?"

"Tell us we're wrong," Trina challenges.

"I don't know if you're wrong or right." I frown at the bag of cocoa powder. "But… it would make sense if that was his motivation, yes. Of course, it doesn't have to be that complicated. He could just *not* be interested in anything more with me."

"Bella," Wilma complains. "Stop it."

"It's possible!" I insist. "And that would be okay, too. At this point, we have too few data points."

"So go get some more," Trina says. "You haven't spoken for three days, right?"

"That's right. He's been busy. And so have I, for that matter." The words only burn a little on the way out. It's not technically a lie. I've been making progress on my thesis and I've been on one apartment tour.

And I *haven't* been wondering why my phone had fallen silent after our brief goodnight text that evening.

Not at all.

"Bella…" Wilma says. "Are you really okay with that?"

"No," I say. "But my freak-out is really very minor. I know for a fact he enjoyed it. A lot, actually. And I know he's busy. So I'm coming up with a strategy."

"I like the sound of this," Trina says. "New lingerie? Phone sex?"

"Show up to his office in nothing but a trench coat?" Wilma suggests.

"Chocolate muffins."

Trina groans as the same time as Wilma exclaims, "Yummy!"

"Your signature move," Trina says. "Bribing people with baked goods."

I start combining the dry ingredients, glancing at the oven. Almost at temperature. "It worked on the two of you," I point out. "And so far it's worked splendidly on him."

"Honey, I think he was always interested in more than just your cupcakes."

That tears a laugh out of me. "You might be right about that."

"But hey, why not? Gives you an excuse to go over there, right?"

"Exactly," I say. "Baking with a purpose."

"You're devious," Wilma says.

"And clever. But let us know how it went this time, okay?" Trina says. "I haven't forgotten that we were the ones who had to *dare* you to go over there."

"And I haven't heard a thank-you yet!" Wilma chirps.

"Thank you," I say. "Thank you, thank you, thank you. I'm your eternal servant."

"That's a bit much. Some cookies would be enough."

"Noted."

"Now scram," Wilma says. "And put on something cute when you go over there."

"Something that makes the 'cupcakes' look good," Trina says with a laugh.

"I'll send you a picture of the outfit later."

"And an update!"

"And an update," I agree. We click off, the giant kitchen falling silent once more. I smile the entire way through my baking. Trust Wilma and Trina to put things into perspective for me.

And they were right. They *had* been the ones to dare me to go over there in the first place. Toast comes jumping onto the kitchen counter to inspect what I'm doing.

"No," I tell him, reaching over to pick him up. He looks at me grumpily, his mission thwarted. "No cats allowed on the kitchen counters." At least not while I'm baking, but I don't add that. It's better to be consistent.

He gives an annoyed meow. "I know," I say. "But only a month and a half left now before your real humans get back. Excited?"

Toast looks spectacularly unexcited and heads off to the living room. Yeah, well, I wasn't too excited about that either, or about the conversation I'd still *not* had with Ethan. The one where I was *not* the Gardners' niece. Every day that passed would make it harder when I finally had to, which was annoying in and of itself, when it wasn't that big of a deal in the first place.

Tonight, I tell myself, putting the muffins into the oven. Tonight, I'll do it. I'll give him muffins and the truth.

What man could resist that?

———

That's not at all what happens.

I ring the bell by Ethan's gate a bit after six p.m. He should be home, and they should just have finished dinner, in time for the girls to watch a bit of TV before heading off to bed. It's all a long string of *shoulds.*

Maria isn't the one who answers. It's Ethan, his voice distant. "Hello?"

"Hi. It's Bella. I made some extra muffins and wondered if the girls want any?"

In the background, a little girl screams, "*Muffins!*" I can't tell if it's Evie or Haven.

"Come on in," Ethan says. "I'll leave the front door open for you. We're in the backyard."

I close the gate firmly behind me and head up the path, stepping into the empty hallway. The house is quiet—he must have unlocked the door with his phone. These Greenwood Hills houses and all their security protocols.

"Ethan?" I ask, walking through the living room. It's a mess of toys and games and a giant plush unicorn I haven't seen before.

I find them outside, by the treehouse. The sight is enough to make me smile. Ethan, lifting Evie up. Haven, leaning out of the treehouse window.

He's so unbearably attractive right then. Strong arms as he holds his daughter. Thick hair, pushed back from his face. Slightly tan skin. A man who exudes everything a woman might want: stability, strength, competence, humor…

"Bella!" Evie calls. She wriggles out of Ethan's arms and comes barreling toward me. "I heard you have muffins!"

"I do." I crouch down and open the container. "Do you want one?"

"Yeees."

I put the lid back on playfully as she reaches for one, and she giggles. "Have you had dinner first?"

"Yes, we've eaten," she says. "Chicken nuggets."

"Chicken nuggets?" I glance past her to where Ethan is trying to coax Haven out of the tree. Maria must have the evening off.

She manages to grab one of the muffins and darts back, her blonde ponytails swinging. "Got it!"

"Yes you did. You have to tell me what you think, too. Do you like chocolate?"

"I love it."

Behind her, a sudden wail rings out. Haven is lying on the ground by the treehouse, Ethan beside her. "Haven? Honey?"

Things move very quickly after that. He carries her inside, telling me that she might have broken her wrist, that we need to go to the hospital.

"What do you need me to do?" I ask. "Do you want me to come? To stay here with Evie?"

Ethan hovers by the kitchen island, one hand on Haven's back as she cries into his shoulder. Evie stares at her father and crying sister with round eyes.

"Haven's upset," she tells me quietly. I wrap my arm around her and she leans into the touch.

"Come with me," Ethan says. "Please."

"Absolutely."

The following minutes are an exercise in careful, diligent patience. Putting the shoes on Evie. Grabbing her toy elephant—he has to come too. Where are we going? The hospital. Is Haven going to die? What? No, absolutely not. She might just have a sprain. Okay. Can I have ice cream? No, not right now. But can I bring my muffin? Yes.

By the time Ethan backs out of the driveway, the kids buckled in and their backpacks in my arms, I feel sweaty.

Haven's crying has become softer now.

"Are you okay?" Ethan asks, looking at her through the rearview window.

She shakes her head.

"Of course not, honey," he says. Everything about him—from his voice to his hands on the steering wheel—radiates quiet confidence. "But the pain won't last forever. And you might even get one of those cool casts, like your friend Kevin, remember?"

Haven nods miserably. "It was green," she murmurs. "I don't want a green cast."

"You can have any color you want," Ethan promises.

From her car seat, Evie starts suggesting all the colors in the rainbow, much to Haven's distraction. By the time we arrive at the nearest clinic, she's settled on either a soft purple or a pastel pink. That's *if* she needs a cast at all.

Ethan parks and we head into the private clinic, all four of us. The receptionist gives a short, professional nod as soon as Ethan says his name and pushes his card over the counter.

"Come with me," she says, smiling down at Haven. "We'll get you X-rayed and looked at right away."

Halfway down the corridor, Evie decides that a fake planter is more important, and I scoop her up in my arms, putting her on my hip. She immediately starts playing with my hair instead.

"Pretty," she tells me, her voice far away. She's looking at the approaching doctor.

Ethan turns to me. "I think it might be best if Haven and I do this part alone. Is that okay?"

"We'll be out here," I tell him. "Won't we, Evie? There's a playroom here."

His exhale is one of gratitude, and then he disappears into the treatment room with a miserable Haven.

Evie and I stay occupied, but it's hard not to let my mind wander to that room. Evie asking questions I can't answer doesn't help, either.

"Will Haven get a cast?" She grabs a few plastic figurines, setting them down decisively on the table in front of me.

"I'm not sure. Maybe. Where was Maria tonight?"

"In town." She hands me a small, plastic dog. "This is you."

"This is me?" I turn the dog over, a tiny Dalmatian. "And who are you?"

She holds up a little firefighter. "Ah," I say. "Good choice."

We play for a little while, Evie completely lost in the imaginary world. I'm *woof, woofing,* when Ethan and Haven finally come down the hallway to join us.

Her arm is in a cast, Ethan's hand on her shoulder.

"Look," she tells us, holding up her arm.

"Purple!" Evie exclaims.

"How are you feeling?"

Haven gives me a small nod. "Okay, sort of."

"She's been given painkillers," Ethan says, smoothing his hand over her hair. "You don't hurt anymore, do you?"

"No. But I feel a bit weird."

"Did it break?" Evie asks, inspecting her sister's arm.

"It's a fracture," Ethan says. "Which means it did break, but only a little."

Haven nods. "And it will heal really, really fast."

"Yes, it will. Come on, let's get home."

I grab Evie's backpack and reach for her hand. She takes mine without question, eyes still on her sister's cast.

"I want one," she tells me.

"Maybe when you're older," I say, which is a beyond stupid reply, but she seems to accept it as normal.

Ethan and I walk out of the hospital, each of us hand-in-hand with a little girl. A smiling doctor stops us when we're almost by the door.

"This is for you," he tells Haven, holding up a giant lollypop. "For being so brave while we applied the cast."

She takes it with big eyes. "Thank you."

"Of course. And for you, little lady…" The doctor hands Evie a smaller lollypop, forestalling any protests. "There you go. You two take care of your mom and dad, now."

Oh, Christ.

Do we correct that? I glance toward Ethan to see his response, but a small voice stops us.

"We will!" Evie chirps, already hard at work unwrapping her lollypop.

Wow.

Ethan shakes the doctor's hand. "Thank you. We'll be back for the checkup."

The four of us get settled into the car, snapping buckles for car seats and seat belts. Adorably, Evie holds out her lollypop to me.

"Want to taste?"

"No, thank you," I tell her. "That's yours. Besides, candy isn't good for dogs, you know."

She blinks at me, and then bursts into delighted little giggles.

"Woof," I say again, tightening the strap around her. "Woof, woof."

From the driver's seat, I catch Ethan watching us with an inscrutable look on his face. He looks away as soon as everyone is locked in and we begin the short drive back to Greenwood.

"Do you want ice cream?" he asks Haven. "You can have some when we get home. And you can choose any movie you want."

"Any movie at all?"

"Yes."

"Okay." Haven's voice brightens a bit. "We should tell Grandma, too. About my cast."

"We can call her as soon as we get back to the house."

"And Mommy?"

The pause in Ethan's reply is slight, but it's there. I glance toward Evie—but no risk there. She's completely absorbed in demolishing her lollypop.

"We can call her too," he says carefully. "If you want, sweetie."

"Okay. Maybe later."

Ethan pulls me aside as soon as we get back home, as Haven runs upstairs to get her favorite stuffed animal. "Thank you," he says, and there's so much emotion in his eyes that I can do nothing but bob my head. They shine with concern and gratitude and relief.

"Of course. What can I do now?"

He glances from me to Evie, who is ambling around in the living room. "Maria has the night off," he says. "That would be fine, but now… I don't want to leave Haven for too long."

"Of course," I say. "Go be with her. I'll stay with Evie and dig through your freezer for ice cream."

His hand squeezes mine once. "Thanks."

I'm a yawning mess when Evie is finally down for the night a long while later. From the murmured conversation in Haven's room, she's not asleep yet, still shaken by the experience of today.

I go downstairs and wash up the bowls, tiredness like a gray haze at the edge of my vision. I had no idea that taking care of children was like this—fun and amazing and absolutely exhausting. It's like I've been vigilant nonstop since I arrived. How does Ethan do it, day in and day out?

But then I think of Evie's little hand in mine, and I understand.

He joins me in the kitchen a while later. The faint lines of his face look deeper, eyes weary.

"What a day," I say softly.

"The worst." He braces his hands against the kitchen island. "She wanted to climb the ladder herself. She's done it a dozen times. Hell, she does more dangerous things than that on playgrounds."

"It happens," I say. "Most kids break something, sometime."

He shakes his head. "I know. But I was *right there,* and when she slipped, I wasn't fast enough. I wasn't even looking."

"You said it yourself, she's done it a dozen times."

"At least she got the color she wanted on the cast," he sighs. "Small mercies, I suppose."

I put my hand on his. "You did everything right."

"I installed a death trap in my backyard," he says, but his voice is somewhat lighter. Driven by impulse, by the darkness in his eyes, I reach over and wrap my arms around him.

Ethan hesitates for only a moment before his arms settle around my waist. He bends his head atop mine and takes a deep breath.

"You did nothing wrong," I mumble into his chest. The scent of him fills me, soap and man and him.

"You're too kind to me," he says. "It keeps tipping the scales. I can't possibly repay you."

"I don't want repayment. And it's impossible to be *too* kind."

He leans back, tipping my head up. There's quiet determination in his gaze. "No, it isn't. I'm sorry I haven't called you since the other night."

"You're busy. I understand that."

"Yes. I've wanted to, though. Every night, I've thought of your body against mine."

Oh God.

Never before has a man spoken like this to me, and in Ethan's deep voice, with his hands on me…

"So have I," I whisper. "All the time."

He closes his eyes, a pained expression on his face. "I don't think you know *just* how tempting you are to me."

I run my hands over his chest. "I don't?" I murmur. "I think you made that pretty clear the other night."

His hands make a deliberate path down my body to grip my ass. "I plan on making it clear again, and soon. I've had a lot of time these past days to think about all the different ways I want you."

I tuck my head against his neck to hide my treacherous cheeks. Ethan must feel it though, because he gives a low snort and tugs me tighter against his body.

"Judging from the way you blush, I'm guessing dirty talk wasn't a part of your last relationship?"

"Not usually." Not at all, to be fair. Ryan had been pretty straight-laced, and after my first wild ideas were shot down, I stopped trying. Maybe I shouldn't have.

He laughs darkly. "Fuck, there are so many things I want to try with you, Bella. To ask you if you've done before. To tell you." He squeezes, emphasizing his words.

I hold on to his shoulders and revel in the strong, hard planes of his body against mine. "I'm looking forward to that," I say. "There are a few things I'd like to try, as well."

His eyes burn on mine, flaring with heady want. "Damn it," he says. "Now all I can think of is fucking you. Right here, bent over the kitchen island and moaning my name. And I can't have that."

My mouth is dry. Parched. Just like that, I want him too, aching for the vision he'd just described—to feel his strength and fiery passion unleashed again.

He closes his eyes. "God, your face. You'd want that too?"

"Yes." I wet my lips, testing out the words. "I'd want you to grip my arms from behind, too. I've seen that somewhere and... what?"

Ethan is smiling, his small, crooked, private smile. "Nothing," he says. "I can do that. I'd *like* to do that. What else?"

"Grip my hair," I murmur. "I like that. And could you... God, why is this so difficult? I've never had this kind of open communication about sex before. Just saying the words is a challenge."

Ethan kisses me again, lingering this time, his tongue gently coaxing mine. I'm breathing hard by the time he pulls back. "I want to hear it all," he says. "Every last thing you want. No need to be embarrassed about it." He rests his mouth against my ear, speaking in a voice that sends shivers down my spine. "I've come several times in the shower these past days, and every time my hand is wrapped around my cock, I imagine it's your sweet pussy I'm inside of."

Holy shit.

My blush is a furious, scarlet thing, even as my body clenches at his words. Ethan laughs. "Was that far enough for you?"

I swallow. "Was it… you have? That's true?"

"Oh yes," he says. "And every night I've wanted to text you to come over."

"Why haven't you?"

"How could I? I only have forty-five minutes before my daughters might wake up with a nightmare; could you be in and out in that time frame? No. That's not fair to you or me."

My mind is still reeling from his earlier words. "I don't think I'd mind," I say. "I'm not exactly suffering in that arrangement, you know. I did *like* sleeping with you."

"Thank God for that," he says, but his eyes dart back toward the staircase, and I understand. It's not tonight, either. He needs to be with Haven—she might be asleep right now, but the painkillers will wear off soon enough.

I rise up on my tiptoes and press my lips against his. I make it sweet and soft, kissing him the way I'd want to if we were *something,* if this was a first kiss after a date.

He kisses me back gently.

"Three things," I say finally. "Number one, I know you have limited time. Forty-five minutes of you is better than forty-five minutes without, so don't hesitate, okay?"

I hold up a second finger. "I'll head home now so you can be with your daughters. Does Maria have the morning off tomorrow, too?"

He nods.

"Then the second thing is this—I can come over tomorrow and make breakfast. We could make a thing out of it, pancakes and waffles and fruit. A kid who's just fractured something deserves that."

Ethan exhales. It's a long, tired thing, but his eyes are filled with gratitude. "You're too kind to me," he says. "Don't protest this time. It's true. I'll have to repay the Gardners somehow for having the good sense to leave for the summer, so I could get to know you instead."

My smile feels brittle. "I'll be back tomorrow. Text me when the girls are up?"

"I will. What about your thesis?"

"That's the good thing about being a student," I say. "My time is flexible."

"What was the third thing?"

I force the words out. "If you ever want to fuck me over a kitchen island, mine is available."

His eyes flash, and then he's kissing me again, a good long while before he finally lets me go. "I'll take you up on that," he murmurs. "Sleep well, Bella."

Guilt erupts inside me the second I close his gate behind me. With every kiss, every encounter, I feel myself slipping further and further into the lie. The time when it was just a tiny, inconsequential thing might have passed.

Because now, having held his daughter's hand at the hospital, seeing the gratitude in his eyes… I'm not sure if it's such an easy thing to shrug off anymore.

13

ETHAN

"Daddy flip!" Evie announces. "Daddy can flip!"

Bella shoots me an amused glance under her sideswept bangs. It's challenging. *Go ahead and try.*

She'd showed up bright and early, a mix for pancakes in one hand and a bottle of maple syrup in the other, just as casually stunning as always. Rosy cheeks and hazel eyes.

I give Evie a half-smile. "You want to see?"

"Yes!"

Beside her, Haven is watching me with wide eyes. I know what she's thinking. She'll ask to try in a second.

"All right, then." I grab the large fry pan and twist my wrist, flipping the pancake high up in the air. After doing an Olympic-worthy somersault, it lands back in the pan.

Evie and Haven applaud. So does Bella, laughter in her eyes.

"Very impressive," she tells me.

"Anything for the ladies," I say.

"Can I try?" Haven says, stepping forward. I push back her honey-brown hair.

"I think you'd need both hands, sweetie. The pan is heavy."

She looks down at her cast and gives a dramatic, pained sigh. I know for a fact she's not in pain, though. I've followed the doctor's dosage orders to the letter. Well, to the milligram.

"But you can set the table," Bella offers instead. "I *know* you can do that one-handed."

"Okay," Haven says. "Can I use the fancy glasses?"

She's asking Bella, who looks at me, her eyebrows raised.

"Yeah, go ahead," I say. "She means wineglasses," I tell Bella. "She likes to drink her water and orange juice out of them."

Bella's smile lights up her face. It's the kind of smile that a man can't do anything but stare at, wondering at his luck. A girl moves in next door who not only wants to sleep with me, but who somehow fit herself into this domestic narrative as well? It's enough to make my mind spin away in *what-ifs* and *could-bes.*

"How fancy," she teases. "Do you have them use linen napkins, too?"

"Yes," I deadpan. "Evie's starting finishing school next year."

"Finishing school, huh?"

"Yes. Manners are really important in preschool. Who curtsies to who, you know."

She rolls her eyes to me, but the smile on her face remains in place. Stupid jokes. Stupid feeling in my chest.

The sound of my doorbell sounds throughout the house. Frowning, I head to the intercom and press down *answer.*

I'm greeted by a familiar face.

"Mom?"

"Yes. Let me in," she says, impatient as always. I do, and behind me, two little voices rise in happiness.

"Grandma's here!"

They scamper off toward the front door, their feet echoing down the hallway. They're more than capable of opening the front door on their own.

Bella bites her lip, looking at me. "Should I stay?" she asks.

It's a split-second decision—whether or not to drag her deeper into my life, as if she wasn't already deep enough. The whole thing feels like it's spinning out of my grip.

"Yes," I say. "Of course you should."

My mother walks into the kitchen with long strides. In her

late sixties, she's still a force to be reckoned with, her permed hair like a helmet.

"Mom," I say, bending down to kiss her on the cheek. "I didn't know you were planning on stopping by today."

Nor so early.

"You text me yesterday and tell me that my oldest granddaughter took a fall," she says. "There's no other place I'd be."

Haven clings to her leg, holding up her cast. "Look, I chose purple."

"Excellent color, dear," Mom says. "It's the color of ambition and nobility."

Christ.

Haven beams at her comment, though I'd reckon she has no idea what either of those words mean.

"Mom," I say, "I'd like you to meet Bella. Bella, this is my mother, Patricia."

My mother's hawk-like eyes focus in on Bella. "Delighted," she says, shaking Bella's hand. "I'm simply delighted."

"So am I," Bella says. "It's a pleasure to meet you."

"Bella is my neighbor for the summer," I supply. "She was here yesterday when Haven fell."

"And now I'm making pancakes," Bella adds, returning to the stove. "Would you like some breakfast?"

My mother settles down at the breakfast table. Haven grabs the seat next to her. "I'd love some," she declares, "as well as the story behind how you two met. But first, Ethan, you're teaching your children how to drink out of wineglasses? What are you thinking?"

I stifle a groan. Trust your mother to be able to embarrass you in front of a girl, even when you're thirty-six and a father of two.

This is going to be a challenging morning.

———

My mother looks at the shut door long after Bella's left. I shake my head at the discussion I know is coming and lift Evie up out of her chair.

"Where did Bella go?" she asks.

"She went home. She has work to do, you know."

"Coming back?"

"Eventually, yes, I'm sure she will. But probably not today."

Evie really only gets the *yes* part of that reply, smiling as she totters off toward the playroom that sometimes masquerades as my living room. "Bella's a doggy," she murmurs to herself. "Woof woof."

What in the world?

"So," my mother says, sinking more meaning into the single word than many authors do in an entire novel.

"So," I echo. "Why don't you just go ahead and say what you want to say?"

Mom's eyebrows rise. "Honey, I don't know enough to say anything. What I have are *questions*."

Sweet mercy. "I don't have an awful lot of answers for you."

She scoffs, like she knows that's not true, and wiggles a little on the barstool. "Awfully uncomfortable, these," she comments. "Why'd you choose them?"

"I didn't choose them."

"Right. Lyra did."

Can I fire a distress signal? If I thought trying to explain Bella and me to my mother was bad, discussing my ex-wife is arguably much worse.

"Where are you going with this?"

Mom makes a tentative spin on the chair, holding on to the island the entire time. "So stupid," she says. "Right. Well, the girl next door seems really nice. She knows how to cook. Kind, too. And she looks at you like... well, she likes you."

I close my eyes. So far, so good. "That's nice."

"Yes, it is. So why don't you take her out on a proper date?"

My eyes pop open again. "You want me to date her?"

"You've been alone for too long. And I include the years you were married to that bitch in that."

121

"Mom." I glance back toward the living room, but the joyful sounds of Paw Patrol drown out our conversation. Haven and Evie aren't listening.

"It's the truth!" she protests, eyes as just as determined as mine. "Let me take the darlings on Saturday and you go sweep her off her feet. You still remember how to, I hope?"

I look up at the ceiling and count to five. It's mildly mortifying to get advice like this from one's own mother, but...

"I still remember," I say. "Thank you."

She smiles and gets up, starting to clear the plates. "Excellent. Saturday it is, then."

I glance back at the living room and what the hell, why not—I'll speak my fears. After all, my mother had raised two sons and done a great job.

"I worry, though... I don't want them to get too attached. They're just now starting to get over Lyra's absence."

Mom's face darkens. "A child never gets over that."

"I know. You know what I mean, though. They don't ask for her that often anymore, they don't cry for her."

She gives a thoughtful nod, but her eyes are ripe with speculation. I know the look. It means she's plotting something. "It seems like they already like her."

"They do."

"Just make sure you go slow, and I'm sure it'll be fine. My grandchildren are strong. Besides, who said anything about marrying the girl?"

"Mom!"

Her smile is wide, and she pats me on the arm as she walks past me to the living room. "You've lived for others for long enough, Ethan. Including your employees. This could be good. Stop worrying so much."

I stare after her, watching as she sinks down into the couch and Haven comes up to nestle against her side.

My hand fists at my side, hard, before I release it and let the tension drain away. A date would make things more serious. It would invite all kinds of potential trouble. But maybe my mother had a point—there was no need to think that far ahead, and Lyra had been years ago.

It's time to try again.

So I call Bella that night, after the kids are asleep and my mother has left, lying on my bed and staring up at the ceiling.

She answers on the third signal. "Ethan?"

"Hey."

"Is everything all right? How's Haven?"

"She's doing great. She's actually starting to look forward to showing off her cast to her friends. We've been discussing who might be jealous."

"Wow," Bella says. "Looking ahead. I like it." Then she sighs. "I'm sorry about this morning. I'm sure your mother had questions for you after I left."

I snort. "Yes."

"I didn't mean to make things difficult for you."

"You haven't." Quite the contrary, actually. "She liked you."

A pause. "She did?"

"Yeah. Your pancakes received stellar reviews."

Bella chuckles. "I hope you didn't tell her the mix came from a box."

"Of course not. I'm a gentleman." I run a hand through my hair, surprised by how... just *happy* her voice makes me. And she hasn't even been away for that long—what, twelve hours? "I have a question," I say. "More like an order."

"An order?"

"Yes. Clear your schedule on Saturday. I'm picking you up and we're spending the day far away from Greenwood."

"I'm being kidnapped?"

"Oh, yes. I can be charming when I try to be."

"So you haven't even been trying?" she asks. "Then I'm in serious trouble."

Her words make me laugh. "Oh, you absolutely are. You haven't forgotten our conversation from the other night, have you?"

"About... us?"

Her hesitance to speak the words out loud makes me smile. Such a charming mixture of bravery and innocence, in a way. "Yes, when I started to tell you about all the things I want to do to you. I want to hear your list on Saturday."

Am I imagining things, or is Bella's voice breathless? "I'm not sure if you're ready for my list."

Her teasing pushes me over the edge. "Do your worst."

"All right, I will. Underestimating me isn't a good tactic, you know."

"I'm scared."

"You should be," she says. "What are you doing now?"

"Lying on my bed."

"Do you only ever call me from bed?"

Oh, the temptation. "It makes it very easy to imagine you're next to me."

Her voice drops. "I see. Anything in particular you're imagining?"

If she insists…

"Well, you're not wearing a lot of clothes in my imagination."

"Ah," is all she says, and then I hear footsteps on hardwood floors.

"Where are you going?"

"To *my* bed," she says.

Are we doing this? Surely not. But… damn if her breathlessness in my ear isn't hot as hell. Can I push it?

A real gentleman wouldn't, but despite my joke, I know I'm not one of those—and Bella has told me she's okay with this. With us.

"I like the sound of that," I say. "What are you wearing outside of my imagination?"

"Pajama shorts and a T-shirt."

The image makes me smile, at the same time as my mind wanders. Her long, fair legs would be on display. "Nice," I say. "But I like you better without."

"I'm taking the shirt off now… no bra underneath."

"Mmm, fuck. I can picture your tits."

"I wish you were here," she says. "Doing what you did the other night."

I undo the zipper to my jeans and look over at my bedroom door. It's firmly shut and the girls are fast asleep upstairs. "What did I do the other night?" I ask.

"Ethan."

"I want to hear you say it." I push down my boxers and close my hand around my rapidly hardening cock. It's so easy to see her in front of me, back arched and those beautiful rosy nipples ready for me.

"Sucked on my nipples," she whispers. There's only brief hesitation in her voice, and damn if it doesn't make me grow harder.

"Yes, I did. Bit them, too."

"I liked that," she murmurs.

"So did I. I want you to touch yourself now," I tell her. "Are you wearing panties?"

"Yes."

"Slide your hand in and touch your pussy for me."

A breathy moan. "Okay."

Imagining her like this is the easiest thing in the world. On her bed, phone clasped to her ear, her other hand working between her legs. "I want you so much, Bella."

"I want you too." Her voice has changed, now, deepened and darkened into something I can't turn away from. "I'm imagining your touch on my skin."

"Where?"

"You tell me," she murmurs. "It's your touch."

"Your lips. Your neck. Your nipples. Your stomach. Your inner thighs. Your pussy."

A breathy sigh from Bella—I imagine her running her hand down her body, just like that. "So greedy."

"For you? Hell yes."

"Just hearing your voice is making me wet," she murmurs. "It's actually... wow, I've never done this before."

"Getting dirty on the phone?"

125

"Yeah."

"That's okay. It's just me, baby. It's just us." My cock slips easily through my hand now as I stroke. "There's nothing you could say that *wouldn't* turn me on."

"What are you doing?" she asks.

"What do you think I'm doing?" I retort. "I'm so hard here for you, and you feel so good around me."

Her voice… her breathy moans in my ear. It's enough to send need pounding through my spine, my legs, my cock.

"Slide a finger inside," I tell her.

"Okay," she whispers. "I wish it was you. My finger isn't big enough."

"Use two."

"Still not big enough."

Fucking hell, at this pace I'm going to explode before she does. I slow down my strokes and bend my knees slightly, my rhythm slowing.

"Tell me how you want me to fuck you," I say.

And she does, in faltering tones, growing stronger by the sentence. "You're inside me… oh, you feel so good, Ethan. So good."

I can see her beneath me, I can feel her around me, and damn if I can't almost taste her on my tongue. Bella is in my ear, but she's everywhere, too.

"I'm close," I tell her. "So close to finishing inside you."

"Do it," she breathes. "I'm close, too."

"Same time?"

"Yes. God, I want you."

"Want you too." My hand speeds up, my cock slipping through my grip, and I'm teetering on the edge. The sound of a long, single moan from her pushes me over. I don't think there's a more beautiful sound in the world than Bella surrendering to her pleasure.

I erupt across my stomach, my chest heaving.

"Fuck," I tell her, when I'm able to speak. "I haven't had an orgasm that strong in… well, since the last time we had sex. But on my own? Can't remember when."

Her laughter is breathless and hot and shy, all at the same time. "I'm glad to hear that."

"How was yours?"

"Electric."

The single word bounces around in my head, even as I close my eyes. "I can't wait to see it again in person," I say.

"On Saturday?"

"On Saturday," I echo. "And Bella?"

"Yes?"

"You're good at it. Talking dirty, I mean."

Her response is sweet. "I have a good instructor."

"Sleep tight, Bella."

"Good night, Ethan." It's not long until I fall into a deep, sated sleep with her voice still murmuring through my mind. Knowing I should stay away, keep my walls up, and yet… feeling more whole than I have in years.

14

BELLA

When the bell to my gate rings mid-Saturday, Ethan has already got his monster of a Jeep running. "Come outside," he calls through the intercom. "Let yourself get kidnapped for the day."

Laughing, I grab my bag and call goodbye to Toast. He doesn't comment, lying on the bottom staircase and watching me through slitted eyes.

"Don't miss me *too* much," I tell him.

He turns his head away resolutely.

I lock the door behind me, initiate the roughly five hundred security protocols through the surveillance app on my phone— Fort Knox could learn a thing or two from this house—and hurry down the path to Ethan.

He's grinning, eyes sweeping over my clothes. "Good look," he tells me.

I glance down at my jeans and hiking shoes. The button-down I'm wearing is somewhat form-fitting, but I'm definitely dressed for a day outdoors.

"You told me to expect something woodsy."

"That I did." He's in dark jeans and a sweatshirt, and with his wide smile and tousled hair… well, he looks like a million bucks. But then again, we can be naked and I'll probably still feel underdressed next to him—that's just the kind of man he is. "Come on, Bells. Get in."

I jump into the passenger seat. It's not just an expression, either, as the car is genuinely so high that I need to jump. Seeing it, Ethan laughs.

"What?" I ask. "You're driving a monster."

"If we're calling names, I can think of a few for your Honda."

"Don't hate on the Honda," I tell him. "She has a proud history and I won't hear any ageist claims against her."

Ethan's smile widens as he puts the car in drive. "You won't hear another word from me—"

"Good."

"—*if* you promise to keep up today."

"Keep up? We're hiking, right?"

He nods. "I have absolutely no idea if you're someone who likes that, so I'm taking a wild gamble here."

I grin. "What would you do if I said I hate trees? And walking?"

He pretends to deliberate for a moment before shaking his head. "This is when having a plan B would have come in handy."

"Good thing you don't need one." I push my seat back and make myself comfortable. "I love the outdoors."

"Thank God." He pretends to wipe sweat off his forehead. "We're not going anywhere challenging, though."

"Think I can't handle it?"

He reaches over to rest a hand on my thigh, the other on the steering wheel. "Bella," he tells me, "I'm learning that underestimating you is a bad tactic."

It gives me a ridiculous thrill to put my hand on top of his. Today is beautifully undefined—I don't know if this is a date, the start of something *real*, or just the two of us spending time together as friends. But I'm going to enjoy the heck out of it regardless.

Ethan sets course to Mount Rainier National Park. The long drive isn't at all unpleasant, either; there's always something to talk about or just calm silence in the car. It feels mature, somehow, the casual comfort between us.

The first major parking lot we drive past inside the national park is almost empty, but Ethan just keeps driving.

"I know just the spot," he says, turning onto a gravel road. As we begin to climb, the drop to my right deepens, trees dwindling in the distance.

"All right, I give. I'm happy you're driving a monstrosity."

Ethan chuckles. "Four-wheel drive *is* a beautiful thing."

We park on a plateau, right next to an old, abandoned groundskeepers lodge. Nestled into a natural grove of trees, it's all but hidden from the valley below. It's a beautiful summer day, the sun peeking out behind clouds.

"We'll start here," Ethan says, pulling out water bottles for us both. The scent of pine and dew is heavy in the air, and for a moment I just close my eyes and take a deep, filling breath.

I open my eyes to find Ethan looking at me. I smile at him. "This is your form of escape, right? Away from work and responsibilities?"

He gives a slow nod. "Always has been."

"Thanks for showing it to me," I tell him.

He runs a hand over the back of his neck, but he's smiling. "Come on," he tells me. "I want to show you this view."

The trail he's chosen for us isn't too hard. It loops up to a viewpoint, the stunning greens of the national park spreading out in front of us like an unbelievably idyllic desktop picture on a computer. The mountain itself crowns the picture in the far distance, complete with a snow-capped peak. It's beyond gorgeous.

I sink down onto a log and take a deep sip from my water bottle. "We didn't see anyone else on this track," I comment. "How come this place isn't packed?"

Ethan's smile is crooked. "Technically speaking, it's not an official track."

"Technically?"

"It used to be, but they've closed it." He reaches around for his backpack and opens it with a swift tug. He pulls out a packet for us both containing a delicious-looking sandwich.

"Courtesy of Maria," he says.

"I'll have to tell her thanks. This looks amazing."

"She's worth her weight in gold," he agrees, sitting down next to me.

I take a bite and savor the taste, the fresh air, the beautiful view and the sunshine. It's a gorgeous place, and perhaps… perhaps this would be the time to tell him about that little lie, the one I'd somehow fallen into telling over and over again.

"Ethan," I begin, but I lose my nerve the second he turns to look at me. It's too beautiful a place to sully. "Isn't this kind of a simple pleasure for a man like you? The newspapers all want Greenwood Hills residents to be sports-car-owning jet-setters."

He cocks an eyebrow. "Perhaps I would have been, if I didn't have children and responsibilities. Like your aunt and uncle, traveling all summer."

I take a big bite from my sandwich and nod, feeling awful.

"But I've always enjoyed the outdoors, even as a kid. My brother and I grew up by the coast and we were constantly in the water. Besides…" He looks over at me, the furrow in his brow back. "I wasn't sure if we wanted to go somewhere with people."

"You'd be recognized?"

"I could be. It's not super common, but it happens, yeah. I'm sometimes photographed too."

And I'd be by his side when that happened, which would take our… whatever this is into something far more. "Makes perfect sense," I say.

His shoulders relax. "I figured neither of us wanted that."

"No, not at all." I could think of little worse, to be honest, than public scrutiny of what was still so undecided. Ethan finishes his sandwich and reaches out to put his arm around my shoulders. I lean into his side, feeling ninety percent amazing and ten percent like a fraud.

"I'll remember this tomorrow," he says.

I can't help needling him. "I should hope so," I tease. "Or do you usually suffer from memory loss?"

"No, you comedian," he says. "And perhaps I shouldn't bring it up, but... what the hell. My ex-wife is planning on coming over tomorrow."

Oh.

"Wow."

"She's the queen of changing plans last minute, so it's not set in stone. But I've tried to prepare the girls for it."

I swallow. "Where does she usually live?"

"No idea. Last I heard, down in Portland, but she travels a lot. She's a proud member of the sports-car-owning jet-setting club you mentioned earlier."

"Right."

He sighs again. "I shouldn't have brought it up."

"No, of course you should've. I'm always here to listen if you need to talk."

He squeezes my shoulder. "Too kind."

I pull back and look at him, wiggling my eyebrows. "How do you know it's kindness, huh? Perhaps I have ulterior motives."

"Right. And what would they be?"

"I couldn't possibly *tell* you, of course. But theoretically, *hypothetically*, it might involve you, and me, and a bed..."

A smile breaks across his face. "Oh, you don't have to be kind to me to achieve that."

"You'd sleep with just anyone, would you?"

"If that anyone were you, yeah." He presses a kiss to my cheek, trailing down to my neck. "So be rude all you like. You won't scare me away."

"What a relief!" I trail my hand through his hair. "I can finally drop this good-girl act."

He snorts again, pressing his lips to mine. "Sorry, Bella," he says when he's finished kissing me, "but it's fairly obvious that it's not an act."

"Shoot." I'm breathless from his lips. "You know my secret now, then."

"That you're good through and through? Yeah, I'm fairly certain of that." He pulls me into standing. "Let's head back down to the car before we do something we shouldn't on this trail."

We talk about everything and nothing on the drive back, and I discover small, banal things about him. That he only drinks his coffee black and that he hates carrots. His first kiss was at twelve, and it was with the neighbor girl—he winks at me when he says this and tells me it's clearly a pattern—but his brother later confessed to having a crush on her. It complicated things for about a week.

I discover big things, too. He believes that his daughters saved him, in a way, from becoming one of those people who dedicate their lives to work, and that he's grateful to them for that.

He asks me things too. About my brother and my parents, about my education, about where I've travelled. And I tell him things about my family and my studies and my dreams. I only speak this freely around Wilma and Trina, but in the car with him... well, the casual comfort is back.

We're almost in Greenwood by the time Ethan looks over at me with a raised eyebrow. "Sooo," he says, drawing out the vowel.

"So," I echo, twisting around to look at him. His thick hair is pushed back and an easy, charming smile is in place.

"Speaking of that list of yours..."

"We weren't speaking of anything remotely related to that."

He reaches out and puts a hand on my knee again. "Everything is remotely related to *that.*"

I look down at his hand, at the long fingers and broad knuckles. "All right. How about I don't tell you the list as much as I show it to you?"

His grip tightens on my knee. "I'd be amenable to that."

"Amenable?"

"Oh yes." He glances over at me again, and this time there's no mistaking the heat in his gaze. "I have about an hour until I've promised the girls I'd be home."

I trace his fingers, one at a time. "Spend that hour at mine?"

"Excellent idea."

"I've been known to have good ones every now and then." Excitement, anticipation, nerves… they all rise up inside me. This is so far out of my comfort zone—the seduction, the exploration. Surely he must have been with women his own age, with far more experience and talent.

But here he is with me.

Ethan wraps his arms around me as soon as the front door closes behind us. Toast is nowhere to seen, but then it's always a coin toss to see if he'll welcome me home or not.

"Who knew I'd be visiting my neighbor's house so often this summer?" he whispers in my ear, walking me backwards.

I wrap my arms around his neck. "Who knew I'd be visiting *my* neighbor's house so often?"

Ethan kisses me deep and slow, his hands moving at the same time, deliciously big and skilled over my body. "Your neighbor is very pleased about the whole thing," he says, pulling my hips against his for added emphasis.

"So is this neighbor," I murmur against his lips. "So pleased that she would probably *not* report you to the homeowners association if you played loud music."

Ethan leans back. "Wow, she must be *very* pleased."

"Very," I agree. "But she wouldn't be against more pleasing."

His dark laughter washes over me, and then he's gripping my thighs and lifting me up against his body. There's such casual strength in the movement. "I remember mention of a kitchen island," he says.

My throat goes dry. "I did mention that."

Ethan walks us into the kitchen, setting me down on the cool marble. His hands make quick work down the buttons of my shirt.

"I remember mention of arm-gripping and hair-tugging,

which I can do," he says, bending to kiss my neck. "What else? Time for you to practice telling me."

I'm about to, but forming words is difficult when his lips are approaching my bra. He pushes the cups down with no preamble, no warmup, his lips closing around one of my nipples. I gasp at the sensation—so sensitive, and he knows it.

Ethan grins, switching to my other breast. He uses his teeth this time, his hands already undoing the button of my jeans. "Come on. There must be more than that."

I lift my hips so he can slide them off me. "Well, you certainly weren't dressed in my kitchen island fantasy."

Grinning, he reaches down and tugs off his shirt. The expanse of wide, muscled chest and a smattering of hair greets me. I look at him, wanting him on top of me, against me, holding me. Anything to feel that chest.

His smile turns crooked. "That impressive, huh?"

"Definitely." Perhaps he's joking, but I'm certainly not. I reach for his pants, but he pushes my hand away.

"Not fair," I say.

"Patience, Bella..." He pushes me back on the counter and spreads my legs easily. His arm curls around my thighs, holding me in place. I'm locked to this moment—to him and to us. His right hand tugs my panties to the side.

I don't protest. Not when he puts his mouth on me, his tongue, his lips. No, I stare unseeing up at the beautifully inlaid spotlights in the ceiling and struggle to contain my breathing.

It's almost embarrassing how much I'm enjoying this. How good he is—how *easy* this is with him. There's barely any thought at all, just complete surrender, and perhaps it's because of his enthusiasm. He handles me like he likes it—like he loves it—and it's so easy to let go.

And when my orgasm finally barrels through me, he's there, holding me and watching me through lidded eyes. Telling me in a rough voice how much I turn him on.

How much he needs me.

So it's not difficult at all to slide off the counter and turn around, my arms braced against the cold marble. And God help me, but I even wiggle my ass a bit.

What's gotten into me? Not Ethan, at least—not yet, and all I can think about is changing that fact.

"Fuck," he growls, slapping down on one of my cheeks. It stings, but only for a moment. "You're so damn beautiful, it's unreal."

"Again," I say.

"This was on your list?"

I open my mouth to reply but all that escapes is a yelp as his hand comes down again, this time on my other cheek.

"Tell me," he says.

"Yes." It had been buried deep, but it had undeniably been there. My ex had never been interested in trying this—nothing remotely resembling rough.

Ethan tugs my panties down, leaving them halfway on my thighs. My entire body trembles in anticipation, in wait, and then… *sting.* Another slap.

"Your skin is gorgeous," he says. "I've thought that from the first time I saw you."

"Peeping from your tree?" I tease, and gasp as another slap reverberates through me. He's not using a lot of force, not at all proportional to the heat rushing through me. But rushing it is, and I arch my back, aching for him.

"I wasn't spying. But if I was, you were exactly the sight I would have chosen. You're so fucking hot, Bella, and I'll keep saying it until you believe me."

He undoes the clasp of my bra, having a better angle at it than me. I throw it to the side and look back at him.

He's gazing in speculation. "Spanking, huh?" he drawls. "Interesting. I wonder…"

He runs his hand between my legs, one finger sinking deliciously deep. "Fuck, you're wet."

I rest my forehead against the cold marble and focus on breathing. Exposed like this… somehow it only makes me *more* aroused. Knowing he's watching and enjoying me. Hearing him say the words.

A zipper is undone. Then he pulls the hardness over my ass, between my legs, teasing me again.

"What do you want me to do now?" he asks.

"Fuck me."

"What? I didn't quite hear you."

"I want you to fuck me. Right here." I force the last word out before I lose my nerve. "*Hard.*"

Ethan groans. "I don't think I'll ever tire of hearing words like that come out of your mouth."

I look back at him. "I said *now.*"

Grinning, he glances down, his hand moving… but he doesn't push in. "Fucking hell. Bella, I didn't bring a condom."

"I'm on the pill," I say, arching a bit higher. I'm practically *panting* with need. Will he just enter me already? *I need him.*

"And you're good at taking it? Regularly and all?"

"Yes, every morning." It's as ingrained a habit as breathing, almost—I've done it for years and years.

Ethan seems to consider. But I wiggle my ass again, spreading my legs wider…

"Fuck," he says, decision made, and positions himself. We both groan as he pushes into me, inch after inch, deliciously deep.

I'll never tire of this.

Ethan reaches for my arms and tugs them back, my chest rising from the cold marble. He thrusts deep and hard, exactly what I'd asked him for.

It's amazing.

"That's it," he breathes. "Right there. Good girl, Bella, right there…"

I'm barely able to reply, busy as I am focusing on my breathing, on the pleasure growing inside me again. Something about this, about Ethan so unleashed and me bent over like this, has me on hair-trigger. And perhaps I won't always want it like this, but right now it's the only thing I want.

His hand slaps down again. "Your pussy is fucking unreal around me."

My concentration shatters with his words. It's impossible to stop my pleasure from cresting, and when he switches a hand from my arm to my hair, giving it a light tug…

My body explodes again. I'm dimly aware of Ethan cursing, of his hips thrusting erratically, of the pulsing deep inside me as he finishes.

And then we're both panting hard, bodies still intertwined.

"Oh my God," I murmur. My legs feel shaky. So do my arms, to be fair. My entire body is jelly.

"You could say that again."

"Oh my God."

Laughing weakly, Ethan pulls out, turning me around and pulling me against his body. My panties are still around my knees.

"Not too rough?" he murmurs.

"No." I lean my head against his chest and breathe in the deep, male scent of him. "That was perfect."

A hand strokes over my hair. "It was. It was also intense as hell."

I nod. It's hard to form thoughts.

Perhaps Ethan senses that, because he smiles and bends down to tug my panties back into place. "Come on," he tells me. "Show me to your room."

"Don't you have to go?"

"Not quite yet." He supports my weight, and once we've made it to my bedroom, I *almost* feel like a person again. A newly fucked person, true, but someone who can remember the alphabet and basic arithmetic. Calculus is probably still beyond me.

Ethan stretches out on the bed beside me and wraps an arm around my waist. I turn into him and take another deep breath again. Funny, how he smells this good.

I think I tell him that because he laughs. "Never been told that before," he murmurs. "So do you. Especially right now."

Closeness and pleasure and *him* are everywhere, filling my head and my chest. Perhaps that's why the sudden spear of guilt is so intense, piercing through my haze of delirious calm.

I have to tell him.

"Ethan," I say, looking up at the edge of his jaw. It'll be easier to meet than his eyes. "I need to tell you something. About me staying here. There's only about a month and a half left, and when I—"

Ethan's arms flex around me. "Bella, please don't, don't say anything at all. Just be here with me until I have to leave. Let's just be us, with no thoughts of the future."

I swallow my words. They go down painfully, their edges sharp. "All right," I murmur, nestling closer against him, holding on while I still can.

15

ETHAN

I'm shocked the next day when Lyra doesn't show up like she said she would. Absolutely amazed—never in a hundred years had I predicted this. She's usually the paragon of dependability.

But I can't tell my kids that, and not just because they don't yet grasp sarcasm.

Haven tugs on my pant leg. "So she'll be here *tomorrow* instead?"

"Yes, honey, that's what she said." On the phone—after I'd given her my piece. She'd laughed, of course, and said that the ways of air travel were beyond her. *I don't control storms, darling.*

"And Bella? Will she be here too?"

I frown at Haven. "No, she'll be in her house. Maybe she can come over for dinner afterwards, though."

Under no circumstances did I want Bella and Lyra to meet. It was just one of those things, like Evie's idea about putting ketchup on ice cream. You *could* do it, but what was the point? No good would come of it.

Haven crosses her uninjured arm over her chest. "So tomorrow, then."

The tone of her voice isn't entirely happy, either. There's something else in it—skepticism. It tears at my heart to see her develop that feeling so early on, and especially against her mother.

A part of me longs to reassure her. *Mommy loves you and she'll be here as soon as she can.*

But I can't bear to lie to my kid, not when it would just raise her expectations again. So I lift Haven up instead, careful not to jostle her arm. "How about we play in the treehouse instead? You can show me the new game you and Evie invented."

She nods, mollified, but the lure of play doesn't entirely soften my own irritation. Who knows if Lyra will even show up tomorrow? And if she doesn't, what will I tell my girls then?

But when the next day rolls around, a black cab does indeed stop outside of my house around midday. I watch with bated breath from the window in my study.

Is it…?

It is. Lyra gets out, a navy dress wrapped snug around her tall, curvy form. Her light-brown hair falls around a face that is just as immaculately done up as I remember. She hasn't stopped wearing her beauty as armor, it seems.

Sighing, I shut the door to my office and head down to the living room. Maria looks up when I enter, the girls playing quietly behind her. They never play quietly—another way this impending visit is impacting them.

"She's here?" Maria asks. There's a furrow in her brow that doesn't surprise me at all. She's heard the girls ask for their mom just as often as I have.

I nod. "All right, girls. Mom is here!"

Evie cheers, racing toward the front door. Haven follows more cautiously, holding her cast close to her chest.

I put a hand on the back of her head. "You okay, kiddo?"

"Yeah." A pause. "Do you think she'll like the purple?"

"I think she'll love it," I say. "Besides, *you* love it, which is all that really matters."

Haven nods once, her small face determined. She shouldn't have to wonder about her mother, but here we are, and damn if I know how to get them out of it without causing more pain.

Evie pushes the front door open and Lyra comes sweeping into the house on a pair of heels and a wind of righteousness, crouching in the hallway to hug both girls.

"Oh, my darlings," she says. "I've missed you both *so* much."

I cross my arms over my chest and try to stop my teeth from grinding one another into dust. I'm not entirely successful.

"Haven, my love, does your arm hurt terribly?"

Haven shakes her head. "It only hurt when I fell, and for a day afterwards."

"I'm sure you were very brave. Did Dad take you to the hospital?"

"Yes, and Bella."

"Bella?"

"She's our friend," Evie announces. "She bakes."

"Well, that's nice."

Evie tugs on her mother's hand. "Come on, I wanna show you my room!"

"Has anything changed?"

"I have a new bed!"

I follow at a distance, listening to the kids chatter to Lyra about all the changes that have happened since they saw her last. For Evie, Lyra is practically a stranger, one who shows up every now and then but whom she doesn't really miss. Haven's the one with the memories, with friends who ask her questions about her parents.

Lyra stays for lunch. Maria serves it without a word of hello to my ex-wife, and Lyra doesn't say thank you. Is the dislike mutual? Why had I been so blind before?

"I brought you gifts, things I've found when I've been traveling," she says, pulling out things from her bag. "This one's for you, Haven." She pushes something that looks suspiciously like a makeup palette across the table. "To play around with and experiment."

Haven inspects it immediately.

"Lyra," I say quietly, "is that makeup?"

She turns to me, warmth disappearing from her eyes. "Yes, Ethan, it is. It's just for fun."

"She's six." I look over at Haven, who has turned the palette over to fiddle with the sticker on the back. Good thing she isn't getting too attached—that thing will go in the trash the second Lyra's left.

Lyra ignores me, pulling out an electronic tablet for Evie instead. "This one has a *ton* of games on it, honey."

Evie shrieks and begins to press at the screen, her sister joining her. My face must have shown the dismay I feel—not only do they already have tablets, but I keep them on *very* limited screen time. These gifts are extravagant and thoughtless.

Is this what the future will be like? Lyra dancing in to town to give them expensive purses and clothes before dancing right back out of their lives again.

She notices my displeasure, because she brings it up the second we're out of earshot of the kids.

"Don't be so prim, Ethan. They're just kids."

"They're not *just* kids, they're *my* kids." I cross my arms over my chest and look over at the girls. Maria meets my gaze and begins to coax the girls to go outside and play. They disappear a few moments later.

Lyra watches them go. "I miss them when I'm away," she says softly. "It's made me think…"

Not this.

"Well, I'm not entirely happy with the custody agreement," she says.

"You agreed to it," I say, gritting my teeth. Our positions had been crystal-clear in the divorce negotiations. Lyra wanted my money. I wanted my kids. She'd even called me the perfect catch —that's what she'd seen when we first met.

So when her lawyer had written out the number, the amount she wanted in order to surrender her custody claims…

Easiest deal I'd ever signed.

Lyra runs her hand through her hair, flicking it back. It feels disgusting now to think that the calculated move had once enchanted me. "Oh, I remember. But deals can be renegotiated."

"Not this one."

Her hand curls around my arm. "So determined, Ethan."

"You can visit any time, but you don't, so I can't possibly fathom what you'd want with custody," I say. It's easy to guess what her lifestyle is like now, too. International travel. Parties. A fast life, the one she'd lived when I met her and the one she'd always wanted to escape back into.

"You know, I'm not a fan of your attitude," she tells me. "You used to be fun. I remember a night in Cabo, many years ago, when—"

"I'm not going down memory lane with you." I shake off her hand. "Come on. The girls said they wanted to show you their treehouse."

"All right." She trails after me as I open the door to the patio. "Do you spend all your time with children, Ethan? That can't be healthy for you. I mean, raising kids isn't exactly a *science*."

I've never been an angry man, nor a violent one. Never had the inclination, but now... Lyra can bring it out so easily with dismissive comments like that about our children.

"Mommy! Look at our treehouse!" Haven calls, and Lyra dutifully heads across the lawn, pausing momentarily in dismay as her high heels sink into the grass.

It feels like an eternity later when it's finally time for her to leave. The girls ask her when she'll be back, to which she says *as soon as I can*, a blatant lie. It could be tomorrow or six months from now, knowing how Lyra is. It might make me a horrible person, but I almost wish it was ten years. A chance for the girls to grow up without having their hopes crushed over and over again.

"I'll follow you to your car," I murmur.

Lyra frowns. She hasn't called her cab yet—waiting curbside won't appeal to her. But I open the front door and motion her out. Maria closes it behind me with soft murmurs to the girls.

"Another lecture?" Lyra asks.

I shut the gate behind us. "No, just a reminder. You're their mother. Visit whenever, but give us enough time to prepare in advance and most of all, stick to what you've said."

She rolls her eyes. "Yes, sir."

I grit my teeth. "Honestly, though, why do you even show up? You got the money. You have no responsibilities. Either be a mother or fully walk away. This in-between state isn't helping anyone."

Lyra looks past me. For a moment, I wonder if she'll actually answer me—if I'll finally get some form of understanding into the woman who'd once set out to ruin my life.

"They're my kids too," she finally says. "Even if I'm not—ah. We've got company."

I turn to follow her gaze, and damn it, but it's Bella. She stops a few feet away and glances between us. There's a Tupperware box of brownies in her arms.

"I'm sorry," she says. "I didn't mean to interrupt."

"You're not. Bella, this is Lyra, my ex-wife. Lyra, this is Bella. She's the Gardners' niece, staying next door for the summer."

Lyra's face clears. "My children have just told me about you. You were at the hospital with Haven?"

"Yes I was." Bella glances toward me again. "She was very brave."

"Oh, I'm certain of that. She has good genes." Lyra's smile turns sharp. "How *nice* of you to swing by to give the girls brownies."

Bella doesn't wither under my ex-wife's stare. She smiles blithely back instead, and in that instance, the difference between them couldn't be clearer to me if it had been written above their heads. A brightly decorated viper in the bush compared to a warm, inviting hearth fire.

"The kids really like them," Bella says warmly. "Well, it was great to meet you."

"Oh, likewise." A black car pulls to a smooth stop next to us, and Lyra turns to press a kiss to my cheek. "I'll see you soon," she tells me, like we're the best of friends.

"All right." I doubt it.

"Goodbye, Bella."

"Bye."

Lyra's cab drives off, and Bella and I watch it disappear. The trees on either side of the street rustle slightly in the passing wind, as if they're sighing in relief.

"I'm sorry," Bella says. "I thought she came yesterday."

"That was the plan, but plans have never mattered much to her. Don't worry about it." I reach for the box of brownies. "I could really use one of these right now."

She smiles crookedly. "I sort of figured you would."

"You know me that well already?"

"I'm trying to." She opens the lid for me and I fish one out. "How are the girls?"

"Happy, for now. Evie doesn't really have any understanding of why it's odd that a mother would go away for so long. Haven… she's more confused."

"Understandable." Bella puts a hand on my arm, and God help me, but I lean into her touch. I'm like a starved man when it comes to it, and I doubt I'll ever be sated. "How are *you?*"

"In need of a glass of whiskey," I say. "It's hard to believe I was ever married to that woman."

Bella nods, but her eyes burn with curiosity. Of course she wonders.

"Come in?" I suggest.

"I'd like that." Her smile softens, and at the sight, something inside of me starts to as well.

It's a long time before we finally settle down on the patio, just her and I, the kids asleep and the evening air warm. The summer sunlight plays softly on her hair, draped like a shimmering wave of brown down her back.

I'm here with her, and yet my mind can't stop tracing the contours of the old wound with Lyra. Over and over the encounter plays. Was I too firm? Not firm enough?

Bella tucks her legs underneath herself. "I wish I knew what to say."

"About what?"

"About today," she replies. "You're preoccupied."

"Right, I'm sorry."

"No, don't be. I just want to be able to help you somehow, and I can't."

I shake my head. "You *are* helping, just by being here. And your brownies, too—they certainly helped."

She smiles. "These were I'm-sorry-your-ex-wife-is-a-bitch brownies, so they'd better. The ones I made the first time were I'd-like-to-get-to-know-you brownies."

I snort. "That makes sense," I say. "These were a bit saltier."

Bella sticks out her tongue at me, and I laugh, moving closer to her. Putting an arm around her feels like the simplest thing in the world, and by far the simplest thing I've done today. She leans into my side, warm and true and somehow so *easy*. It makes it simple to say the words. "All right," I murmur. "So you want the whole sordid tale?"

"If you want to tell it," she says.

"I don't, really. But it might make you think slightly better of me."

She looks up. "What do you mean?"

"Can you honestly tell me you haven't wondered why I was married to Lyra? From what you've heard so far?"

Bella bites her lip, but the answer is in her eyes. "A bit."

"Just a bit? Good."

"Well, she *is* very beautiful."

I snort again. "And she knows it. Well, I met her at a party out of state. She was witty and charming, and one thing led to the other. She was pregnant two months later."

Bella's eyes widen. "Wow."

"Yes. On purpose, too, as I discovered years later. She'd lied about taking birth control entirely."

"Oh my God," Bella says. "That's despicable."

"Yes, well, I'm inclined to agree. We got married shortly before Haven was born." And Lyra had never wanted the pictures displayed anywhere, either, because of her noticeable baby bump.

"Did you want to get married?"

I run a hand over my face. "Yes and no. It felt like the right thing to do. The kid was ours and I… well. I owed it to Haven and Lyra to give it a shot. Marriage, I mean. We signed a prenup, because at the end of the day we hadn't even known each other a year. She hated that, but…"

Bella nods slowly. "But it didn't work out."

"No. She was never interested in being a mother. We argued a lot." Everything had been a fight, by the end. She wanted more parties. More time away from me. More money in her account. "And not too long after Haven, she got pregnant with Evie. I do think that was a genuine mistake on her part—she didn't want to be pregnant again."

Bella puts a hand over mine, threading her fingers through mine. "But you wanted Evie."

"Of course I did. How couldn't I, after having held Haven? Evie arrived nine months later and the marriage collapsed soon after that."

Fights.

I can't do this anymore.

Lyra packing up her things.

"I'm sorry." Bella's voice is thick with sincerity, and for the first time in a long while… it doesn't grate. It doesn't feel pitying. There's none of the implied *we-suspected-it-all-along* that I'd gotten from my mother or my brother. They'd apparently known she was a gold-digger from the start.

"You haven't heard the worst yet," I say, glancing behind me to double-check that the patio door is completely locked. The next words are difficult to speak out loud. Difficult to even consider without anger rising up to put me in a chokehold.

Bella squeezes my hand. "I haven't?"

"It all came out in the divorce settlement. It was so blatantly obvious, with her on one side and me on the other, that all she'd ever wanted was money. She was the one who made the offer.

She would relinquish her custody if I agreed to scrap the prenup."

Bella's drawn-in breath is audible. "You can't be serious."

"Dead serious." My voice feels detached, far away, floating somewhere over the burning rage in my stomach. I will always try to keep my daughters from finding out about that, but one day they'll draw the conclusion themselves, and hearing them ask about it will break my heart more than Lyra ever did. "She told me straight out that she'd lied about birth control with Haven for that purpose."

"She trapped you?"

"Essentially, yes." I reach for my glass of whiskey and knock it back, but it does nothing to quell the tension inside me. "Joke's on her, though, because I was dealt the best hand. I can always make more money, but the kids are irreplaceable."

Bella is silent for a long while. So long that when I look down at her, I'm shocked to see that her eyes are glittering, sparkling with unshed tears.

"Bella?"

"I'm sorry. I know it's… wow. You're strong, Ethan. And kind. And a far better person than I am, for being able to be civil to her today. I want to slap her now."

It takes me a moment to absorb the impact of her words. It's been an age since I've felt anything but a fool over my blindness in that marriage. Someone who'd easily been played. I'd walked straight into her trap.

Seeing Lyra and Bella together had made it all so clear. Bella values her studies and her future, baking and hiking, children and animals—at least the cat she's taking care of.

And her face is an open book.

"Bella," I say. "You've seen the truth. I'm a dad who either spends too little time with his kids or too little time at his job. I promised to read your thesis and I haven't even managed to follow up on that. I have no idea what I can realistically offer you in terms of the future… but I want to try."

Bella cups my face between her palms, the skin soft against the stubble on my cheeks. Her eyes are wide. "To try?"

"Yes, to try and date you properly. To be an us, whatever that means. We'll figure out the details along the way."

I haven't been nervous in a long time. But I'm nervous now, watching her beautiful hazel eyes, the unlined skin of her face, the kindness in her smile. She's so young, and so smart, and so gorgeously unattached. She could be with anyone. Anyone at all that isn't me, with a truckload of baggage and two kids.

"I want to try too," she murmurs, and the smile that breaks across her face… it takes my breath away.

I catch her lips with mine. She laughs as I bend her back, as she stretches out on the loveseat and wraps her arms around me. I can't remember the last time I felt as hopeful about the future as I do now, so I grip her tight, as if I can keep both her and the feeling close by arms alone.

16

BELLA

I rearrange my bangs in front of the hallway mirror for the fiftieth time, my hair long down my back—and thank God for that, because for some reason I've gone with a backless dress.

One I'd bought years ago on sale, and later realized was not only unpractical but basically useless. Not only was it risky, as it was just fastened with a tie around my neck, but it was light blue. When did I go to events that called for dresses like these?

Tonight, apparently.

I take a deep breath and push an offending tendril of hair to the side. Ethan and I are going to a party—and we're doing it *together*. "Easy peasy," I tell my own reflection. "He likes you, you like him… nothing could be simpler."

The bell to the gate rings and I grab my purse in one hand, bending to say goodbye to Toast. My hand disappears in the cat's thick gray fur.

"Wish me luck?"

He butts his head against my hand and lets out a small, warm purr. I scratch behind his ear. "What's this?" I ask. "Are we becoming friends?"

Toast winds around my leg before disappearing down the hallway, probably offended by the mere suggestion. "Don't worry!" I call after him. "I won't tell anyone!"

Then I lock the door behind me and head down to meet Ethan. He has his back to me, his navy trousers expertly fitted, contrasting with the blue shirt that stretches taut over his shoulders.

I pause with my hand on the gate. "Sorry," I say, "but I'm looking for my neighbor? Single dad, usually wearing shorts?"

Ethan's smile is wide and carefree, the one that always manages to take my breath away. Will I ever gain immunity? I doubt it. "You've only seen me at my worst, haven't you?" he asks.

"If that's been your worst, I'm not sure I'm ready for you at your best."

His gaze wanders over my form, down my neck, my dress, my espadrille wedges. "You've been holding out on me too," he says. "Are you planning on opening the gate or am I doomed to admire you from a distance forever?"

Laughing, I push it open, stepping out onto the sidewalk and into the waiting crook of his arm. "I wouldn't doom you to anything."

Ethan presses a kiss to my temple. "You're stunning."

"And you're *sure* this isn't overdressed for a barbecue?"

"No," he snorts. "Trust me, Cole and Skye rarely do casual. This might be called a barbecue, but it's really their version of a summer party."

Perhaps he notices my nerves, or he can anticipate them, because he tugs me closer. "Sure you want to go? I don't mind staying home. I know what being seen together with me can mean, sometimes."

"No, no, of course I want to go. I was just wondering if *you're* sure, actually," I say. "You'll get questions from your friends, you know."

Ethan's smile is a slash of white. "As opposed to the lack of questions I got when I was single, you mean?"

"I guess I'd forgotten about that."

"And so what if they have questions? I meant what I said… I do want to try. And being my date to a party is part of that."

It's a statement, but Ethan's deep voice makes it a question. It's the same question he's been asking me all week—either with his words or his touch. *Can we make this work?* And at every turn I've said yes, yes, yes. This time is no different.

I slip my hand through his. "All right, then. I'm ready."

"We have one stop to make first."

"We do?"

He tugs me along toward his house, the gate already half-open. "Someone is *very* excited about seeing you in your dress."

Haven comes running down the hallway toward the open front door. "Bella!"

"Haven!"

Her eyes widen as she takes in my dress. I wonder if I should pull my hand out of Ethan's, but he keeps his grip firm around mine. Has he spoken to them yet?

"You look so pretty!"

"Thank you," I tell her. "Do you like the color? It's not purple, but it's pretty close."

"No, no, it's still pretty," she assures me. Her eyes snag on our intertwined hands. "Daddy, are you taking Bella to a ball?"

He reaches out and musses her hair. She darts back, shooting me a *can-you-believe-this-guy?* look. I bite my lip to keep from laughing. "It's not a ball," he says, "and I'm not a prince."

Haven rolls her eyes and looks straight at me. "I know Daddy's not a prince, but you look like a princess."

"Thank you," I tell her, because just like that, Haven has banished my nerves entirely. The only thing that really matters beyond Ethan is his daughters, and if they're fine with us, I can handle whatever questions his Greenwood Hills friends might have.

Ethan keeps his hand in mine on the walk over to Cole's house. The summer air is warm, and the sun won't set for hours still. It's the perfect evening for a party.

I push the faint, incessant guilt to the back of my mind—but only for tonight. I'll tell him tomorrow. And besides, house-sitter, the Gardners' niece... does it really matter so much, in the grand scheme of things? Ethan has been coming over nearly every evening this past week, and the things we've spoken about, the things we've done… He'll understand when I tell him.

We pause outside of a house that is the size of a small castle. If I thought mine or Ethan's was imposing, this is…

Ethan snorts beside me. "Big, isn't it?"

That's an understatement. It looks like the kind of house people who've never been to Greenwood Hills *think* are in Greenwood Hills.

"Wow," I say.

"It's even worse on the inside. Come on, let me show you." He keeps his hand in mine as we walk up the massive driveway, nodding to some of the people milling on the front porch.

It *is* even worse on the inside. Double staircases, marble floors, interior design that looks *too* casually thrown together to be anything but planned—likely the work of an interior designer. No one actually *owns* fourteen coffee-table books.

Skye sees us first and reaches out to hug us both. "Thank God," she says. "Familiar faces!"

Ethan raises an eyebrow. "It's that bad?"

She glances over her shoulder. "Not at all. Just… well, a little, actually. I've just spent the better part of an hour debating publishing models and while that's fascinating, I could use an escape."

"Is Isaac upstairs?"

Skye's eyes warm. "Yes, and I can't wait to sneak back up there later. Oh, I didn't mean that how it sounded. Please don't take offense."

Ethan shakes his head. "None taken. I know the feeling."

"I bet you do." Skye gives me a wide smile. "I'm so glad you could make it too, Bella."

I meet her smile with my own. She hadn't even glanced down at my hand, still intertwined with Ethan's. "So am I. You have a beautiful home."

"Thank you. A bit on the large side, though, isn't it?"

I must look as shocked as I feel, because she laughs. "Oh, I know what it looks like. I'd shave off a few square feet myself, but that doesn't work when your husband develops properties for a living."

"Poor you," Ethan teases, and Skye laughs again.

"Yes, I'm really struggling here. Come on, you two. I'm guessing you want to bypass all the unnecessary mingling?"

Ethan nods. "If possible?"

Skye winks at us. "Of course it is. Having a lot of square feet does have some perks, you know."

She leads us through a gigantic kitchen and out through a back door. We emerge to the side of the crowded patio, following her down a few steps to a sunken lounge. Sitting on the patio furniture are people I recognize. Blair, Nick, Cole, all sharing a drink. From across the lawn, the sound of soft live music drifts toward us.

Well, this is certainly *one* kind of barbecue, I guess. Ethan wasn't kidding when he said they didn't do casual.

We have a seat on the empty loveseat. Blair grins and nods to our intertwined hands. "Good to see you two took our advice," she says, blonde hair like a golden waterfall around her face. She's still as unbelievably gorgeous as the first time I'd met her.

Nick elbows her gently, and she gives us a chagrined smile. "Sorry. I know these things take time, and I shouldn't push."

"I don't think we took *too* much time, did we? It's been two months since I moved in?"

Ethan rests his arm behind me on the couch and takes a sip of the drink just offered to him. "Something like that, yes."

Cole shakes his head. "I can't believe your luck, man. The perfect woman just moves in next door? That just doesn't happen. I feel like you haven't worked for it enough."

Ethan snorts, but he doesn't object. "Can't say I disagree."

"How about you?" I ask Cole and Skye, who's just sat down on the armrest of his chair. "How did you two meet?"

"Well," Cole says, "it's a rather long story."

"It's very short," Skye protests. "He was trying to tear down property that I was trying to protect."

Cole mutters something in his glass that sounds an awful lot like *that's not how we met*, but Skye ignores him completely.

"That sounds complicated," I say, "and very intriguing. What happened next?"

They launch into their story together and I listen, nestled into the crook of Ethan's arm. It's clearly a telling they've perfected, because they know when to pause for the other's part. It's as thrilling to watch as the story itself.

From there, the conversation flows easily. It's not awkward at all, actually, being here with Ethan's high-flying friends. I'm certainly aware of the difference between us—I have nowhere to live and they probably all own multiple houses—but it doesn't make me self-conscious the way it had when I first met them at dinner. They're people, I'm people. Not to mention that Ethan likes them, and I trust his judgment. Not once has he lorded his money or status in a way that's made me uncomfortable.

Cole stops by my side later, a glass in his hand. "You're the Gardners' niece, right?"

The pulled pork slider I've just swallowed turns to lead in my stomach. I can't reply.

By my side, Ethan speaks for me. "Yes, she is."

"Some of their close friends are here, I believe. Craig and Joanna Robson. Do you know them? They're over by the fire pit."

"We can go over and say hi," Ethan offers, finishing the last of his own slider. "I don't mind."

Oh no.

No, no, no.

"Thanks for letting me know," I tell Cole. "I might talk to them later, but for now, I need another one of those burgers."

"So do I," Cole says, motioning to one of the waiters. "Isn't my caterer the best?"

"Yes, and you're the humblest," Ethan says, accepting another of the sliders. Somehow, neither of them pick up on the panicked sweat that must have broken out across my forehead.

The second it's just the two of us again, I grip Ethan's hand tightly. "Do you want to head out soon?" I ask. "I think I've had enough miniature burgers and crooning jazz music to last me a week, possibly longer."

Ethan tips my head back and kisses me, right there in front of anyone who might be looking. "Thought you'd never ask," he says.

The sigh of relief that escapes me as we leave Cole's mansion behind is tinged with heavy guilt. All it would've taken was one word to the wrong guest at that party for the innocent lie to come crashing down around me.

And it would be so much worse if he didn't hear it from me.

"Ethan," I say softly. "Tonight was amazing. This whole past week has been, actually. Absolutely amazing."

He fits his arm tightly around my waist. "I'm happy to hear it," he murmurs. "It's been amazing for me too."

"I want you to know that meeting you was… well, one of the best, most unexpected things in my life. I had no idea when I moved here for the summer that this would happen between us. It's been the best surprise." I swallow, forcing the next words out. "That's what I want you to focus on."

He unlocks the gate to his house, pulling me along up toward his front door. The sudden change in direction disrupts my flow. "We're going to yours? What about the kids?"

"Yes. You're sleeping in my bed tonight."

"What about the girls? Won't they be surprised when I'm here in the morning?"

"You often come by for weekend breakfast anyway," he says, unlocking the front door. The second it closes behind us, he wraps his arms around me. "You can't say things like that to me, Bella, not without living up to them. Stay the night with me. Let me show you just how good of a surprise this has been for me too."

My arms tighten around his neck. The fierce sincerity in his voice has dealt a withering blow to my resolve, but it makes one final, valiant stand. "Ethan, I need to—"

He presses his lips to mine and swallows the truth I'd

planned on laying out for him, meeting it with soft heat and strong, gripping hands. The truth is better spoken in daylight, after all.

The dark is for lovers.

He lays me out on his bed, strips me slowly, even as I do the same to him. Tonight there are no discussions about lists or wants or fantasies. There's just us and the sound of our breathing.

And when he spreads my legs and fills me up, when I cradle him against me and run my nails gently down his back, it's different than it's been before. We make love without words this time, but we've never spoken louder.

Ethan shudders in my arms when he comes, burying his head against my neck. We lie like that for a long, long time.

"Stay," he murmurs. "I love having you in my bed."

I wrap both my arms and legs around him, fighting against the tears that prick at my eyes. He might have said *bed,* but the word I hear is *life.* And I feel the same way.

"I love being in your bed," I whisper, desperately hoping that I'll still be invited after tomorrow, when the truth meets the cold light of day.

17

ETHAN

Bella groans and turns over in bed, pretending to put a pillow over her head. She mumbles something that sounds like *it's so early.*

Laughing, I pull the cover up around her and press a kiss to her bare, smooth shoulder. "Sleep a while longer, then."

She grumbles again but doesn't try to keep me in bed—not that I would've been averse to her trying. But there are sounds from the hallway outside of my bedroom that are easy to recognize.

I pull on a T-shirt and a pair of jeans and open my bedroom door to two girls, one in a tutu and the other in nothing but her nightie, dancing around with the theme song to Paw Patrol playing in the background.

"Morning!" Evie chirps. It's one of those small Evieisms—she's never quite figured out the point of adding *good* to good morning or good night.

I scoop her up and ruffle Haven's hair. "Did you guys just get up?"

"Yes. Maria is making breakfast, but she says we have to wait for Bella, too." Haven tries to peer around me into the dark of my bedroom. "Is she still asleep?"

"Yes. Let's let her wake up slowly. Why don't we go grab some orange juice?"

When Bella finally emerges, she's showered and sheepish. The expression on her face makes me chuckle. "I'm sorry," she says. "I thought I was used to early mornings, but apparently not."

"You slept in for thirty minutes. It's hardly a capital crime."

Maria hands her a cup of coffee, the smile on her face just a tad smug. "Good morning."

"Good morning," Bella says earnestly. "And thank you for preparing breakfast. Can I help with anything?"

"You can sit down with the girls," Maria tells her. "Sir?"

I nod and lift Evie up from where she'd been trying to climb on the drawers to reach the fruit platter. "Come here, kiddo."

She wails in protest and goes completely limp in my arms—the newest tactic. It makes it damn near impossible to put on her clothes or brush her teeth, but it won't help her here.

"Won't work." I tell her, plopping her down in her chair at the breakfast table. "You'll get food in a minute."

"Patience," Haven tells her, with all the pretentious experience of being the older sibling.

"We'll all get food in a minute," Bella says, smiling at me from the other side of the table. It throws me off for a second, but then warmth spreads through my chest. It's odd, this… or perhaps it's odd that it *isn't* odd, not at all. It feels right.

The girls are going to get attached. Hell, they already are. But maybe that's okay. Perhaps she's here to stay—and perhaps letting someone new in is the right thing to do. The girls can't live in Lyra's shadow forever. Maybe I shouldn't either.

Evie pulls Bella into the living room immediately after breakfast. "Can you help us?" she asks, holding up the makeup palette Haven had gotten from my ex-wife. "I want a butterfly on my cheek."

Bella looks over at me. Her expression is a mix of *help me* and *what do I do?* I grin and shake my head at her. *You're on your own.*

"I'll try," she tells my youngest, "but I'm not good at drawing. Okay, have a seat here…"

By the kitchen island, Maria is humming to herself as she wipes off the marble. When she notices me watching, she shoots me a not-so-subtle thumbs up. "Great job," she tells me.

Well.

"Thanks." If both my mother and housekeeper approve… perhaps my own apprehension is needless.

It's midday by the time Bella and I get a moment alone together. The girls have run out to play in the treehouse, with Maria to supervise. It's a Saturday unlike any I've had in years—with no pressing demands to work, with an adult in the house that isn't my family, with possibility hanging in the very air.

Bella pulls me into the living room and down onto the couch. I wrap an arm around her and breathe in her scent. Shampoo and perfume and something else, warm skin and woman. I want to hold her like this forever.

"Ethan," she murmurs.

"Mhm?"

She pushes me back, a hand on my chest. "I need to tell you something."

"All right." My fingers twine through her hair, soft and silky.

"Remember when we first met?"

"Of course I do. You came over to introduce yourself with your I-want-to-get-to-know-you brownies."

"Yes, right." She takes a deep breath. "And you asked me who I was, what I was doing here over the summer. Well, you kind of assumed, actually. And—"

The sound of the bell to the gate rings through the entire house, amplified by the built-in speakers. "Shit," I say. "I'm sorry, I can tell this is important."

She nods. "But it can wait. Are you expecting someone?"

"Not at all," I say, heading to the hallway. The face on the intercom is as familiar as it is inconvenient at the moment. "You're here?"

My younger brother's voice echoes back to me. "Yes, and you're there. Glad we've established that."

The snide asshole, probably flown in from New York or Tokyo or wherever he's been for work, and never a call in advance.

I open the gate for him and turn to Bella, who's already gathering up her things.

"You don't have to go," I tell her.

"Yes, I do." She presses a kiss to my cheek. "I don't need to force my way into *every* friend or family event you're having. That's not exactly nice, is it?"

"You're not forcing your way into anything."

"Still," she says. "I left my thesis on your bedside table. Don't be too harsh in your critique, all right?"

"I can't wait to read it."

She smiles at me, and it's her normal kind smile, but it's tinged with something else that I can't place. What had she been meaning to tell me, exactly? A thousand options race through my head and none of them seem pleasant.

But there's no time for that, because the front door opens and Liam steps in. He's in a suit, no tie, his hair a mess. "Finally," he says, "I though… oh. Hello," he says to Bella. The same height as me, the two of us dwarf her in the hallway.

She gives him a half-smile and extends a hand. "Hi there. I'm Bella, Ethan's friend."

He shakes her hand. A light shines in his eyes—one I remember from our childhood. "Ethan's friend? How nice. I'm his brother, Liam."

"A pleasure."

"Likewise." His gaze meets mine with a wink. "And why didn't I know you had a new *friend,* Ethan?"

"Why didn't I know you were coming to town?"

Liam waves that away, like it doesn't matter, and reaches up to undo the top button of his shirt. "Wasn't sure I was until I boarded the plane. Now, beautiful Bella, are you telling me that my big brother has finally found himself a girl?"

I groan and reach out to brace myself against the wall. Trust Liam to have as impeccable timing as he did social skills. A skilled-as-hell investor, he'd developed an oversized ego to match his oversized trades.

I build things. Companies. Tech. My money comes from creation. Liam's? His comes from trading, and damn if you didn't have to be an asshole to pull off that confidence trick.

Bella laughs, but it sounds a bit forced. Damn it. "I think you'll have to ask your brother about that," she says. "But for the record, I'm all in."

Liam's eyebrows shoot even higher, looking over at me now. "Did you hear the lady?"

"I did," I say, unable to stop the smile from tugging at the corners of my mouth. Whatever she'd been about to tell me earlier, she's all in. *All in.*

Liam finally lets go of Bella's hand. "And you certainly live up to your name," he tells her.

"All right, did you come here just to hang in the hallway?" I ask.

He shakes his head at Bella, as if I'm not there. "He's completely forgotten his manners. Do you think he's a lost cause?"

She laughs. "He has potential, but's it's been close at times."

"Good thing he has you to pull him back from the brink."

Bella looks over at me, laughter in her eyes. Whatever she sees on my face draws it to the surface, and it fills the air between us, light and lovely. "Happy to," she says. "I was actually heading out. It was nice to meet you."

"Sure you can't stay?" Liam asks.

"I'm sure, I have work to do. Besides, you have nieces to attend to."

"Yes," I say. "Do you feel like being a canvas for makeup? They need someone to try out their new designs on."

My brother looks suitably alarmed at that.

But as it turns out, he's safe. Evie and Haven attack him with questions instead as they show him the treehouse and Haven's cast. They even perform a dramatic reenactment of Haven's fall and laugh as Liam pretends to catch her.

163

I do have to give it to my little brother—for all that he's never here, when he *is* here, he's all in. He stays for a few more hours, but I don't manage to get a real conversation going, one about his job or his plans for the future.

It's late that evening when I finally open Bella's thesis. She had indeed left it on my bedside table with a small post-it note on top.

Be honest, she's written in looping cursive.

I lie back with an arm under my head and start to read. She's a great writer, succinct and clever. I've made it nearly halfway through when my phone rings.

I answer without looking at the caller ID. "It's good," I tell her. "Really good. Especially your use of—"

"I'm not your little girlfriend."

My voice breaks off. "Lyra?"

"Yes, it's me."

Silence.

"What? No, how are you? How nice of you to call?"

I grit my teeth. "What do you want?"

"Right down to business as usual. But that's all you care about, Ethan, isn't it? Business?"

"If you called just to have a fight, I'm more than willing to hang up."

"So testy." She clicks her tongue. "All right, I'll get to the point. You see, I've been thinking a lot since I last saw you. About one thing in particular—your cute neighbor girl."

I put down the thesis. "Whatever you have to say, I don't want to hear it."

"You don't? Oh, this I *do* think you'll want to hear. You see, meeting her got me thinking. I spent a lot of time talking to neighbors when I lived in Greenwood. You never had time for that sort of thing, of course." A delicate pause. "Or for me."

"Lyra," I warn. "That is not the truth."

"Well, I spoke to Mrs. Gardner several times. A nice, if somewhat severe, older woman. And one thing I remember *very* clearly."

Lyra pauses, like an actor before delivering a particularly juicy line. I have no patience for her dramatics. "All right? And what was it?"

"Neither she nor her husband have any siblings. I remember, you see, because she often complained that they were the only ones able to take care of their elderly parents."

It takes me a moment longer to compute this information than it should. No siblings. And no siblings meant… no nieces and nephews.

"You understand, right?" Lyra asks. "This means your girl is a little liar."

There's no response to that. None at all, not against the pounding of my pulse or the anger at Lyra's obvious glee. Because I can't believe it. It's such an outrageously stupid lie, and Lyra is not above lying herself, just to stir things up.

I hang up without responding, unable to face Lyra's gloating. Dazed, I glance down at Bella's thesis, at the carefully scribbled post-it note. *Be honest.*

There's no way she's been lying to me about this. Why would she? Why else would she be staying in their house?

A loose sheet of paper peeks up out of the neatly stapled work in my hands. I tug it loose, and find that it's a letter. It must have gotten caught amongst the other pages.

Reading the title takes me several tries.

Application for Washington Polytech financial aid.

Applicant: Miss Bella Mary Simmons.

The rest of the words blur together in a haze of thoughts, one moving faster than the other.

If she had lied… why had she? Perhaps she's been hired by the Gardners? She might actually be the live-in housekeeper, the cleaner, the stewardess. Lying about that made no sense, not unless you took into consideration an artfully placed document about her need for money in a binder meant for me.

This has to be what she'd tried to tell me earlier. She's going to ask me for money.

Around me, the world gently collapses.

18

BELLA

In terms of work, that day is a complete waste. The words on the screen in front of me swim—it's no use. I can't focus at all. No, my mind is on Ethan, on spending the night in his bed, on his words last night.

I run a hand through my hair and try to shake the wide, stupid smile on my face. It refuses to budge, like it's been welded in place. This thing with Ethan and me is better than anything I've had before. Realer than reality, none of the pretense, just the two of us.

And as soon as I get the chance to tell him the truth, there won't be anything between us. The longing to come clean is nearly overwhelming now. To meet his eyes and have him know all of me, the same way I want to know all of him. I text him and let him know that I'm free that evening, after his brother has left, but he doesn't respond.

The doorbell to my gate rings instead. Toast barely looks up from his perch on the couch—he's gotten used to Ethan's evening visits. I head over to the foyer and press the door to the gate without looking, unlocking the front door too.

It's him, because of course it is. His thick hair falls over his forehead, nearly hiding the furrow in between his brows. How I long to erase it in laughter or pleasure. That might be my goal in life, I think. Just keeping that furrow at bay.

"Hey," I say, reaching for him. He lets me pull him inside. "Has your brother left?"

"Yes, a while ago."

"It was really nice to meet him."

Ethan nods once, his arms at his side. By this time, he's usually wrapped them around me, sometimes carrying me off unceremoniously to the sofa or the bed.

"Good," he says, but his tone says it's anything but. "Bella, I just heard that the Gardners don't have a niece."

My breathing chokes off for a second.

And then I'm babbling. "Oh Ethan, I wanted to tell you so often, but I was afraid of how you'd react. That's no excuse, of course. I should've, of course I should've. I tried to tell you this morning."

He's so still he might be a statue. "So you're *not* family?"

"No, I'm not."

"Then who are you exactly?"

"I'm house-sitting for the Gardners this summer. They needed someone to watch the cat, and the house, and water the plants and run water in the pipes… it's like a summer job."

"You get paid to live here," Ethan clarifies. The furrow in his brow is deeper, now. No erasing it in sight.

"Yes, I do."

"Was that so unthinkable to tell me? Why lie?"

My chest feels like it's caving in on itself. I don't know where to start, how to approach this, and my words just spill out. "I had two friends visiting, Wilma and Trina. I think I've told you about them? It was a few days after you'd seen me topless by the pool. They dared me to go over and introduce myself, and I was nervous. You assumed I was related to the Gardners' somehow and I just rolled with it, because it felt silly to say that I was a house-sitter. You so clearly had your life together and… well. But I had no idea what we'd become, Ethan. None at all."

He holds up a hand. "Your friends dared you to come over?"

"Yes."

"Why?"

"I mentioned that you were attractive. They wanted me to take a risk—I hadn't really spoken to a man after Ryan. And you work in the industry I study, so they told me to give it a shot… Ethan?"

He turns from me, a hand on the front door, and the tension in his shoulders would be visible from space. My words trip over each other in their rush to get out.

"It was a white lie, and it grew from there, until it felt impossible to undo. I'm so sorry about that. Everything else I've told you has been the complete truth, I promise." My chest isn't just caving in, it's imploding, leaving me a hollow mess inside. Damn my tongue and my inability to find the right words.

Ethan doesn't turn. "Did you put your financial aid application in your thesis on purpose?"

"What?"

"The document. Stuck in the thesis you left me. Was it on purpose?"

Oh God. One of the letters must have gotten caught amongst the pages, stuffed as they often were in the same bag. The conclusions he must have drawn… "No, absolutely not."

He opens the door and heads out into the warm evening air.

"Ethan?"

"I need time," he says.

I follow him out on the front lawn. "Okay," I say. "I'll be here. And if you want to—"

"No, I don't want to talk." He pulls open the gate in my overwrought, wrought-iron fence. "You lied to me, Bella. For weeks."

And on that note, the gate locks behind him and he's off, out of my temporary property and perhaps permanently out of my life. I sink down onto the lawn and try to keep from crying. But I don't succeed in that, either.

19

BELLA

"So you haven't spoken to him since?" Wilma asks, the concern on her face threatening to undo my calm composure.

"Nope."

"And it's been over a week?" Trina challenges. "How can he be so hurt by this? It just doesn't make sense to me."

"It makes perfect sense," I say. "He doesn't trust people easily, not after his divorce… and then I went and lied to him."

"I wonder what he's told his kids," Wilma muses. "They must be asking where you went, all of a sudden."

Sighing, I reach up for one of the packets of cocoa powder on the high shelf in the kitchen. With only two weeks left in the house, I'm tentatively starting to arrange my meager possessions into boxes. Perhaps it's early to be packing, but I'm so stressed by the radio silence from my neighbor-turned-lover that I have to keep myself busy somehow.

"I don't even want to think about that," I say. "And I'm not sure he'll forgive me—ever." The fear has been my only companion in the past week and a half, as I've given him the space he asked for.

"That would be crazy," Trina protests. "Of course he will. From what you've told us, this was real. It was great. If he's as smart as you think he is, he'll see that."

"He might. But he could also decide that I'm not worth the trouble. What good is loving someone if you can't trust them?" I'd had a lot of time to think it through in the past few days—all the opportunities I'd had to set him straight and not taken. It's a peculiar kind of pain, when it's entirely of your own making.

Wilma shakes her head. "You can't speak like that. You have to *believe* he'll come around."

I snort, but nod anyway, mostly for her benefit. It's a discussion we've had a million times. Me, rational, logical—insisting wishing for something doesn't help it come true. Her, a strong believer in belief itself, in good vibes and the universe and The Secret.

"Maybe he will," I say, lifting up one of the cardboard boxes on the kitchen island. "Maybe he won't. But it doesn't change anything in the short term. I still have to find a place to stay."

"You can stay with one of us, of course," Trina says. "And I'll come with you apartment hunting this weekend. You're visiting a few places on Saturday, right?"

"Yes. Thank you, honestly. Both of you."

Wilma smiles. "That's what friends are for. I haven't forgotten who patched me back together after Ben and I broke up."

"Not to mention you and Ivan," Trina supplies, a smile on her lips. "Or when you were convinced you failed your entrance exams. Or when we were at that party and you got—"

"All right, all right, we get it." Wilma reaches out with her fingers splayed, ready to pinch Trina's arm, but she dances back.

"We're here to support Bella!" Trina says. "No fighting!"

Laughing, I step in between the two of them, holding up my arms like a judge in a boxing ring. "Not in this house, you don't."

"So protective of the house," Wilma says morosely, "and not of your friends."

"Of course. Material objects are forever, right? That's the saying?"

"*Friendships* are forever." Trina gives me a push and I laugh, nearly tripping over Toast. He gives a disgruntled meow and looks up at me expectantly. I glance over at the time on the oven.

"Right, food time. He's like an alarm clock, this one. He knows on the minute when it's time for him to be fed."

"Smart cat," Wilma says, sinking back into her kitchen chair. "By the way, how have the sleeping aids I gave you worked out?"

"The non-sleeping-pill-sleeping-pills?"

"The organic, natural, herbal remedy sleeping aids, yeah."

"Surprisingly well," I say. "I've been sleeping much better these past two months, and much deeper."

"*Yes*." Wilma makes the universal sign for success, an elbow tugged downwards, and shoots Trina and me a victorious look. "Another win for 'untested and scientifically dubious medicine.'"

"It worked this time, yeah," I allow. "But I do feel very hormonal. That's not a side effect, is it? Like, my breasts are tender all the time. And while I usually get nauseous sometimes around my period, it's never been this bad before."

Wilma frowns. "They're not supposed to affect that side of things," she says. "Sure you're not just about to have your period?"

"No, I had… actually, I don't know when I last had my period." It feels like a long time ago. Longer than it should have been, longer than it usually feels like.

"Bella," Trina says carefully, "you don't think you could be pregnant?"

"No, of course not," I say. "I'm on birth control. I take it every morning, like clockwork. I'm like Toast with his food. Never miss a day."

"Good, because that's not what you need right now."

"Definitely not. It's probably nothing," I say, waving my hand dismissively. "I'll sort it out."

And that's that. It's not until later, when they've left and I start mentally calculating the days, that I realize my period isn't just fashionably late. It's the kind of late that would be downright rude to the host.

I'm not always very regular, but has it ever been this late before? And once the idea takes root, it's impossible to get out—like when you leave the house and can't remember if you've turned off the curling iron or not. The thought of pregnancy niggles away in my brain until I can't focus on anything at all.

"I'll just get one little test," I tell Toast, grabbing my car keys. "Just one little test. It'll be negative, and then I can stop worrying."

I get in my trusty little car with its new battery and pray it'll start. It hasn't given me grief this summer after I visited the mechanic, but of course this would be the day it acts up.

Not today, I repeat. *Not today of all days.* And my Honda hears me, or perhaps Wilma is right and the universe does listen to your wishes, because I back out of my driveway without any trouble.

No, the trouble starts when I drive down the quiet street and meet an achingly familiar Jeep. I slow my car to a crawl, and amazingly… so does he.

Two windows roll down. One by the driver's seat, revealing Ethan with both hands clasped tightly on the wheel. There's no smile on his face, his jaw tense.

The backseat reveals the cutest little six-year-old ever to live, with two ribboned pigtails. "Bella!" Haven says. "Where have you been?"

"I'm sorry I haven't been around, sweetie," I say, refusing to look at her father. "I've been very busy."

"Can you come over later? I'm going to a birthday party and I want braids, but Daddy can't do braids, and Maria isn't home tonight."

It takes everything I am to shake my head. Thankfully, Ethan spares me from answering. "Bella is busy tonight, too," he says. "She has school, you know. She needs to study."

Haven's face falls, and she shoots her father a glare. He can't see it, but judging by its potency, I'm sure he can feel it through the seat.

"That's right," I agree. "But I'm sure I'll see you again soon."

It's a lie, because I'm not sure at all, not judging from the way her father is frowning. He looks over at me, and for the first time, our gazes lock.

His brow is furrowed, his eyes narrowed with conflicting emotion. I can't tell if he misses me or wants to strangle me. Or himself. Or us both.

"Ethan," I murmur.

He shakes his head. "We can talk later," he says, rolling up their windows. I lift my foot off the brake and like two ships in the night, our cars start moving again. Haven waves cheerily from the backseat and I wave back.

I manage to keep my composure for roughly five more seconds before my eyes well up, and by the time I park outside the pharmacy, I have to give myself a few minutes before I can go inside.

I can't possibly be pregnant. This can't be happening, because if I am… there's no way Ethan will ever look at me softly again.

When I return to my oversized, over-empty mansion, Toast greets me by the door. He winds his way in between my legs and gives a soulful *meow*. I glance down at my watch, but it's not mealtime yet.

I scratch him under the chin, sniffling. "Thank you," I tell him. "You're a lot of work, but I like you."

He butts his head against my leg one last time. *You're welcome.* I imagine him saying. *But don't get used to it.*

I don't make it further than the guest bathroom on the first floor. There, under the soft lighting from directional spotlights, I'm faced with the truth.

I'm pregnant.

At least if the four different pregnancy tests I've bought and taken are to be trusted, and considering there's *four* of them… I can't rationalize it away.

Pregnant.

How? Had my birth control pills expired? I race up the stairs to my bedroom, as if solving this problem might somehow solve the other one, the one involving unexpected motherhood.

My hands shake as I look on the back of my birth control pills. Finding the expiration date and... no. They're not expired. Not even close.

What's happened? How have they failed?

My gaze snags on the green bottle of sleeping aids that Wilma had given me. A bunch of leafy herbs are pictured on the front.

Still trembling, I reach out and grab the bottle. Pills rattle inside. I scan the back... St John's Wort, chamomile, ginger. And below, in the tiniest font known to man.

Should NOT be taken in conjunction with hormone-based birth control.

I sink down onto my larger-than-life bed, in my larger-than-life house with my larger-than-life problem.

I'm pregnant. I'm pregnant. I'm pregnant.

And it's a fucking *herb's* fault.

Which isn't comforting at all, because it's not really true. It's my fault for not reading. For not researching. For assuring Ethan that I was on birth control and had the situation handled when I didn't.

My stomach sinks with the realization that he's not going to handle this well. He's not going to believe me, not after knowing how Lyra had trapped him. And combined with my previous lie... What will he think of me?

My stomach drops out from under me entirely, and I race to the bathroom, violently ill for the first time during this pregnancy.

It won't be the last.

20

BELLA

The knowledge is irrevocable. It weighs on my mind every second of every hour, pulling me from sleep, from rest, from study. I spend that night staring up at the ceiling, trying to come to terms with the unexpected.

Pregnant. A child.

I would be a mother in nine months, and Ethan a father again.

And right now I'm the only one in the entire world who knows.

The knowledge feels almost suffocating, combining with fear. How am I going to do this? Be a good mother and keep up with my studies?

But I dismiss that thought fairly easily. My studies could wait a few months if they had to—children couldn't. And hadn't I always wanted to have kids one day… Was it really so different, having them now or in five years' time? A small, surprised glow of happiness starts to form inside me, living right alongside the fear and the panic. I'm going to be a mother.

I have to tell Ethan. That's the first thing on my mind the next morning, as I try to formulate a strategy. *Tell the child's father, step one. Call my mom, step two. Find a place to live, step three.*

Easy enough. What could possibly go wrong?

I'm eating breakfast and strategizing tactics for step one when my doorbell rings, which almost cuts off my air circulation. Has he beat me to it?

He has, because when I open the gate, who comes walking up with his back straight and face determined? No one but Ethan.

My hands start to shake, and uselessly, they flutter toward my still-flat stomach. I knot them tightly together.

"Hi," Ethan says, his voice low. "Can I come in?"

"Yes, of course." I push the door open further and he steps inside, standing strong and tall in the center of my hallway. Well, not *my hallway* much longer.

We stare at each other for a few moments.

"Well," he says, his lip curling wryly. "We've really made a mess out of this, haven't we?"

Relief so heady it nearly makes my knees buckle sweeps through me. He might not trust me, but he's not coming here to tell me he never wants to see me again.

"Yes," I say, "although it was of my making."

"Yes, but I didn't react the way I should've, either." He pauses, frowning. "Bella, are you okay? You look tired."

Great, thanks. I've just been having an existential crisis for the past fourteen hours. I wring my hangs and nod toward the couches in the living room. "Do you want to have a seat?"

Puzzled, Ethan follows my lead. The furrow in his brow is deeper than it's ever been before. "Bella?"

"I have to tell you something. Something else." I knot my hands together in my lap and pray to any and all gods listening for strength. For finding the right words. Because maybe, if I can just phrase this right…

"All right," Ethan says. His voice is an ocean of caution. "Tell me."

"I discovered something yesterday. And I know what you might think when you hear it, but your first assumption won't be true, because I didn't plan it at all." My voice wavers twice, but so far my eyes are clear of tears. I can feel them waiting in the wings, though, ready for a cue only they know.

"What is it, Bella?"

I take a deep breath, fear roiling in my stomach. "I'm pregnant," I say, and then my words trip over one another on their way out. "You see, I took this herbal sleeping aid all summer, and apparently it interfered with my birth control. I've Googled, and it's well-known in the medical community, but *I* didn't know, and I didn't read the small print properly."

Ethan has become a statue again, frozen marble, strong lines immortalized in stillness. He gives no impression that he's going to speak soon, or perhaps ever again.

My hands feel sweaty. "I took the tests just yesterday. Four of them, actually. This is a complete surprise to me too. Ethan, I don't want you to think… it wasn't intentional." That's the cue, apparently, because my eyes well up of their own accord. *Showtime!*

It takes forever until he speaks, and in the silence, the faint hope I'd harbored weakens and sputters out entirely. His voice is weary.

"And I'm the father, I assume. Fucking hell, Bella, I didn't want more kids, especially not now."

"I know." I'm nodding furiously. "It's the worst possible timing, I know that. Same for me with school."

He's silent again, for so long that I have time to count to sixty twice. Wondering if I should keep explaining, if I can only make him see… But when he opens his mouth, I realize he's just been gathering steam.

"You told me you were on birth control." It's the voice he uses when he deals with people he wants to get rid of—I've heard him use it with his ex-wife.

"I am. But the herb in the sleeping aids decreases its efficiency. It was actually on the bottle, but I didn't read the fine print. That's on me." Desperate, so desperate to be understood, I continue. "It's called St. John's Wort. The herb. You can search it online."

He nods again. Falls silent.

My heart beats a war drum in my chest.

"Where are you going now? After you move out of here?" Ethan asks. Polite interest in his voice, nothing more.

"I'm looking at places on Saturday. If I don't find anything right away, I'll stay with a friend."

"All right. Well, you have my number. Call me if that doesn't work out or if you need anything." He stands, and from his back pocket, pulls out his wallet. Counts through the bills. Puts a stack of them on the living-room table.

"For all the medical appointments," he tells me, "and the vitamins, for everything like that. I know it's costly."

I can hardly see the bills through my tears, can barely hear him through the audible sound of my heart breaking.

This can't be happening. "Ethan…"

He pauses by the hallway. How has he made it all the way over there in the span of my heart cracking?

His gaze is courteous, but there's no emotion on his face, like he's shut me out entirely. Like I'm now a stranger.

Like I've betrayed him.

The words spill out of the crack in my soul. "What about us?" I ask. "Is there any way you could forgive me? For lying about being their niece…"

Ethan looks away, his jaw working. "That lie seems almost minor now in comparison," he says calmly. "Did you get inspired from Lyra's story, or was this always the plan? Were you aiming for this from the first time you came over to introduce yourself? I'd have to assume so, since that's the first time you lied to get closer."

I can't get enough air. It's all been sucked out of this room, out of the space between us, leaving it an empty vacuum.

"Ethan, that's not at all—"

"Spare it, Bella." He shakes his head. The disgust on his features… it might be aimed at me or at himself or at us both. Probably us both. "You might be having my child, but I'm not about to trust you again. I'll be in touch."

He heads toward the front door, pulling it open. I stumble after him but only make it to the foyer before it slams behind him. Somewhere deep in the house, I hear a cat yelp at the sound.

Slowly, ever so slowly, I sink to the floor. The stone is cold against my skin and my tears, when they fall, glisten on the hard surface.

One thing is inevitable in life, and it's that time never stands still. The days keep turning, despite the internal state of panic I'm in.

Most days I spend ignoring my thesis in favor of pregnancy research, apartment hunting, packing up my belongings and ensuring the Gardners' house is in pristine condition for their arrival. I'm to be out one day before they arrive, which includes coordinating with the cleaning crew to do a final sweep of the house.

All these tasks are good. They keep me busy—too busy to focus on the fact that my baby's father hates me. That I have no idea at all how I'm supposed to break this news to my parents, to my friends.

That I might eventually have things like preeclampsia or something that's called lightning crotch.

My visit to the OB-GYN isn't for several *weeks* yet—she'd laughed when I said I thought I should come in right away. "Between week six and eight," she told me, "you're welcome to come in for your first appointment. Before then, I can't really see much." And then, the first person to say it, she added, "And congratulations, Bella."

I'd cried after I hung up the phone, but I do that a lot these days.

The hardest thing was to be quiet around Wilma and Trina. I joined them for drinks one evening to celebrate Trina's new appointment as an undergraduate teaching assistant, and had to blame a headache for my choice of drink.

"How's Ethan?" Wilma had asked, her hand reaching out to land on mine. "Have you been able to get through to him?"

"No. That ship has sailed entirely, I think."

"Stubborn, infuriating man," Trina had said. "Do you want us to knock some sense into him? We could, you know."

"Greenwood Hills security might get to us first," Wilma mused. "We'd have to go incognito."

"Exactly. Bella, if you lend us your trench coat, we'll go pummel your man for you."

I'd laughed, touched and warm and sad all at once. My heart ached to tell them the truth, but it still felt too big for me to grasp myself. I couldn't even imagine saying the words out loud.

I'm going to be a mother.

I'd kept my hand on my stomach for the rest of the night, a quiet determination growing every time I'd repeated those words in my head. *And I'm going to do the best job I can.*

So by the time I'm set to move out of the Gardners' mansion in Greenwood Hills, it's real to me, just as real as the new and painful morning sickness that has started to make an appearance. I hope it's just passing through, and not here to stay.

I keep the trunk to my Honda Civic open and carry bag after bag out to the car. I tuck my handbag in on top and I'm just narrowly able to close it.

There. An entire summer—and entire life, it feels like—all packed up.

There's no sound from the other side of the hedge. It's empty, quiet, just like my phone has been. Ethan hasn't been in touch, and I've been too afraid to contact him. He'll do the right thing, but knowing he'll do so begrudgingly, thinking I tricked him…

The shame of it makes my cheeks burn.

I walk through the house one last time, attic to the basement, making sure everything is in place. Expensive vases in their correct spots, check. Kitchen cupboards empty of my items, check. Saying goodbye to Toast… not check.

"Toast?" He's not upstairs, not in any of his normal spots.

"Toast?" He's not downstairs, sprawled on the couch or waiting by his food bowls.

I rush out the front door and shut it firmly behind me. Had I forgotten to do that while I carried my things? Had he finally managed to make his big escape?

"Toast? Toast!" The entire yard is fenced, but he's a cat. In the fight between the two, I knew which one I'd put money on. I walk around the property, calling his name, panic increasing with each passing minute. This can't be happening, not today, not when I have to leave, and not to Toast.

It's one thing too many.

"Toaaast!"

I look under the lounge chairs and by the pool. The gardening shed, too. Nowhere. Gone.

A deep voice calls out from the treehouse. "Has the cat disappeared?"

Ethan. Watching me from his side of the lawn, just like the first time we'd seen each other.

I nod miserably. "I think he snuck out when I was loading my car."

"And you haven't found him?"

"No."

He withdraws from the window, only to return a second later. "I'll come help you look."

My heart is pounding by the time he's at my front gate. He walks in with a single nod to me, striding around the perimeter of the property. I follow him.

"He's been gone for about an hour at least."

"I'm guessing your 'aunt and uncle' would hate it if he's gone?"

"Yes." Hate might even be an understatement. Toast's well-being had been key in the house-sitting manual I'd been given. All instructions began and ended with him. How could I have been so stupid?

Ethan and I are quiet as we look. A truce, of sorts, even if my body feels like a live wire, taut with his presence.

"How are the girls?" I ask, my curiosity overcoming my caution.

"Good." Ethan's voice is clipped. And then, reluctantly, "They're wondering why you stopped coming over."

"What did you tell them?"

"That you're getting ready to move and you're very busy."

I nod, slowly. Makes sense. And yet, one day, we'd have to talk to them. They'd be getting a baby brother or sister, after all.

Perhaps Ethan hears my thoughts in the silence, because he drags a hand through his hair. "I don't know, Bella," he tells me. "I don't know."

"That's okay," I say. One problem at a time.

Cat today. Baby tomorrow.

But by the time the sun starts to set, Toast is still nowhere to be seen. Ethan has to return to the girls, and I walk him to the gate, right past my fully packed Honda.

"Let me know if I can do anything to help," he says.

"You've already helped," I say. "Thank you for looking with me."

He nods once, glancing toward the car. "Text me when you're settled into your new place. I'll come over, one day. We have... things to go over. Logistics. Preparations."

"Okay. Yeah, I'll do that." The furrow on his brow is killing me, making me feel like a personal failure. I haven't helped smooth it out at all—I've only made it deeper.

We'll be okay, I tell myself and the baby. *Your daddy is a really good man. He'll come around.* But try as I may to crush the small kernel of doubt, a flicker of it remains.

"Bella..." Ethan says.

"Yes?"

"There's something moving in your car."

"Oh!" I open the trunk and immediately start digging through my bags, and yes... there's an annoyed hiss and then a gray head peeking out of one of my bags.

"Toast!"

The disgruntled cat lets me pick him up. "You'd been hiding in my packing, you rascal?"

He doesn't confirm or deny, choosing silence instead—a clever move. "Oh, thank God," I say. "Thank you, Ethan. I truly can't thank you enough."

He nods again. "Sure. Drive safe, Bella."

"I will. Ethan?"

He pauses by the gate, big and solid and real and further out of my reach than he'd ever been before. His gaze is heavy. "Yeah?"

"I'm truly sorry about this situation. Whether you believe me or not regarding the rest, I hope you'll believe that. I never wanted us to be like this."

He's quiet for a long moment. "That," he says finally, "I think I can accept."

He disappears, out of my driveway and back to his own house, where his existence will continue as it was before I came into the picture.

Toast purrs contentedly as I carry him back up to his palatial house. I press a kiss to the soft, warm fur on top of his head. "Goodbye," I murmur. "I'll miss you so much."

21

ETHAN

"Daddy," Evie wails from her car seat. "Let's gooo."

"Just a second." I stretch to my full height, peering above the hedge. I'm just barely able to make out the shape of a sleek, silver Jaguar on the driveway. The same car that's always parked there when my neighbors are home.

No beat-up Honda Civic in sight.

"*Daaaddy.*"

"Yes, yes." I close Evie's door and settle into the driver's seat. Haven is quiet in the backseat, playing with a doll she's holding.

I see them when I back out of my driveway, right through the slats in their fence. Mr. and Mrs. Gardner, walking down the familiar path toward their garage.

They see me. I raise a hand in hello, which is nothing we've ever done before. Why am I starting now?

My car crawls forward.

Mr. Gardner, his gray hair perfectly coiffed, raises a hand in a hesitant hello back. The car continues down the street. If I'd spoken to them more, I would have known Bella wasn't the real deal.

Haven gives a dramatic sigh. "I don't like our new neighbors."

"They're not new," I correct. "They've lived there for years, you just haven't noticed."

She glares at me through the rearview mirror. "They *are* new," she protests, "because Bella lived there before."

My hand tightens around the wheel. Bella, my salvation, and Bella, my ruin.

"She was only living there temporarily."

"Tem-po-rar-ily," Haven pronounces, pouring as much disdain as is possible for a six-year-old into the word. It's clear she doesn't find my side of the argument very convincing.

"Yeah, I know," I say. "For what it's worth, I agree with you. I don't like them very much either."

Not in comparison—not even now, knowing what I know, when Bella's name turns to ash on my tongue and the memories feel like wounds.

Haven hoots in the backseat, content with her victory. Evie, having followed this conversation carefully, asks the one thing she's picked up on.

"Bella is coming back?"

Haven saves me from responding. "No, silly," she says. "Her and Daddy had a fight."

"Bad Daddy," Evie says, her voice one of deep reproach.

Sometimes I think parenthood is like being trapped in a madhouse for years, desperately trying to stay sane.

"We didn't have a fight," I lie, breaking one more of the rules I'd tried to live by for so long. *Be honest with your kids.*

"Then why are you so grumpy?" Haven asks, and after a millisecond's pause, she exclaims, "Aha! See?" like she's just received confirmation.

I shake my head, turning the car onto my mother's street. Thank God she's been a Greenwood Hills resident for as long as I have.

"I'm sorry if I've been grumpy," I say, parking the car on the curb. "Bella and I were good friends, and then she had to move away."

This, Evie understands. "Daddy's sad?"

I exhale slowly. Daddy's pissed, actually. Furious. Offended. Shocked. But I'm forced to lie *again,* because Bella has ensured she'll be in their lives, now as the mother of their half-sibling.

"Yes," I say. "Daddy's sad."

Haven reaches forward and puts her good hand on my shoulder. "Don't be sad. You still have us."

I put my hand on hers and feel like an indecisive balloon, caught between inflation and deflation. My anger dissipates like smoke in the wind. "And you two are all I'll ever need, baby girl."

Haven's hand slips from underneath mine. "Grandma!"

A second later she's unlatched her seat belt and struggles with her door, my mother laughing on the other side as she pulls it open.

"Hi there, honey!"

The girls wave cheery goodbyes to me as they bound up my mother's driveway, hand in hand with her. I have everything I need, truly. I have a fantastic mother, two beautiful children, a company that's thriving and a job that I love. I can handle another kid.

Hell, that part is probably the easiest; I know from experience that holding your child, seeing him or her for the first time… yeah, that wouldn't be difficult at all.

No, the difficult part would be facing Bella over and over and over again. It wouldn't be like with Lyra. No, every time I'd see Bella, it would be like seeing my own doomed hope.

She'd never sneer at me or laugh like Lyra did.

And somehow that felt worse.

The gates to Cole's mansion slide open when I approach, allowing me to park by his house. A glance at the watch tells me I'm a few minutes late, and I find him and Nick on the back porch. A laptop is placed on the table, but that's the only sign that this is a work meeting, the two of them reclining with sunglasses on.

I shake my head at them. "All you two are missing is a pair of pina coladas with tiny umbrellas."

Cole pushes up his sunglasses. "Are you offering to make us two, Carter?"

"In your dreams." I sit down on the lounge chair opposite them. "Is Skye around?"

"Upstairs, working," he says. "She has a deadline next week."

"New book?"

"A new *chapter* to her editor," he says. "Books aren't that fast to write. I should know, because I once said that and got my head bashed in."

"Your hotels aren't fast to build either," Nick points out. "Learn some humility."

Cole throws his hands up. "It's my one flaw."

"One?"

"Yes, one. Without humility, I couldn't possible admit to more."

I snort. "You said this was a business meeting. To the best of my knowledge, though, we're not in business together. Nor do our areas overlap."

Nick's grin is crooked. "Not *yet*, they don't."

"We've been talking," Cole continues, "about creating a holding company."

I lean forward. "Oh?"

"Yes. A capital venture firm, of a sorts. Not the kind Nick runs, but with more focus on investing. We all have investments of our own, of course," Cole says. "This one would be more for our own amusement. It would allow us to invest in companies off the beaten track."

I run a hand over my jaw. "One we'd own jointly?"

"Yes, we'd all invest an equal share. The management would report to us, since we'd constitute the board."

Nick nods to me. "And we'll hire a known, expert capital investor to run the whole thing. He'd have his own team."

I find myself nodding along. My own investments are solid, A-grade. Long-term, and all with the help of a private financial manager. This, though… it would be fun. We could have a say in the placements.

"He?" I repeat. "Do you already have someone in mind for the position of chair and manager?"

Cole grins, like he's already told a joke. "Your little brother."

My laugh is surprised. "No, no way."

"He's one of the best investors in the country," Cole says. "You don't think he'll accept?"

"I wouldn't be so sure of that, no. He's been distant for years, and he's never in Seattle. He really only cares about making money."

Nick raises an eyebrow. "And that would be a bad thing how?"

I run a hand over my face. Having Liam's smug face around on the regular… "Mixing family and business never ends well."

"We'd take the heat off of that," Cole says. "Any bad news would come from us."

"Think about it," Nick offers. "It's your call, in the end. We just figured it might be a good solution."

"Right. Thanks." I look past the two of them to the tennis court in the distance, the perfectly mowed lawn, the impossible homeliness of Cole's palace.

"Why are you so morose, anyway? I thought you'd dance at this suggestion," Cole says. "The girls are all right?"

"Yes, absolutely." I run a hand over the back of my neck. "Man, it's such a fucking clusterfuck of things. I don't even know where to start."

"Start at the beginning," Nick says.

But that's impossible.

The girl next door tricked me into becoming a father again. She actually lied to me about who she was the entire time, too. Fun, right?

There's no way I can pour out all of my embarrassment on a silver platter and share it with them, not while it still feels like it might choke me.

"It's Bella," I say simply. "She wasn't who I thought she was."

"Ah." Cole's voice is delicate. "Should have recognized the look on your face right away."

"You wore it yourself long enough," Nick tells him.

Cole holds up a hand. "You wore it the longest out of all of us. Just because I couldn't recognize it at the time doesn't make it less of a fact."

Nick ignores his future brother-in-law and turns to me. "Not who you thought she was? That girl was as transparent as glass, man."

"And she clearly liked *you*," Cole says. "Sweet, too."

"Have you tried saying you're sorry?" Nick asks. "Hurts like a motherfucker to admit, but it does the trick every time, even when you're not."

"Didn't need to hear the last part," Cole remarks.

I grit my teeth at their well-meaning advice. "There's no solution to this. She's a bit of a manipulator."

"*Bella?*" Cole asks. "We're talking about the same girl who blushed when we joked about how you were both single?"

I reach for the computer on the table. "Don't we have an investment company to create?"

They exchange a glance, and the conversation about my morose state is thankfully left behind. Not forgotten, though. No doubt they'll ask again, and again, and again, until I'll finally be forced to relive the entire humiliating ordeal.

Transparent as glass.

I'd thought so too, once, watching her cheeks flush beautifully.

Turns out she lied with her body too.

22

BELLA

I pace back and forth in my new living room. It's a fairly simple thing to do, considering it's the size of a shoebox and still unfurnished. *Get a couch* is currently number seven on my list of tasks, right under things like *research pre-natal vitamins* and *tell my friends and family I'm pregnant,* but above such trivial things like buying renter's insurance.

Ethan is going to hate it. The surefire knowledge only adds to my pace as I try to wear down a path on the linoleum floor. He'd texted that he specifically *wanted to see where I'm living,* and I didn't see the point in denying him that. His kid would live here too.

The apartment might be tiny, but it's still a godsend. I'd contacted the landlord seven minutes after the post appeared online, and Trina and I had been there bright and early the next morning.

She'd rolled her eyes when I'd told her it had charm. *I think you need to look up the dictionary definition of that word,* she'd said.

But I can see potential in these walls, in the corridor-like kitchen and the bedroom that's just big enough to fit both a bed and a crib. It's just under my budget, which is good, because I'll need every penny I can when the baby gets here.

"Our baby," I tell my stomach. It's still mostly flat, but when I press my fingers against it, it feels harder—almost like I've grown abs. "Your father is going to love you," I say, "even if he'll never love me. No worries on that score, though. Won't ever hold it against you."

It'll take years until my baby will be able to reply, but the conversation still feels reassuring—like we're in this together.

I look at my phone to check the time. He's late. He's never late. A loop back down to the mirror, yes, my hair still looks good, I return to the living room to pace. It's not a particularly good way to pass the time, but the knot of nerves in my stomach won't let me relax.

The doorbell rings and I open my front door with the greatest pretense of calm I've ever managed to pull off.

Ethan's green eyes meet mine. "Hey," he says.

"Hi." I take a step to the side. "Come on in."

He steps past me into the apartment. The scent of *him* hits me, familiar shampoo and sweater and man. I knot my hands together in front of me.

"This is the place," I say, clearing my throat.

He looks around, his face completely devoid of his usual easy smile. It's clear in the silence that he sees the things I've tried to ignore. The cracked paint. The crooked windowsill. The giant stain on the floor.

"You're renting this?"

"Yes. It's centrally located, has loads of natural light, and a parking spot."

I sound like a realtor.

Ethan nods once, striding through to the kitchen. He eyes the rickety chairs and kitchen table like he's spotted an adversary in a boxing ring. One second, two seconds, but then he surrenders and has a seat on one of them. His long legs barely fit in the space.

"Have a seat," he tells me, like it's not my kitchen and my rickety kitchen chairs. "We have things to discuss."

191

"Yes, we do." I sit down opposite him and clasp my hands together on the table, like we're about to have a business meeting. "Have you researched St John's Wort? That it can interfere with birth control?"

His jaw works, but his reply is smooth. "I have. It can."

The tone makes it clear that he still doesn't believe me—that he can't let go of his suspicion that this was premeditated. For the love of God, he had been the *least* premeditated thing I'd ever done in my life!

"Have you been for a check-up yet?" he asks.

"I'm going tomorrow, actually. I'm six weeks along now." Six weeks of being pregnant, six weeks since I'd been in his arms and he'd looked at me like… like we had a future.

Like we could have a life together.

"Good." Reaching into the inner pocket of his jacket, he pulls out a folded wad of papers. Unfolding it, he starts laying out documents on the table, one after one. "My lawyers have been working on these the past few weeks," he says. "Would you be okay with joint custody?"

I swallow. "Yes."

"I'll pay for all of the medical expenses, birth, health insurance, all of that, both for you and the child." Another document pushed over to my side. "Schooling and college as well. Money will be made available in a trust, only accessible by me or by the child, when they come of age."

"Okay." My voice sounds feeble, lost in the explosion of legalese and documents on my wobbly table. Perhaps it'll crumble under the weight—I feel like I might.

"A monthly allowance for you. I don't want my child or the mother of my child to live in a place like this."

"A monthly allowance?"

"Yes." He pushes another piece of paper over to me. There are numbers on it, one highlighted in bold, but I can't pay attention to that. Not when it feels like I'm losing my dignity and my heart at the same time, both of them sliding further and further out of my grasp.

"I don't want a penny," I say.

He grits his teeth. "*Bella.*"

"I don't, truly. I don't want an allowance, or for you to dictate where I live."

"Don't be stubborn about this."

"Stubborn? How can I not be? This was never what I wanted. *This,* between you and me. Documents and coldness and… and… monthly *allowances.* Don't you think I know that you're only doing this because you have to, but you'd rather it never happened?" I shake my head. "But I can't feel that way. This pregnancy was a complete surprise to me. I'm scared senseless, I have no idea what I'll tell my parents or my friends, or what to do with school. The only thing I know is that I want to give this child everything I can." My throat is closing, but I force the rest out, too. "Nothing has changed for me, Ethan. I still hope you'll forgive me."

He closes his eyes, like the tears clouding my vision are too hard to face. "Bella, you lied to me. About who you are. About your birth control."

"Not about birth control," I whisper. "And never about who I am. I'm a graduate student. I like to bake. I'm a tolerably good hiker. For Christ's sake, I want to work as a systems engineer—you *know* that, Ethan. Why would I want to become pregnant in the middle of that?"

He shakes his head once. "You know exactly why."

"I'm *not* Lyra," I say. My tears have given way to a startling, righteous anger. How dare he think I'd put myself in this position just for money? "I'm just *not.* So stop comparing me to her."

His eyes open with clear irritation. "Why the first lie, then? Why pretend to be their niece?"

"I have asked myself the same question over and over these past few weeks. I was nervous and flustered and you were, well, *you,* and you suggested that and it sounded good. I gave a half-nod and then I was trapped, and I was too embarassed to set the record straight after that. It's honestly just as stupid as it sounds."

"You want me to believe that, but Bella..." He pushes away from the table, his chair creaking ominously. The alleyway kitchen looks minuscule with him braced in between the cupboards. "I can't, okay? I just *can't*."

Despair and anger, both in equal measure, threaten to choke off my words altogether. Getting them out should earn me a medal. "I lied about being their niece. I'll always be sorry about that. But I didn't lie about birth control, and I don't want your money. That has *never* been part of why I care about you."

His shoulders are tense, like he's preparing for blows, but he's not moving toward the door. Not yet. "You're entirely too likable on your own," I tell him. "You're a fantastic father. You're brilliant at what you do at work. And you're so funny. No one makes me laugh like you do."

My words hang in the air between us, him not moving, me not speaking. My heart feels like it's about to beat out of my chest.

"Ethan," I murmur.

It breaks him out of the spell. He strides out to the living room, right to the front door. It doesn't take him many steps.

I follow. "I was with my ex for six years," I tell him, wrapping my arms around my chest, trying to keep myself from unraveling. "And I thought I loved him—I thought I knew what love was. But I was wrong, because being with you, Ethan... it felt like coming home."

He's still not looking at me; his hand is on the doorknob. The words might feel like they come from the very bottom of my soul, but there's no telling if they're even reaching him.

"Don't leave me alone in this." My voice breaks, but I'm beyond embarrassment. "I don't want your checks. I want you to come to my doctor's appointments with me."

He shakes his head once. "Damn it, Bella, *I can't*."

I grip hold of his arm with both my hands, willing him to look at me. "What can I do to make you trust me again? What can I say?"

His voice sounds just as defeated as mine. "I don't know, Bella. I don't know."

He pulls the front door open and my hands fall limp to my sides. It closes with a decisive snap behind him as he leaves, taking my hope that I'd one day be forgiven away with him.

23

ETHAN

"Grandma! Look at me!" Haven crouches down on the grass, tucking her legs and arms underneath her. "Evie?"

Her younger sister obediently puts the two plastic crowns on Haven's back, the golden crests upwards. "Look! What am I?"

My mother squints at her oldest grandchild. "A royal stone? A stone queen?"

"No!"

I clear my throat. "Are you a hedgehog?"

"Yes!"

"It's her new favorite animal," I stage-whisper to Mom. Louder, "that was very inventive, honey!"

She tosses the crowns off and grins. Evie grabs one of them and runs off, shrieking, looking behind her to make sure Haven is giving chase. She is.

I take a deep sip of my glass of lemonade. Maria's recipe, and just as invaluable as Maria herself. She's sitting down the table from us, tucked under the parasol, a book in hand. I can tell she's watching the girls over the top edge of the page.

"A hedgehog," Mom comments. "Of all the possible animals."

"The week before it was a hippopotamus."

"Goodness. You need to get these girls a pet. Something fluffy."

"Don't say that when they can hear. Haven's been pushing Operation Canine since, well, she learned to speak."

"A hamster," my mother suggests. "Small, furry. It'll tide them over until you have time for a dog."

"I'll never have time for a dog." I take another deep sip of the icy drink. With work and now another child on the way... no time at all.

Bella had her check-up last week. I'd called her after, our conversation brief and focused on the child. Everything looked good, she'd told me. Healthy heartbeat.

I'd shut myself in my office after that phone call, my head in my hands with emotion. *Healthy heartbeat.* Another baby. My baby.

"Ethan?"

I blink, refocusing. "Sorry?"

"You're a million miles away." My mother clucks her tongue, the way she did when I was young. It's been twenty years since I've heard that sound. "I just asked if you've heard anything from Liam since he visited?"

"No, nothing."

She frowns, shaking her head. "Weird."

My little brother's frequent absences and lack of communication is a sore point for us both, but I know it hits her harder. "He'll probably visit again soon. He often has business here, after all."

"Yes, you're probably right." She raises a hand to shield her eyes from the sun. "I thought I'd see Bella today again. The neighbor girl?"

A billion different responses race through my head. "She's moved away," I say finally.

"Well, not out of the city?"

"No." I can sense her frowning at me, but I keep my gaze locked on my kids playing in the treehouse.

"They had a fight," Maria offers, without looking up from her book. "They're not talking."

Oh, Lord. "No, we—"

"A fight?" my mother asks. "Ethan, what could possibly have been big enough to justify a falling out? Fix it."

"That's not—"

"He hasn't been happy since," Maria supplies, ratting me out to my mother. I shoot her a warning glare, but she ignores me soundly, flipping the page of her book. "I don't know what happened."

"Ethan, explain yourself," my mother demands.

I look up at the sky and take a deep breath—save me from the meddling of women.

"She turned out to be more like Lyra than I'd expected," I say, wincing internally at the memory of the quiet tears running down her cheeks last time we met. Lyra never did *that*, except in fits of dramatics.

Maria scoffs.

Mom just raises her eyebrows. "Ethan, you can't be serious."

"I'm dead serious."

"That girl didn't have a single manipulative bone in her body. What's worse, she seemed like the kind of person who could *be* manipulated!"

I grit my teeth. "Trust me when I say that she does."

"I won't, not until I hear the full story." Her voice is the same one I'm using—the one that brooks no argument. Carter stubbornness in action, and it's a face-off. "What happened?"

Maria puts down her book and heads down to where the kids are. Effortlessly giving us privacy.

I clear my throat. "She lied about who she was. She said she was the neighbor's niece when she was actually hired to house-sit for the summer and take care of the cat."

"Ah," my mother says, and a whole world is contained in that word.

"Just say what you're going to say."

"Well, I'll say that she was probably intimidated. I know you don't always think so, sweetie, but you're sometimes rather impressive. Has she apologized for it?"

"Yes." Profusely, actually. And explained it. And on some level, perhaps I could understand it—*that* lie, anyway.

"And?" Mom asks. "That's it? That's the whole reason you're not talking?"

I shake my head, my teeth grinding together. No one, I've told no one, and it's… well. It's too much to keep to myself.

"Well, she's pregnant."

My mother is silent. The times I manage to strike her speechless are rare, but I don't take any pleasure from this particular moment.

Her eyes are wide. "You're having another child?"

"Unplanned, but yes."

Her eyes grow hazy with tears, the widest smile spreading over her face. I can't help it—I smile too.

"Oh my God," she says, "another grandchild. A baby! And how was that not the first thing you told me today, Ethan? You let me babble on about Liam and my book club and *groceries*!"

I laugh, reaching over to hug her. "Mom, it's still early days, and it's complicated."

"This part is very simple, though. You're having another kid. Are you happy?"

I haven't really thought about it in those terms. *Happy*. But when I don't let my thoughts speak and just listen to what's inside me… "Yes," I say. "Really happy, actually."

Mom wipes at her eyes. "Why on Earth isn't Bella here? Move her in with you! What are you waiting for?"

Ah.

"She said she was on birth control," I say. "Clearly, she lied."

My mom grows still. "Did she tell you that?"

"She denies that she planned it, of course. Says she took some herbal medication at the same time that interfered, something called St. John's Wort." I shake my head, turning away from the look in my mom's eyes. "But I won't be dragged into the same arrangement as with Lyra. The kid, I'm happy about. Not Bella."

Thwap. My mom hits me on the back of the head, and not gently, either. "Ouch. What was that for?"

"For being an idiot," Mom says. "You're telling me that the girl I met—who was clearly keen to make a good impression on me, and on you, I might add, looking at you like she thought you'd hung the moon—is somewhere in the city all alone, thinking you hate her? The mother of my future grandchild?"

"Erhm. Yes, I suppose."

She leans away from me, arms crossing over her chest. Rare are the times I've seen her truly angry. "Did you investigate? Ask her OB/GYN to confirm any of her story? Or did you jump straight to your own conclusions?"

Damn it. "Mom, she *lied.*"

"About some things, but not about all. And now you've left her on her own to deal with a mistake that the *two* of you made together."

"I know how—"

"I never thought I'd have to have this discussion with you. You're thirty-six years old!"

"I'm well aware of that, but—"

"You were interviewed in the newspaper last month! A full-page spread!"

"What does that have to do with anything?"

"You're letting Lyra win if you do this." She puts her finger n my chest, the eyes I've inherited staring back at me. "She was *one* woman. She doesn't speak for all of us. And I'd bet my finest racehorse that the only thing Bella has in common with Lyra is her gender."

"You don't have a racehorse—that's not an expression." I run a hand through my hair, looking away from her. Her words are hitting too close to a truth I'm desperate to believe in.

"I might. What do you know?" Mom huffs out an annoyed breath. "Tell me more about her. What was she like?"

"She was very good with the girls," I say. "Even when she clearly had no clue what to do, she was good." In the distance, Evie shrieks with laughter, the sound like a balm to my senses.

Mom leans back in her chair, knotting her fingers together in her lap, like they've done all the pointing they've needed to today. "What else?"

I wet my lips. Wonder if I've chosen the worst possible person to confide in. "She was kind. Truly kind, not the polite type of kind."

"She was?"

"Yes. And funny. Quietly strong, too, the kind of brave you don't see, but it's there, underneath the surface." I bury my head in my hands, arms braced against the patio table. "Christ. Have I really gotten it all wrong? Messed it up completely?"

"You might've," my mother says. "But if she's all that you've just described, I think you still have time to fix it."

The running of feet breaks me out of my thoughts. Evie sprints into my arms, climbing onto my lap. I lift her up.

"What's wrong, baby girl?"

"Daddy's sad again," she says, her weight warm in my arms. "I could see."

"Daddy's not sad," I protest.

"He's just contemplating his past failings," my mother murmurs.

I glance at her, but she just shrugs, unrepentant.

Evie puts her hand on my cheek. "Not sad anymore," she declares. "Come play with us?"

I stand, bouncing her a little bit in my arms. "Sure. Are we playing magical treehouse?"

"Yes."

Walking down the lawn with her, I make a decision. Honesty. That's what I'd always tried to adopt with my kids, and perhaps it's time I started extending that value a bit further. "Evie?"

"Mhm?"

"What do you think of Bella?"

"Really nice."

"Nice?"

"Yes. And good cookies."

"She *makes* good cookies, yes, that's true." I smooth a honey-brown curl back from her forehead, my mind racing ahead. "What would you think of her coming over more often?"

24

BELLA

"Wow," Wilma breathes. The amazement on her face doesn't seem fake, either—does she really find this picture as fascinating as I do?

"It's amazing, right?"

"It really is." She puts the picture down between us on the floor, as I'm still sans couch, and we both stare at the black-and-white sonogram. "I'm still in shock, Bells."

"Oh, so am I! I still can't grasp that that little girl is inside me," I say. "Or guy, I suppose. And it's so early still. My OB/GYN told me it'll look much more like a baby later on."

"I didn't even know they did ultrasounds this early," Wilma says. "Well, to be fair, I don't know anything at all about pregnancies. I know your belly gets big, and I know they last for nine months, but that's it."

"You're right on all three counts, actually. It's early for an ultrasound, but I think it's because of Ethan's health plan." His name only burns a little on the way out. "The new clinic I'm at is fantastic."

"Has he seen the picture?"

"No. I considered sending it to him, but I also asked him to come to the check-up with me, and he didn't."

Wilma lies back on the floor with a dramatic sigh. "The man is an idiot."

I sigh. "The problem is that he isn't, though. He's probably been retracing all of our conversations and finding patterns to fit his theory."

"You can be a clever idiot."

"Something you know from experience?"

Wilma lifts her head briefly to stick her tongue out at me, before settling back down. "You can't tell me you aren't angry with him, Bella. You can't possibly be handling this as serenely as you seem to be. I know you—and you're not one to back down from a fight. Wow, this crack in your ceiling is legit."

I glance up. "I called the landlord about it, but he said it was part of the old building charm."

"Well, it's not so charming when old buildings come down around you and you're buried in rubble."

"No hating on my home."

"Calling it a *home* is a bit of a stretch," Wilma points out. "And don't deflect. You're angry at him?"

I keep my eyes on the wide fissure in the plaster and try to keep my own cracks at bay. "He's dismissing everything we had because of this pregnancy. It's like he's seeing what he wants to see, instead of the truth. Of course I'm angry at him."

"Good." Wilma's voice is determined. "Better angry than sad."

"I'm both."

"Both is also good."

"Have you started studying psychology and not told me about it?"

"No, I'm just an armchair expert. Do you have any dreams? I could interpret those."

"Sadly, I'm all out."

"Dang." She looks down at her watch. "Trina should be here soon with the take-out."

"Awesome."

"I'll have to point out the crack in the ceiling to her."

I groan, because Trina is an architect student. "You know exactly what she'll say."

"Oh yes," Wilma says, relish in her voice. "She'll say it's structurally unsound. But look at it this way—she might be able to get your landlord to lower the rent on those grounds."

"Yippie. Also, what the heck am I going to tell my parents? You're very welcome to come up with suggestions."

"They come to town next month, right?"

"Yes."

"Tell them the truth," Wilma says, grinning at my expression. "Yes, they might have apoplexies, but what else can you do?"

"Conceal it for eighteen years, never visit, become—"

The sound of my phone ringing echoes through the still mostly empty living room. I reach for my bag, thrown by the front door.

"Ten bucks it's Trina who can't remember our take-out orders," Wilma says.

I chuckle, fingers closing around my phone. But the name on my screen isn't our friend at all.

"It's Ethan."

Wilma straightens. "Shit."

My heart in my throat, I answer. "Hello?"

"It's me."

"Hi."

"We have a lot to talk about," he says. "Are you home? Can I come up?"

"Now? Like, right now?"

Wilma's eyes widen, and then she's nodding. *Yes,* she mouths.

"Yes, now." Ethan's voice is the embodiment of polite, cool professionalism. "Unless you're busy, in which case I can come back later."

You're not busy, Wilma mouths, already standing to grab her purse. I wave at her. *Stay.* But she shakes her head.

205

"Bella?"

"Okay. Yeah, okay. Are you downstairs?"

"I'm in the area. I'll be there soon."

"All right."

He hangs up without another word. I sit staring at my phone, my heart racing. It isn't until Wilma heads to the front door that I come to. "He wants to talk."

"I heard," she says. "Bella, this is great."

"It's probably about contracts. I didn't sign them the last time."

She put a hand on my shoulder. "Whatever it is, just remember that you have the right to be angry, to be furious, to be sad, anything and all of that."

"Thank you."

"Good luck, babe. And call me *immediately* after."

She disappears down the hallway, the low heels of her boots steady on the floor. They're far steadier than the beat of my heart.

I snatch the sonogram picture from the floor and clutch it to my chest. It feels like armor—like my strength. Funny, that. In so short a time my life has reoriented itself entirely around this child, like a planet changing its source of gravity.

Ethan had to be close, because I'm still sitting on the floor when he knocks. In his hands is a Tupperware box with small, irregular chocolate squares.

They disrupt my thoughts—I don't even say hello. "You brought *brownies*?"

"The girls and I baked them this morning." And then, perhaps because he can't resist, he adds, "Maria didn't help us."

I take it from him. "Impressive."

"Marginally, perhaps." Ethan's eyes slide from mine to the image I'm clutching, and the faint smile fades from his face.

"Is that...?"

"Yes."

"Can I see?"

I hand it to him, and for a long moment he just studies it, a finger tracing the small shape. For some reason the sight of him clutching the tiny picture makes me want to cry. I swallow the emotion down.

"It's really hard to make her out yet," I murmur. "It'll be clearer on the next ultrasound."

Ethan nods, and I realize I'd forgotten that he's done this before, that of the two of us he's the one with more experience. "A girl?"

"Oh, I don't know. Too early to tell, but I just think of the baby as a girl." In my head, she already has Ethan's honey-brown hair and green eyes, fitting in with her older sisters.

Ethan just looks at the image, his head bowed. I rock back on my heels and can't help but notice the circles under his eyes, the unusually tousled thickness of his hair.

"Bella," he says finally, his gaze meeting mine. "I don't know where to begin."

I swallow. "Why don't you begin at the beginning?"

"How pragmatic."

"Engineering student," I say, the old joke slipping out.

His lip curls. "Engineer."

Hope soars inside me.

He hands back the picture, but there's reluctance in the gesture. "I can send you a copy," I say.

"I'd like that."

Sounding more sure than I feel, I slip my hands into the pockets of my slightly-too-snug jeans. "Starting at the beginning, huh?"

"Yes."

"How far back are we talking here?"

He rubs the back of his neck. "I'll fast forward from the Big Bang, but pretty far back."

"Wow."

"I really wish you had a couch."

"It's going to be one of those conversations, huh?"

"I'm afraid it might be." Ethan looks up at the ceiling, exhaling, like he's gathering strength. And then, "Do you know there's a gigantic crack in your ceiling?"

"It's not important."

"It strikes me as very important."

"The place is safe. They wouldn't rent it otherwise."

His scoff tells me he thinks I'm an idiot. "Landlords do plenty of shadier things than that. And you refused to let me find you a better place to live?"

I cross my arms over my chest. "You can't ask me to accept your charity. Knowing what you think of me, too? Absolutely not."

"Bella, I don't—"

"It *was* basically charity."

"You're right. I've been an ass." Ethan spreads his arms wide, and like his frame, like his voice, they fill the small space. "From the second Lyra called me to tell me the Gardners had no niece, I've been an ass."

I blink. "That's starting from the beginning?"

"No. I got distracted." He shakes his head. "For so long after Lyra, I shut down. I wasn't… I didn't look for love. I hadn't looked for it actively *before* her, and after that, well… There were women, but nothing lasted, because I never allowed it to.

"And then you walked over with those damn fudge brownies. And I wanted you, even though I knew I shouldn't let myself."

I have to swallow before I can speak. "Because you thought you couldn't offer me a relationship?"

"Yes. And it wasn't because of a lack of time, or because of the girls." He puts a hand to his chest. "It's because I wouldn't let you in. Not really. But you didn't walk away. You kept coming, as irresistible as you'd been the first time, and I decided the risk was worth it. Because I knew there was a risk, and in the back of my mind, I was always waiting for the other shoe to drop."

I wrap my arms around myself. "And then it did."

He nods. "And then it did. And it was like a confirmation of everything I already knew, that relationships weren't for me, that women weren't to be trusted. But lost in that realization as I was, I left you alone with this, and I'm more sorry than I can say. It's inexcusable."

I wet my lips. "You're right. This is a couch conversation."

His laughter is short, surprised. "Told you it was."

"Ethan, what you thought I did was pretty inexcusable, too."

"You're being too kind to me again," he says. "I've been an ass. Be angry at me."

"I have been."

"Good."

"But not just at you. At myself, too. At your ex-wife for putting these thoughts in your head."

"I'm the one who listened to them. But I won't, not again, not where you're concerned."

I shake my head. "Don't say that."

"Don't?"

"We're going to have to learn to trust each other again. It won't be an overnight thing, but we have to." And then, because I haven't said it before, and because I can't resist, "We're going to be parents together, you know."

And the answering smile on his face makes the knot inside me loosen. "We are."

"And I plan on being very, very, very involved," I add. "Comparatively speaking, you know."

"To my ex-wife?"

"Yes."

"I wouldn't have it any other way." Ethan steps closer, the solid wall of him now inches away. "That's not all I came here to say."

"It's not?"

"No. But the next part might come off as a bit desperate."

I laugh, pushing my hair back. My emotions feel scattered and my defenses flown wide. "I'll try not to judge."

"Thank you," he says, mock serious, and then actually serious, as he reaches up and catches a stray tendril of my hair between his fingers. "The truth is that I've missed you, Bella. What you said about needing to learn to trust is right. We need to re-learn one another again. We need… well, *I* need to have you close."

A thousand responses flit through my mind. Some kind, some sappy, some… well. "More papers for me to sign?"

"Christ no, not now, not ever."

"I would, though. Whatever you need to feel secure."

Ethan's hand flits to my chin, tilting my head upwards. The space between us feels like it's alive, humming with anticipation and closeness. It's been weeks since we touched last.

Weeks.

"Do you think you can forgive me, Bella?"

"No," I murmur. "Because you're too late. I already have."

A smile ghosts across his lips. "My heart damn near stopped after the first word."

"Sorry. Is that dangerous for a man of your age?"

His smile is full-blown now. "Teasing me while we're having this conversation is very unsportsmanlike. I can't retaliate at the moment, not while I'm begging."

"Sorry. I'll behave."

"Please try to." His thumb smooths over my lower lip, the roughness soft over my skin. "Move in with me, Bella. With us."

My breath comes out in a surprised huff.

"I know I'm asking a lot," he says. "What I told you about having little to offer wasn't *entirely* self-defense, after all. I come with two energetic kids, a complicated, pain-in-the-ass ex-wife, workaholic tendencies, and plenty of trust issues."

"And a very nice treehouse," I murmur. "You come with that too."

"Is that a selling point?"

"Oh yes." I wet my lips. "What about the girls, though? What would they say?"

"They love you," he says, hand cupping my cheek. I fight the urge to lean in to the warm touch. "They have since you first met them. But we'll go slow, for all of our sakes."

I grip his shirt, as if to make sure he's real. Everything he's saying… it's what I've wanted to hear for weeks. "Ethan, I need to know. Is this just because I'm pregnant? It's okay if it is. I'd understand that. But I need to know where *we* stand, the two of us."

"I deserve that question," he murmurs. "I'll admit that the baby forced me to reconsider certain things. Without that, I don't know if I'd have worked through this as quickly as I have. It would have been… *easy,* so to speak, to dismiss you and not open up. But even if you hadn't been pregnant…"

"Yes?"

He looks away, something like embarrassment crossing his face. "I got annoyed at Maria for changing my sheets, the ones you'd slept in."

"You did?"

"And I couldn't eat a baked good without thinking about you. Looking for you on my morning runs. It might have taken me longer to come around without the baby, but I would've, Bella. I missed you too much."

My hands flatten against his chest, soaking up the feel of him. "Oh."

"That's it? My grand declaration, and I get an *oh?*"

I tap my index finger against him. "Patience, Ethan."

He gives a long-suffering sigh, but there's something else in his eyes. Tentative happiness—hope. "I've never been good at that."

"I've missed you too," I say. "More than I expected, and far more than was good for me."

"I'm selfishly very glad to hear that." His other hand comes up, tangling in my hair. "What about my question? Will I get an answer to that?"

I wet my lips. "I already said I forgive you."

"No, baby. About moving in."

It's not fair, asking me that with his mouth so close to mine. "In time," I murmur.

"Hmm. I'll take that, for now."

"Good." I stretch up on my tiptoes. "Because that's all you're getting. For now."

He bends his head, warm breath against my mouth. The faint pause is a delicious thing. I'm the one who breaks it, pressing my lips to his. They're warm and soft and as he kisses me, it's like coming home.

25

ETHAN

Several weeks later

Bella flips over to the last page. "And this section? You didn't have any comments on this one."

I skim through the final paragraphs. "That's because it's excellent."

"And you're not just saying that?"

"I'm not just saying that. I've been honest with the feedback so far, haven't I?"

She nods, her fingers stroking down the page of her thesis. With only weeks until it's due, Bella is polishing and re-polishing and re-re-polishing. "It's good," I tell her. "A few final adjustments, but after that, it's good."

"You're telling me to stop tinkering with it."

I chuckle, rising from the kitchen table. "Yes, that's exactly what I'm saying. Do you want more frozen yogurt?"

"You're an enabler," she says. But she holds out her bowl. I mix the flavors she likes from the freezer and when I return, I scoot my chair close to hers.

"Pregnant ladies get what pregnant ladies want."

She hums in displeasure around her spoon.

"What?"

"Pregnant *ladies*. I sound so old."

"You will be a mother in a few short months," I point out.

"Yes, but that's the *fun* kind of old."

I roll my eyes at her. "You'll be a young mom, comparatively. Twenty-four is well below the national average."

Bella takes another bite of the fro-yo. Her hair is braided down her back, but little tendrils have escaped, framing the beautiful cream of her skin. My hand aches, wanting to reach out and pull her close.

But we've been good so far.

Very, very, very good. She hasn't made any signs that she wants more than occasional kisses, and I haven't pushed.

Trust. Time. Go slow.

It's driving me insane, but I'm sticking to the program.

"I don't know when I should start applying for jobs. I'll be done with my studies right around the time this little guy comes out." She puts a hand on her tummy, beautifully rounded. "It seems pointless to start until a while after that, but…"

"You have time," I say. "All the time in the world, in fact."

Her gaze locks with mine. This is getting close to things we haven't discussed yet, things like money and the future of our relationship.

I'll never offer her a contract again, but she'll never want for anything—not if she'll let me take care of her. It's been a long time since I've wanted to take care of anyone except my daughters, but with Bella, the desire is bone deep.

"I want to work," she says. "Eventually, after the baby. It's what I studied for."

"Of course you do. It would be a shame for the industry, too, to lose someone like you." I tap her thesis on the table. "It's not quite Nobel-prize worthy, but it's close."

Bella rolls her eyes, smiling. "You're ridiculous."

"Yes. A tad biased, too."

A sound upstairs. Bella pauses, and we both wait for the footsteps down the stairs. They don't come.

"Evie sometimes knocks things off her bedside table," I say. "She's a very active sleeper."

"Ninja dreamer."

"Exactly. I'll go check on her."

Bella nods, diving deep into her dessert. I pause with my hand on the back of her chair. "It's late. Stay the night?"

"If your master plan is that I'll sleep in the guest room so often that I eventually forget I have my own apartment, just know that I'm on to you."

"Of course you are," I say. "Doesn't mean it's not working."

Bella smiles up at me. Pregnancy has given her a near-perpetual flush in her cheeks, and something about her eyes, her hair... it's different, subtle, beyond the more obvious changes in her body. Impossibly, she's even more beautiful.

"It's a brilliant plan," she says.

"One you should stop actively opposing."

Her hand comes to rest on mine on the back of the chair. Slender, warm fingers. My body tightens at the faint contact. "I'll stay the night."

"Thank God. I was seconds from begging."

She shakes her head, taking her hand off mine. "Flatterer."

"The guest room is made up," I add, innate politeness forcing me to. *But so is my bed,* I want to add. *Stay with* me.

So far she hasn't. Not once.

"Thank you."

And later that night, when I'm lying in bed staring up at the dark ceiling, I go over all the fifteen reasons I *shouldn't* get out of bed and walk down the hallway to her room. Things like space and time and privacy and boundaries and trust and forgiveness and pregnancy. Lyra had hated being touched when she was pregnant—she hated being pregnant at all.

Bella has been different at every turn, but maybe...

I don't dare push it. Push us. This is too important.

But then, around midnight, someone pushes my door open just a smidge. I sit up in bed.

"Yes?"

"Daddy?"

It's Evie, her nightie bunched around a shoulder, her curls a halo around her head.

"Are you all right?"

"Yes. Bad dream." She's half asleep, still, the way she often is the few times she wakes up in the night.

I pull back the covers and lift her up. She curls in my bed with a sigh and I smooth a hand over her fluffy hair. She's asleep in seconds. From experience, I know the dream will be forgotten in the morning.

All in good time, I think. For now, I have all three of my girls under the same roof, and that's more than enough.

———

Bella stays over once more that week. Every time she agrees feels like victory, especially since the girls love it, too. They're very hard to get into bed at a reasonable hour when Bella's around to play with.

"Wouldn't a dog be nice around here, Bella?" Haven asks her, glancing in my direction to make sure I'm overhearing. "Wouldn't you just *love* one?"

Bella chuckles. It's not the first time she's been subjected to Operation Canine. "A dog would be nice," she says, "but they're a lot of work."

Haven's smile dims. I had to give her props, though. She knows I'll do a lot to make sure Bella is happy—her question had been strategic.

I put my hand on the back of her head. "Perhaps one day in the future. When you and Evie are older."

"Everything is always when we're older."

"Not everything," I say. "You used to ask for another sibling. Remember how I said 'maybe when you're older'?"

She eyes Bella's tummy. The girls hadn't been able to believe there was actually a baby in there until Bella started to show.

Now that she does, they *understand* it, but they don't really have a solid conception of it.

I'm still having trouble grasping it some days, to be honest.

"Is it a boy or a girl?" she asks Bella. It's only about the fourteenth time she's asked.

Bella musses Haven's hair. She hates it from me, but she tolerates it from Bella. "I still don't know. Your dad and I have decided not to find out. We won't know until he or she arrives."

Haven rolls her eyes. She doesn't understand the decision. Neither do any of our parents. *But what about the gifts?* Bella's mother had asked me, the first time I met her. *I don't know what to get!*

But Bella had been firm, and I'd agreed with her. This baby had been a surprise from the beginning.

Let it be a surprise to the very end.

That didn't mean that Bella didn't *suspect,* only that her suspicions changed pretty much weekly. I was getting whiplash from keeping up with the ever-changing pronouns.

"We should head upstairs," Bella tells Haven. "It's getting late. We should finish the book we started yesterday."

Haven slips her newly non-casted hand into Bella's and pulls her excitedly up the stairs. Her patience seems infinite. I keep waiting for the furrowed brow, the irritation, that she'll take me aside and say it's too much. Becoming a first-time mom is enough for anyone—becoming a stepparent at the same time…

But she's never complained, and I'm in awe.

We've just said goodnight when I hear an excited call from her bedroom. "Ethan! Ethan, get in here!"

I'm down the hall and opening the door to her bedroom in seconds, in nothing but my boxers. "Are you okay?"

Bella is sitting on the side of her bed, hair loose, a hand on her stomach. "Come feel this—he's kicking."

"He is?" I fall to my knees in front of her, putting my hand softly on her tummy. She grips my wrist and moves it slightly to the left.

"Right here," she murmurs. "Come on, give your dad a high five…"

I keep my hand pressed close. She's in one of my T-shirts and her skin is warm through the thin fabric. And then I feel it. A movement, slight but unmistakable.

Bella grins down at me, tears in her eyes. "Wow."

"Wow," I echo, putting my other hand on her stomach too. "Do you feel it? Inside?"

She nods. "It's so distinct, I can't imagine what it'll be like when he's bigger…"

"We're back to he?"

She looks sheepish. "Yes. I know I change my mind often, but now I'm sure again."

I can't hide my smile. "Do you feel okay? It doesn't hurt?"

"No, not at all." She puts her hand on top of mine. "He's stilled now. Maybe he just wanted you here."

I can't think of a single intelligent thing to reply to that.

"I know I wanted you here, at least," Bella continues, a blush on her cheeks. "Do you think you could stay the night with me?"

"Yes." Dear Lord, yes.

She scoots back up the bed, giving me a glimpse of those fair legs and a hint of purple panty, and then she disappears under the covers. I slide in behind her, and I don't hesitate for a second in reaching for her.

She settles into the crook of my arm with a soft sigh. "I've missed this," she breathes.

I run my hand over her silky hair and try to focus beyond the warm weight of her body against mine. *Months, Bella. It's been months.*

"So have I."

I wrap my other arm around her, bending my head to rest it against the top of hers. She smells like my soap, having used my shower today. It makes me inordinately pleased.

Her hand smooths over my stomach and every muscle in me locks in place. "I knocked on your bedroom door the last time I was here."

"You did?"

"Yes." Her voice is abashed. "I'm sorry. I just wanted you to hold me, and I couldn't fall asleep. But you already had someone in your bed."

"Evie?"

"I couldn't tell if it was her or Haven."

I grip her tighter. "I can hold you now."

She turns her face toward my chest, her lips grazing over my skin. I stare up at the ceiling and force myself to stay relaxed. But her lips continue up to my neck, and it's impossible.

"Kiss me good night?" she murmurs, a hand on my chin, and dear Lord…

I kiss her and I do it properly, coaxing her warm mouth open, my tongue sweeping in. Perhaps goodnight kisses should be chaste, soft things, but there's nothing chaste about this.

Bella kisses me back, her hands on my bare chest. She lifts one of her legs to drape it over me and oh fuck, the pressure on my aching, hard—

She pulls back.

"Ignore it," I say. Can she hear the desire in my voice? "I know you're not ready yet, that we're taking it slow. I can wait."

In the darkness, I can't make out her expression. But then her hand moves downwards, over my chest, my stomach, beneath the elastic band of my boxers.

There's not a part of my body that could have stopped her, and least of all *that* one. I hiss out a breath as her hand closes around me.

"I don't want to ignore it," she says. "Silly man, I've been waiting for you!"

"Waiting for me?"

"To feel like you trusted me again. I didn't want to rush you."

I open my mouth to respond, but the words die as her movements speed up. For a long few seconds I can do nothing but breathe.

"You have no idea how that feels," I murmur. "Or how long I've wanted you."

"The second one I know pretty well."

I wiggle my T-shirt out of the way and up her body, and she stops stroking long enough to slip out of it. There's brief hesitation in the air as I put my hands on her. "Bella?"

"My body is different," she says, voice soft, almost apologetic. "I know that."

"Yes, it is." I weigh her full, firm tits in my hands, bending my head to take a nipple in my mouth. The soft swell of her belly against me is wondrous. "You're even more beautiful. It's not fair, really."

She laughs, but the sound dies as I use my teeth, transformed into a gasp. "I remember some things," I murmur.

"So do I." Bella shifts so she can stroke me at the same time and I damn near come right then, her soft breast in my mouth and her hand on my cock.

Proudly, I exercise restraint, reaching into depths of character I didn't know I had. And when she finally begs me to, when I reach into her panties, she's the kind of wet that I know I'll dream about for years.

"Ethan," she murmurs. "*Please.*"

I run my hands over her naked body, wondering how to do this best, how to not hurt or harm. Finally, I settle behind her, lifting her leg and keeping my arm around her. "Just like this, baby," I murmur, guiding myself. "I can't wait to be inside you…"

Pushing in is like coming home—there are no other words for it. She twists her head to kiss me, my hand between her legs to ignite her own pleasure, my hips thrusting… the idea of there being space between us is laughable.

I always want her this close.

I grip her as tight as I dare when I shatter, my body curved around hers and still buried deep. Her soft, encouraging moans are the most beautiful sound.

"Move in with me," I mumble against her neck. "I'm very close to begging."

Bella surprises me then. She doesn't say yes. She doesn't say no. She just relaxes against me. "Oh, I love you, Ethan."

I close my eyes at the words, at the emotion that threatens to split me in half. Just when I thought I had nothing left to give, she proves me wrong.

"Christ," I whisper.

Bella chuckles. "Still just me."

"I love you too," I murmur. "Far, far more than I should, probably, but if there's a way to stop I hope I never find it."

"Me neither," she whispers, twisting to kiss me. "Can I move out of the guest bedroom now?"

Laughing, I pull her close. "Baby, you are never sleeping in here again."

BELLA

Lucas Edwin Carter was a surprise down to the very last moment, which made sense, since he had been nothing but surprising from the time he was two lines on a pregnancy test.

We're at a farmers' market with the girls when another round of Braxton Hicks contractions hits. Ethan is at my side, arm around my waist. "Another set of false ones?"

"I think so, yes. Who knew labor was so much fun that your body had to simulate it for weeks beforehand? Oh. Ouch." I grip his arm, resting my face against his chest. He smells good.

"Not right now, sweetie," he tells someone who's hopefully not me. "Bella will be fine, but she's in a bit of pain right now."

"Baby pain?"

"Right, pregnancy pain."

No, I want to object, labor pain. The contractions have never been quite this painful before—and have they ever gone on for quite this long? I'm about to open my mouth to tell Ethan that perhaps this is different, when the contractions release me from their fiery grasp. The pain is gone.

"Okay," I murmur, releasing his arm. "We're good. We're good."

The furrow in his brow is back, concern in his eyes. "Are you sure?"

"One hundred percent." My voice is more certain I feel, but I've learned that's another part of pregnancy. You're asked to self-assess all the time, as if you have a direct line of communication with the baby—as if we keep up a text conversation.

Ethan eyes my stomach with a fair bit of skepticism. He's the one who wants to go to the hospital at every hint of a contraction, has been more nervous than me since I entered the ninth month.

Better safe than sorry is his constant refrain. It's gotten us admitted to the hospital twice so far only to be sent back home.

"I'm not going in today," I tell him.

"Fine." His hand rests on my low back as we continue walking through the market, looking at the best early spring has to offer.

And then the second contraction hits.

And then the third one.

And they're not at all like the ones that have come before. Ethan steers me toward the car, calling for the girls to hurry up and swearing under his breath.

"This was a bad idea," he mutters, glancing at me.

I gasp with sudden relief as a contraction lets go of me. "I wanted to go to this market. Did you get the local honey? The organic one Skye told us about?"

"No, and we're not turning back to find the honey stall."

I stop dead in my tracks, and he's forced to stop beside me. "Ethan, that was the whole point of us coming here!"

He looks up at the sky, like he's asking it for strength. Perhaps he is. I glare at the perfect line of his jaw. "We are *not* turning back," he says, "but I can send someone to get it for you? Would that make you feel better?"

"That's just wasteful. Don't worry, I'll be super quick." But I'm not quick, because as soon as I turn, another contraction strikes me.

If the other ones were Little League, this one is Varsity.

My nails dig into his arm and I'm gasping. "No honey."

"No honey," Ethan repeats. "Bella, your water just broke."

I look down at the leggings that have been my home for the past few weeks. It takes me a painfully long moment to compute that what he's saying has actually happened. "Oh God. How didn't I notice that?"

He leads me toward the car. "We're going to the hospital, and I don't want an argument about it."

I'm still stuck on the water breaking. "I really thought I'd notice it."

"You were in the middle of a contraction."

I breathe through my nose in the front seat, listening to the familiar hustle and bustle of Ethan fastening the girls' seat belts in the back. They're unusually quiet. I should ask about that, but then pain hits me again and I pretty much forget my own name.

Ethan calls his mother from the car, and she's on the curb outside her house when we arrive.

"Come here, girls," she tells them. "You'll stay with me for the night."

Haven hesitates with her hand on the car door. "Good luck," she tells me. "I hope you're not hurting too much."

Oh no.

I give her a wide smile and reach out to clasp her hand. "Thank you, sweetheart. I'm not in too much pain at all. We'll see you tomorrow, okay?"

"Okay." Her dad kisses her on the head and lifts her out, and then we're off again, Evie already dancing up the driveway in the rear-view mirror.

Ethan handles everything in the hospital, my go-to-bag on his shoulder. For a crazy few seconds I almost feel like Haven with a broken arm, when Ethan had shown his insurance card and the arm was in a cast within the hour.

But I doubt this will be as quick.

We're escorted down the hall and another contraction hits. I want to scream for painkillers, for an epidural, for *something*, but the hospital is calm around me and perhaps that only happens on television, so I settle for leaning on Ethan.

"We're almost there," he says. "You'll get to lie down soon."

"Okay."

We get a private room, but I'm mostly focused on the bed and the nurse waiting with a smile. "Shall we count those contractions together?"

So we do, and in short order I'm changed into a gown, attached to a machine that measures the fetal heart rate, and they check how open I am. Apparently more open than they'd suspected, because they administer an epidural without me having to dramatically demand one. And then we're left there, Ethan and me and our unborn baby.

"The painkiller is kicking in," I tell him a while later.

"I can tell."

"Come here." I pat the side of my decadently wide hospital bed. He takes a careful seat on the very edge, like a little baby bird. The absurd analogy makes me want to laugh.

He smiles at my smile. "Something funny?"

"Yes. A lot of things. Like the fact that I won't exit this room without a baby."

"Wild, huh?"

"Very." In so many ways. Innumerable ways, actually. I stare unseeing at the screen by the end of the bed and think about all the things that can happen after this.

I'm so underprepared.

"You okay over there?"

"I'm fine," I murmur, trying to breathe. It turns out breathing through my pain was nothing compared to my panic.

"Bella?"

"I've been preparing for *this* moment, but not for what happens after. I've read all the pregnancy books but not the motherhood books. I'm not ready."

Ethan grips one of my hands, but I don't want it right now. I'm too busy panicking. "You know," I accuse him. "You're the perfect father, and you have *heaps* of practice. But what if I screw up on the first day? What if I don't know how to hold him, or to help him with his homework, or what if he's allergic! And I give him peanuts!"

"Bella—"

"No, I take it back. I don't want this."

Ethan's eyes are clouded with concern, but through it all, he forces a wide smile. It's the one I like best—the one that says everything is going to be all right because he's there.

"So it's a boy now?"

I shoot him my best death glare. "I'm convinced now. I *know* it."

"We'll figure out how to raise him together," he says. "And no one knows what they're doing until they do it. That's just life."

"Not making me feel better."

Laughing, he puts his hands on either side of my face. They're cool against my skin.

"Bella."

"Ethan."

"Focus on this. One thing at a time. I might know how to do a lot of the other stuff, but I've never done *this*, and I'm in awe of you."

"You are?"

"Oh yes. Seeing you over the past few months, too… you're magnificent, and stronger than I could ever be. The rest will be a piece of cake, and I'll be right there with you."

His eyes widen as mine tear up. "Bella?"

"Excellent speech," I sniffle. "Did you practice it beforehand?"

"No. Should I have?"

"No," I say. "You nailed the delivery."

He smooths my hair back. "Done panicking?"

"Yes, it's officially over." I settle back into the bed and nod toward my bag. "I brought some stuff for us to entertain ourselves with while we wait. Skye told me there might be a lot of waiting."

He grabs my bag, grunting at the weight, and looks through it. His voice is incredulous. "You packed a book on molecular physics?"

"I've always wanted to learn more."

"Wilma's thesis?"

"She asked me to read through it and comment on any mistakes."

"You brought *this?*" He holds up a tome of a book, written by one of the literary greats.

"I saw it in your study. I've never read it. It's a classic, come on. Don't look at me that way."

He puts the entire bag down, contents and all. "Have I told you lately that I love you?"

"Hey, the bag isn't *that* bad."

"Sure it's not," he says, grinning. "We're not here for a vacation. But if you want to read Tolstoy in between contractions, I won't stop you."

I mutter something about how I'm at least *trying* to be cultured and Ethan bends to kiss me, breaking off my protests.

But his kiss is soon broken off in turn by another contraction. And then another. And it's not long until our doctor returns, a smile on her face.

"Looks like someone's getting ready to meet their baby," she tells me.

If I've ever doubted the theory of relativity before, I'll never do it again. Because time warps and bends and speeds up and slows down in the coming hours. Or is it days? Weeks? An eternity?

Because there's no telling how long my labor is. It's a blur of pain and orders and breathing. Of faces. Dearest is Ethan's, close to mine, telling me things in a deep, calm manner. I barely make out his words, but his voice is heavenly.

Or at least I *thought* his voice was heavenly, but then a wail cuts through the air that is infinitely preferable. I see two tiny, blood-covered feet before my screaming baby is pulled away.

"I can only see his feet," I half-sob, half-cry. "I love his feet."

Ethan isn't next to me anymore, his face focused on the bundle. "Wait till you see the rest of him."

"Him? It's a boy?"

The nurse returns, placing the tiny, ruddy-faced baby on my chest. "A boy," she confirms.

"Hi," I whisper to him, to this beautiful, mushed, minuscule human being who is somehow part me and part Ethan. "I've waited for you for so long."

He looks up at me and I look down at him and my tears don't stop. I doubt they ever will.

"Ethan, look," I breathe.

"I'm looking," he murmurs, bending so his head rests next to mine. "I'm looking, Bella."

"He's asleep?"

"Yes." Ethan stretches out beside me, and we both watch the crib at the foot of the bed with bated breath.

Not a peep.

"Thank God." I stretch out fully for what feels like the first time in days. Not even at gunpoint could I come up with a single part of my body that isn't sore.

Ethan slides his arm underneath my head. "I practically had to bar the door to keep the girls out."

I smile at that. "They want to play with him?"

"Yes. Haven gets that he's not big enough yet, but Evie doesn't."

"Yesterday she snuck a doll into his crib when I looked away."

Ethan groans. "Was it her purple-haired one, at least?"

"Oh, you bet it was. She means the best." Both the girls did. The other day they'd sat next to me and watched him as he slept, and I'd answered all their questions to the best of my ability. Certain questions, like *how did you and Daddy make him?* had been difficult to answer.

We picked him up at the baby store, I'd felt like saying, but I'd mangled a short reply about how it could happen when two people loved each other. Anything more elaborate than that and I'd need Ethan as backup.

"Your parents just called," he tells me. "They arrive in town next weekend to meet him."

"They'll be taking a ton of pictures," I warn. "Prepare yourself."

"Oh, your mother told me she already has a scrapbook planned," Ethan says, sounding pleased by the thought. His meeting with my parents a few months ago had gone far better than I'd hoped. My parents, apprehensive of the whole situation, were immediately at ease in his company. I understood the feeling perfectly.

"Both of our brothers need to meet him, too," Ethan says.

"Wyatt is dying to," I say. "Has Liam accepted your offer to work with you on the new company?"

"No, and I don't even know what city he's in." There's more in his voice than he's letting on—I know the distance between him and his brother pains him. "He said he'd think about it. Cole is planning to speak with him, and I'm not sure Liam is prepared for that. He'll be steamrolled."

Laughing weakly, I turn onto my side and bury my head against his chest. Through all of this, the long nights and my panic and the difficulty with latching, Ethan has been here. Something about the sheer strength of him, his wide smile, his competence, makes for the best anti-stress medication on the globe.

"I'm so very, very happy I did all this with you," I tell him.

His other arm comes around me, somehow avoiding all the bits of me that hurt. "That's good," he says, "because I can't imagine doing it with anyone else either."

"I love you," I tell him. "I'm sorry for being so crazy the last few weeks."

"That was your right." He presses soft kisses to my forehead, my cheeks, my closed eyelids, my mouth. "You'd look so good in white."

I burst into laughter. "Ethan Carter, you never stop trying, do you?"

"I never will. Marry me, Bella."

I smile against his jaw, burying my face there. "You're relentless."

"Don't you want to?"

It's the first time he's asked that particular question, though he's been mentioning marriage for months. I lean back and meet his gaze with my own, and there's no fear or concern there. No hint that he's asking out of a misguided feeling of responsibility.

"I do," I whisper, running my finger along his cheek. "I really, really do."

His smile could light up a stadium, but it's just me here, and I'm hit with the full force of it. My heart leaps into overdrive.

"I love you," he murmurs.

"I love you too," I whisper. "But perhaps a small ceremony? Just the five of us, and our parents."

"The five of us," Ethan repeats. "I think that might be the best phrase I've ever heard."

"Sounds good, right?"

"Yes," he says, and then groans. "But it might become the six of us."

I put my hands flat against his chest. "Hold on there, stud. I'm not ready to be pregnant again."

"Haven asked me for a dog yesterday."

"You agreed?"

"She chose a very weak moment. I was sleep-deprived and holding Lucas and there was absolutely nothing I would have said no to. We should be lucky she didn't ask me for a pony."

Laughing, I pull him closer. "Some could say the same about your proposal here, choosing a weak moment."

"They're not remotely comparable." He kisses me again, soft and sweet. "You should get some sleep."

"We both should. The girls won't be back for hours."

"Remember when Cole called me a lucky bastard because my perfect woman moved in next door?" Ethan murmurs.

I fight against my impossibly heavy eyelids. "I remember thinking he was wrong, because that was the way it was for me," I say.

"He was right." Ethan's arm tightens around me. "Because you've given me everything I've ever wanted, including the things I'd never thought to ask for. And I'll never stop loving you for that."

I swallow against the sudden tightness in my throat. "You're taking the words right out of my mouth," I murmur. "Because that's the way it is for me."

His lips find mine, and kissing him is home, safe and thrilling at the same time. "We'll just have to agree to disagree," he says, pulling the comforter up and over us. I snuggle closer to him and close my eyes, the feeling of his arms around me all I need. From the foot of the bed, there's a small cooing sound from our sleeping son.

The one who was as unexpected as he will be loved, born into a home with two clever older sisters and two parents who love each other very much—because I hadn't lied to the girls when I explained how Ethan and I'd made him. I'd just simplified a tiny bit.

AUTHOR'S NOTE

Thank you so much for reading!

Ethan and Bella will be back, because the Seattle Billionaires series isn't over yet… Liam Carter will get his story told in January 2021!

Billion Dollar Catch is book three in the series. Read about Cole and Skye in Billion Dollar Enemy, or about Nick and Blair in Billion Dollar Beast, both available on Amazon.

ABOUT OLIVIA

Olivia loves billionaire heroes despite never having met one in person. Taking matters into her own hands, she creates them on the page instead. Stern, charming, cold or brooding, so far she's never met a (fictional) billionaire she didn't like.

A voracious reader of romance, Olivia picked up the pen a few years back and what followed was nothing short of a love affair of her own. Now she spends her days giggling at the steamy banter she's writing or swooning at their happily-ever-afters.

Smart and sexy romance—those are her lead themes!

Join her newsletter at www.oliviahayle.com for bonus content.

Connect with Olivia

facebook.com/authoroliviahayle
instagram.com/oliviahayle
goodreads.com/oliviahayle
amazon.com/author/oliviahayle
bookbub.com/profile/olivia-hayle

Printed in Great Britain
by Amazon